PRAISE FOR WM SHAKESPEARE

"The great master who knew everything."
  Charles Dickens

"England's Homer."
  John Dryden, The Essay of Dramatick Poesy

"The Soul of the age, the applause, delight, the wonder
of our stage."
  Ben Jonson

"That King Shakespeare, does not he shine, in crowned
sovereignty, over us all, as the noblest, gentlest, yet
strongest of rallying signs; indestructible."
  Thomas Carlyle

"I will praise any man that will praise me."
  William Shakespeare

BARTHOLOMEW DANIELS

ROTTEN AT
THE HEART

*Being Wm Shakespeare's account of his first adventure
as an unwilling intelligencer in service to the Crown,
as relayed from his recently discovered journals by
Bartholomew Daniels.*

EXHIBIT A
An Angry Robot imprint
and a member of the Osprey Group

Lace Market House,
54-56 High Pavement,
Nottingham,
NG1 1HW,
UK

Angry Robot/Osprey Publishing,
PO Box 3985,
New York,
NY 101853985,
USA

www.exhibitabooks.com
A is for As you like it

An Exhibit A paperback original 2014

Cover by Nick Castle Design
Set in Meridien and Caslon Antique by Argh! Oxford

Distributed in the United States by Random House, Inc., New York.

ISBN 978 1 90922 343 1
Ebook ISBN 978 0 85766 344 8

Printed in the United States of America

9 8 7 6 5 4 3 2 1

For Brian Etheredge, my late good friend who, I think, would have been amused.

INTRODUCTION

Being a brief account of how Bartholomew Daniels came to be in possession of these earth-shattering historic documents written by the late William Shakespeare.

An estate sale in Evanston, one of the big old houses along Asbury. I was looking for chairs, really. Should have known better than to shop for furniture in that neighborhood, even used. But the place had books, a lot of books. I am a sucker for books.

I could just make out the chalky ghost of white paint stenciled on the lid of the olive steamer trunk wedged into the corner of the room:

Lt Thomas McBride, US Army
8th Air Force, 482nd Bomb Group
Alconbury, Huntingdonshire, England

The trunk was full of books, old ones. Leather bindings, some of them with raised bands across the spines, the Coptic method. I took out a few, paged through them. They weren't mint. The whole trunk gave off a musty smell. Some of the covers had a little mildew. I could see some mold along the edges of the pages here and there. They covers weren't warped, though. They hadn't been soaked, just gotten too damp. Wherever this trunk had been stored, it hadn't always been dry. Basement maybe.

All the books were from British publishers: Chapman & Hall, Methuen, some smaller houses. A couple from the nineteenth century, but most of them from the Twenties and Thirties. Not first editions, at least not famous ones, but, by a quick count, forty-some books, in decent repair. Seal them up with some kitty litter and baking soda; that would take care of the smell. I could deal with the mildew. These could be worth something.

"Great-grandpa's." The girl in the glasses. She'd been by the door when I came in, sitting at a card table, reading *The Heart of the Matter* by Graham Greene. I was predisposed to think well of her.

"Lieutenant McBride?" I asked, pointing at the stenciling on the lid.

She nodded. "He was a new literature professor at Northwestern, just married. He knew how to fly. He signed up when the war started. Great-grandma, she begged him not to, but..." her voice trailed off, she shrugged. "Anyway, he never came home. The army shipped his stuff back, including a trunk full of books. I guess maybe she couldn't deal with them at the time, maybe she never could, maybe she just forgot about them. But the trunk's been down in the basement forever."

I looked around the room. A library, clearly, and built as one. Floor to ceiling bookcases on three walls. A bay window facing the front with a small desk tucked into the alcove. All the shelves were crammed with books.

"Not like she needed more books, I guess," I said.

The girl smiled a little. "No. She'd been one of his students his first year. A little bit of a scandal about that the way I hear it. But they married. She was pregnant when he was killed. She was an English professor at Northwestern, too, for decades. Unusual for a woman, at least when she started."

The girl pointed to a picture on the desk. A handsome woman: dark haired, partly gray, pulled back. In her mid-forties I'd guess, sitting on the corner of a desk in front of a room full of students, her hand in mid-gesture, her passion plain on her face. Most of the kids were in *Leave it to Beaver* togs, but there were a couple in jeans, a few guys with long hair. The Sixties, just as things were changing.

I looked around the room, out the doorway into a living room that was bigger than my apartment and furnished with antiques mostly.

"I guess the professor thing used to pay better."

The girl smiled. "She came from money. And her son, my grandfather, well, he didn't go the professor route. He was all about business. Him and my father." A little distaste in her voice at that. She looked around the room, wistfully, it seemed. She held up the Greene novel in her hand, a finger marking her place. "I guess I got the recessive gene."

"That's one of my favorites," I said.

"You've read Greene?"

I nodded. "The scene at the beginning, when Scobie comes home and tells his wife he's been passed over, then gets her to pick at some meat–"

The girl interrupted. "'It had always been his responsibility to maintain happiness in those he loved. One was safe now, forever...'" she looked at me expectantly.

"'...and the other was going to eat her lunch.'" I said.

She smiled, but a sad smile. For anyone who understood that passage, it would have had to be.

"I was fifteen," I said. "That was the first time a book broke my heart. They've been doing it ever since."

Her smile got a little happier. "Are you a professor too?"

I shook my head. "Writer."

"And you want to buy great-grandpa's trunk of books."

I shrugged. "Probably can't afford them. I was hoping I could afford a couple of chairs."

She laughed softly, her smile brightening a little. "Forget the chairs. When I said she came from money, I meant it. Most of the furniture ought to be in a museum. And dad got valuations on every stick of it, trust me on that." Her smiled faded a little. "But I guess it's hard for him to imagine much value in books. He just wants to get rid of those. The trunk has a yellow sticker – best offer. I'd rather see those go to someone who has a heart they can break."

I pulled out my wallet, took all the bills out of it. "I can give you a hundred and twenty seven dollars," I said. I dug into my front pocket. "And thirty-seven cents."

Her smile brightened again.

"Deal.

I got the trunk home, horsed it up the stairs, unpacked the books.

I almost missed the box – the broad, flat wooden chest under the moldering blanket that was folded under the books. The box was maybe four or five inches deep, rectangular, almost exactly as wide as the chest, maybe half as long. It fit snuggly in the bottom and it was heavy. Even when I turned the trunk on its side, it took a bit to work it loose. When I did, I could hear something sliding around inside.

The wood was almost black with age – and dirt. The corners were capped with bronze gone green with tarnish. The chest latched closed in the front, not a lock, but the latch was rusted in place. I tried to force it with a screwdriver, slowly adding pressure, but I didn't want to damage the mechanism. The chest might be worth something.

I sprayed some WD-40 on a cloth, rubbed as much as I could into the latch, the rust turning the rag an ugly brownish orange as I did. Once the cloth started coming away clean, or close to it, I tried the latch again. A hint of movement maybe? Or wishful thinking? I rubbed in more WD-40 and left that to work for a while.

Got another rag, some lemon oil went to work on the wood. Ten minutes and the rag was almost solid black, but the wood was a little lighter. Another rag, another ten minutes, and I could see the wood pretty clearly. Oak, and with a very fine grain. Fine enough to get me a little excited.

Funny thing, being a writer, you're always looking up some kind of obscure crap for some reason. A few years back, I had some half-assed idea about somebody stealing a Stradivarius. Story never worked out, but I learned that part of the reason for the unique quality of the sound from those instruments was the density of the wood. Something about the climate at the time, the little ice age, and how trees grew more slowly, making very fine grained wood.

Could be nothing, but it could mean that I was looking at a chest that was at least a few hundred years old.

I felt the writing before I saw it, just one line carved into the lid of the chest, very worn, very faint. I took the lampshade off , held the light at a shallow angle, tried to make out the words. **No**? **Non** maybe? An **s**, something that started with a **D**. Three words, it looked like. I got a pencil and a piece of paper off the desk, tried to make a rubbing. **No** or **Non**, then **Sanz Dr** and then a portion I couldn't read, but whatever the **Dr** word was, it ended with a **t**. A quiet alarm was going off somewhere back in my writer brain, something I'd read. I got up to grab the laptop, ready to start Googling.

But then the latch on the front of the chest fell open, just like that.

Papers. The chest held papers. On top, a letter dated October 13, 1943.

Dear Marion,

I'll continue my superstition. It is my firm belief that God will not take me so long as I have an unfinished letter to you. We fly tomorrow, so I will start this tonight, certain that I will return to it.

Some excitement I hope. I got into London for a couple of days, so of course I had to find a bookstore. The one I found was heartbreaking. It had been hit during the Blitz and lay torn open, a women and two young children sitting in front of makeshift shelves on the sidewalks selling what stock they'd been able to salvage. I found some lovely titles, well, dozens of them, actually.

Then I spotted the box. A wooden chest of apparently old manufacture. I didn't know what was in it, as the latch on it was intricate and frozen with age. The women claimed never to have seen its contents. But she was anxious to be rid of it, calling it the fountain of her sorrows. Something her husband, who had owned the shop, had found. Something he had risked his life to save, running back into the shop only to be killed in its collapse. The box survived, he did not. It took some doing to get that latch open, I can tell you that.

I'm going to save the surprise of what's inside (or at least of what I hope it is) until tomorrow night. Surely fate will not prevent my sharing such news! I will give you this hint. Three words are carved into the lid, faint now with age, barely able to be read, and they are in French. (As bright as you have always been, that may be hint enough for you.) It's crazy, all of this. What I'm thinking can't possibly be true. I overpaid, I suppose, for the box and the books. It's probably nothing. But we all need distractions, and the war makes so many things seem so meaningless.

Good night, my love. I go to sleep dreaming of your embrace.

Then just a few scrawled lines, written in haste.

It's morning and I only have a moment. Jesus, it's Schweinfurt. I know you can't hear me, I know you haven't read this yet, and when you do, I pray that it's because I've mailed it, not because you're opening this box. But pray for us. Pray for us all.

OK, I'll finish tonight. I swear to God I will.

He didn't of course. Neither did six hundred other airmen.

The feeling of eavesdropping, of trespassing, of my eyes being the first to see the last words of a man now almost seventy years dead, dead more than three times longer than he'd been alive, that invested the box with a more sacred weight as I set the letter aside and lifted the first, large sheet.

The paper itself sent a tremor through me before I'd even read the words on it. Minutia from the attic of my writer brain again.

Before the 1800s, almost all paper was made from cotton, not wood pulp. Fabric would be soaked and treated until it broke down into individual fibers. The fibers then would be lifted from the soaking solution in a kind of trayed sieve. The mesh of the sieve left marks on the paper called chaining. I could see the chaining marks here. Deckle edging, inclusions, papermaker's tears – all the hallmarks of old, hand-laid paper.

And then I read the words.

It wasn't easy at first. The ink was old, often faded, the writing sometimes barely legible. Some of the language was archaic and the spelling had the random, quasi-phonetic nature common before the nineteenth century, complete with the odd silent letters added as a homage to a word's Latin or Greek roots.

It was more like translating than reading. I sat on the floor with a notebook, working my way through the first page. The writing was large, centered, formally spaced, almost like a cover sheet.

These pages being a true account of my adventures as an unhappy intelligencer in service to Lord Carey, the Second Baron Hunsdon and Lord Chamberlin to Her Majesty Elizabeth Regina, kept so that these troublesome truths might have a home should e'er I need their record for my protection.

And then a signature. The signature was easy. I had seen it before. So have you.

Wm. Shakespeare

There's more, of course. Experts are checking the paper, the ink, the chest. Shakespearian scholars are pouring over the syntax. Lawyers from the girl's family are suing me.

But I'll let all that shake out as it may. That's not my province.

My province is stories. I know a good one when I read it. This is one hell of a story. And this Shakespeare guy, he can write a little.

So, I give you his tale, crudely wrenched by my undeserving hands into this more accessible form. A tale of murders done to serve both God and Mammon, of crowns and capital, of banal deeds and heroic sacrifices. Of friends and hearts both betrayed and embraced.

A tale of a time more than three centuries distant, but a time, I fear, too much like our own.

A tale I have entitled, stealing from the Bard's own work, *Rotten at the Heart*.

Bartholomew Daniels

ROTTEN AT THE HEART

by

William Shakespeare

As edited by Bartholomew Daniels

"An evil soul producing holy witness
Is like a villain with a smiling cheek,
A goodly apple rotten at the heart."
The Merchant of Venice, Act I, Scene III

CHAPTER 1

The theatre is my only solace, the warm, unclean bosom of the stage. To write, there is joy in that. But it is a kind of possession, a transient madness and always pursued alone. It leaves me spent as though used, and roughly, by the Muses that others imagine to be my servants.

When I have finished a night's work, and it is almost always the night's work due both to life's usually day-lit demands and the sense that my fictional imaginings are best pursued alone and in the hours of dreaming, I find myself thus. Unkempt, my clothes sweated and askew, my fingers stained with the fluid of this endeavour, and my breath often coming in heaves and starts. I am like a woman after a man has fulfilled himself, has emptied his seed into her and then rolled away, leaving his stink on her sheets and his sweat to dry on her skin, the matter for him finished but for her, sometimes just begun. That same sense that a miracle may have transpired, that I will issue forth into the world something new and complete that no other could author, but whose authorship comes only at the solitary cost of long labour and suffering.

Such is the cost of my writing. But at the theatre I am one with my fellows. I find in those drawn to the stage a kinship of spirit that thins that fog of thought and imagining in which I am too oft enveloped. A fog that blinds me to the easy commerce most men seem find in one another's company and that makes me feel apart and unwelcome in their society.

At the side of the stage on the gentle afternoon of a summer's day, neither over-hot nor stormy in its temperament, but fair and graced with breeze.

How I wish I could return to that moment from this side of the gulf that now divides my life between the days before and the days since. For having in the interim witnessed horrors previous unimagined, and having been made party to schemes of such cruel cost and aimed at such innocent subjects and for such banal reasons, I find my previous philosophies useless. Any thoughts I held concerning the world's goodness or its capacity for love, for charity or even for mercy, have proved too fragile against these stern lessons. I can only hope to create some world anew in which those too-scarce graces can prove strong enough to stand.

On that last day of an easier lived life, I was leaning on the wall at the edge of the stage, comfortable with my fellows and feeling light and careless, even with James Burbage, the company's leading player, in both his cups and his temper.

That July day was Dick Jenkins's first in rehearsals, Jenkins being the new boy player the company had hired to replace Henderson for the woman's parts, as

Henderson's voice had finally dropped in timbre even if in face and form he was still the comeliest woman on the London stage. Henderson had been Burbage's favourite, so Burbage all that day had carried on as though Henderson's inevitable adolescence were somehow the product of Jenkins's nefarious agency. Finally, Jenkins, so discomfited by Burbage's constant pique, misspoke a line.

"Am I to feign affection to this?" shouted Burbage, waving at Jenkins. "He opens a mouth that I am, in but a few lines, expected to kiss, and vomits out gibberish. At least Henderson's ass was hairless. Look at this woolly carbuncle. Even a Sodomite would balk at saddling this mare."

Burbage stomped to the side of the stage for another cup of sack. Jenkins stood centre stage, his face quivering.

"Mind not Burbage," I called from the wing. "Rehearsals offend his vanity. His pride is swollen even larger than his talent, and he believes his every utterance deserves an audience. It is ever so with actors."

"It's the hairless ass he misses, Will," called John Heminges, another of the company's actors and shareholders, from across the stage. "With Burbage in his drink and Henderson in his dress and paint, I think they oft confused the bounds of life and art."

Burbage drained his cup and hurled it at Heminges.

"Perhaps we should take a razor to Jenkins's haunches and put our esteemed player in a better spirit," I answered.

Burbage guffawed a laugh, his original distemper largely pretended anyway. "You may shave what you like, Will, but you'll still lack the steel to do it harm. Your name may say 'Shakespeare', but at the brothels they call your shaft more akin to the quill you wield than to any spear." Burbage grabbed his own codpiece. "The ladies do, however, desire my Lancealot."

The company, those amused and those not, broke into laughter, knowing it the only way to tease Burbage back to work. For Burbage, the adulation of a crowd was like the sun unto a flower.

Burbage strode to centre stage as though truly for an audience, grasped Jenkins by the shoulders, and kissed him firmly on the lips. "I shall learn to love thee, boy, even if my lance shall not."

The rehearsal concluded, I sat alone at the small desk in the theatre's stores, and considered our accounts. Our troupe, The Lord Chamberlain's Men, was the leading company in London, but leading that pack of late meant only that we would be the last to ruin. Only a few years hence, we – along with the other companies of players, the bear baiters, the brothels, and all other entertainments – had been forced from the city proper. For in the city, the power of the Puritans was ascendant, and their joyless philosophy saw no distinction between an actor and a whore, considering any activity that might grant a man a moment's pleasure a festering infection that diverts his soul from the constant worship of their harsh god. The city, too, in concern of the recurring bouts of plague that still sprung to flame from the smouldering pestilence that underlay its burgeoning population, hoped our relocation outside its bounds would lessen the threat. And so we current kept our theatre in Shoreditch, while many of the other companies were across the river in Bankside.

The company owed the lease, the shares, to the owners – of which, thankfully, I at least was one – and the wages to the other players. Given three new plays to be opened in the coming weeks, we would again need to buy the costumes and other accoutrement attendant to a successful staging. Our revenues had always scarce bested our expenses, but too often now that slim margin fell to the wrong side of the balance.

Thankfully, I had a correspondence from Henry Carey, both the Baron Hunsdon and the Queen's Lord Chamberlain. He had been in poorly health, which was a grave concern, as his status as our troupe's namesake and patron was in truth our greatest asset. If this note was evidence, he was some recovered, and requested a series of performances at court, as the Queen herself enjoyed all manner of amusements – her tastes much vexing those Puritan ministers who desired to drive from life every pleasure. A curious religion to me, so sure that we are most of us damned and yet still preaching such poverty of spirit that, on the day we wake in hell, we will find our sufferings not much increased from the dour life that they require.

Word from Carey was most welcome, both as a sign that his health was recovered and so his patronage secure and because our investment in performances at court was minimal and the payment for them generous. With these, we might steal a march on the forces of penury, whose armies of late seemed always at our gates.

Which left the conundrum of my personal accounts. I had the expenses of two households, my own in London and that of my wife and children in Stratford. And from Stratford, too, word of a new suit targeting my father. His barely disguised Catholicism left him vexed by the taint of recusancy, which eroded his station and left him prey to any who might press a claim, for he was forced to balance the benefit of a vigorous defence against the attention his opponents would surely bring to his religion. At least his closet Catholicism was better tolerated in the hinterlands than it would be in London. Here, for me, any stench of Papistry could mean ruin.

Yet I am no Catholic. On matters of religion, I am convinced that any attempt to reduce to human custom and practice the will of a God infinitely exceeding the capacity of our understanding is folly. At best an innocent folly that encourages some charity and blunts the less holy impulses of our animal natures. In common practice, a banal folly buoying the hearts of men, who hear in the pause between each beat the empty echo of their own mortality, so that through all history they have hewn gods of every nature from dead stones and then prayed to their creations, imagining that a deity of their own making can somehow bridge that abyss which, at death, awaits us all. In its worst and most common practice, religion is an invented madness purposely infected into people to drive them to hate and to mould them to the ambitions of charlatans. It makes the world into a model of the hell they pray against in service of the trivial and transitory desires of the princes of the earth, whether those princes are adorned with crown or mitre.

Also on the desk I had a long-awaited response from the College of Heralds. My father, years ago and at the time still the bailiff of Stratford, had sought the armorial bearings and coat of arms that would make him, officially, a gentleman, and me, therefore, a gentleman born. But the application had languished as my father's fortunes reversed, until I, some months prior, and, at the time enjoying an uptick in fortune that I had foolishly presumed to be permanent, had renewed that claim. Now came word that, with only payment of the final licence, the arms would be granted.

When teased by my fellows about my pretendings to stature, I would swear my aim only to be to secure for my father that standing that I did feel his by right. And, as should be with any good fiction, that lie was true – for to be finally named a gentleman would comfort my father greatly and provide some bulwark against the stream of claimants who now found him an easy meal. I did even admit my own desire for the practical advantages the status of gentleman would convey, as it would allow me to stand on even ground with the landlords and merchants with whom I had daily truck. It would allow me to adorn myself in honest in such finer clothes as oft I wore only on stage without risking the attention and fines of Her Majesty's agents, as their Sumptory Laws forbade commoners from wearing certain fabrics and colours so that their betters could ready distinguish those deserving their courtesy.

With the half-measure of these some-true lies I deflected inquiry into the hypocrisy of my appetites. But I cannot conceal from myself the venal ambitions of my own heart. I cannot forget that, as a boy, I did sometimes hate my own father for falling from his station at just such time as I might first taste its benefits, knowing full well I had done nothing to earn them by merit. Did hate my mother and the name Arden, which was the well-spring of the faith to which they did so stubborn cling, to all our ills, to no benefit that I could discern and with no blessing of philosophy to which, even now, I could lend credence. And I still remember the brickbats from the university playwrights, their amusement at my poorer Latin, at my occasional lapses in manners, and at my constant attention to matters of business – for I had not their wealth to pursue theatre as a diversion or a passion alone, but instead needed to make from it a livelihood.

So, in those moments when, in conscience, I confront the truth of myself, I must confess that the coat of arms is not for my father, and not even for the mercantile advantages to be gained as a gentleman, but is instead a reflection of my own naked lust for standing. A lust I have so oft lampooned in the characters I write. But I had been a more optimistic man when I took up the cause of our family arms anew, and now understood that cost of the licence was likely beyond my means forever. I pretended to a status I had done nothing to earn and could never afford.

We can know our own ills, but that does not mean that we can cure them. And if my own golden calf is a simple scroll adorned with a shield and a scribbling of Latin, then it is hubris at the least to imagine myself the better of those who cling instead to a cross or a crucifix. We are each adrift on our own boundless ocean and must cling to any flotsam of hope on which we can gain purchase, for despair yawns in the deeps and would have our meat in its fearsome jaws should e'er we let go.

The daylight was failing. A month past, I would have bolted to the borrowed rooms where I had found a kind of Eden in the arms of a young mistress. But of late what I had done to earn the fruit of that now despoiled apple, and the cost to us both of its conniving acquisition, had become too plain. The pleasures I gained from her favours were now so stained with shame that I could scarce keep my own company knowing first how I had made hers. And so, despite the girl's entreaties, I had these past days foresworn her bed.

Too dark now to read the ledger. I could start a candle, but candles are expensive. I resolved to retire to my quarters. I would burn a candle there in service to my writing, and since that service would provide saleable product for our company, at least the candle would earn its wage. The play was the thing. Though at current I was flailing for an idea on which to anchor one, wasting not only candles, but also ink and paper on failed and fitful starts.

As I closed the ledger and returned the papers to their drawers, Burbage burst in, staggered with drink, his face pale. His mouth gaped, and he choked for a moment as he tried to speak.

"Calm yourself, man," I said. "What news has thee so?'

"It's Carey," Burbage said. "The Lord Chamberlain is dead."

CHAPTER 2

"How are you called, Shakespeare?"

I was awakened early the morning next by a herald from Somerset House, home to the late Lord Chamberlain and his family. The herald bore a summons to meet that evening with George Carey, the eldest son and second Baron Hunsdon. I was glad that it was the Baron's herald and not the Baron himself who witnessed my state, as I was askew after a long night with Burbage and the company's other shareholders during which we tried to blunt this insult to our fortunes with what drink we had at hand and then, having exhausted that, sorely depleted the stores at the tavern closest.

Now I stood at Somerset and in the Baron's company, having borrowed from our troupe's stores the attire to costume myself into a semblance of propriety and hoping that this prompt attention from the late Lord Chamberlain's heir signalled good fortune.

"My lord?" I said.

"Your name, man. How are you called?"

"Will most often, by those who know me well, but as you like it."

Carey grunted. "By which to say, should I prefer to call you a spotted ass, you would pretend no offence so as to retain my favour?"

"By which to say, my lord, that my name is William, and whether Will or Willie or Bill, they all fall as easy on my ear, and that I am sure that the truth of your reputation – which is that of a fair and gentle man – would preclude you call me by any name to which I could not in honour answer."

Carey barked a gruff laugh, and poured from a silvered jug two measures of claret, holding one out to me.

"Can you in honour drink?"

I smiled and accepted the goblet. "In honour, yes, and even again when honour is out of earshot."

Carey sat in the chair nearest, but as he made no invitation that I do the same, I kept my feet.

"And so you are clever," he said.

I gave a long nod, as if to bow. "As a shepherd has naught to sell but his mutton, I have naught but my wits. And as I am not yet starved, they do find some commerce, but in a more common market than your grace would frequent. I do fear that my wits might taste stale compared to the finer meats of your habit."

Carey gave me a long and inscrutable look, an appraising, then drew a swallow from his goblet. "I suspect you know well enough the quality of your mutton, sir, and I suspect also you have found few voices which please you as well as your own."

"I had, sir, until I made your company, but I am now better served to hear yours."

Carey rose from his chair and made a slow circuit of the room. A decade older than me, a half-head taller, he was a powerful man gone some heavy now. But still with muscled shoulders and arms that no doubt could cleave well with a blade. His clothes were of fine material and yet simple manufacture with little of the excess adornment common to his station. I feared to learn whether his plain dress was due to some Puritan sensibility or from mere simplicity of habit. But thought, too, this. My experience with men of his rank was either at court or at our theatre when they graced our performances, but in either case, public occasions for which they would dress to proclaim their station. Ours was a private meeting and in his quarters and it sudden seemed likely that his dress merely reflected what little effort my rude company required.

His passage of the room complete, he stopped before me, just enough distant that I could not say his intent was to intimidate, but also could not say other.

"You are concerned, I assume, for the future of your company?" he asked. "Having lost the weight of my father's favour?"

I cleared my throat. "As a shareholder of the company I am, of course, bound to consider its interests. But I would not so sully your father's memory as to broach such matters so close in wake of his passing. There is time enough, always, for business, but this time should be reserved to the fond memory of your father."

Carey stood stock still a moment, considering me. Then he spoke, a harsher air to his voice. "Did you think I summoned you that we might embrace my father in fond reminisce? Do you imagine, sir, that, should I wish some company to celebrate my memories of him, I would reach first to you? A commoner, and not even of my personal acquaintance?" He looked darkly at me for a long moment with eyes that held both anger and hurting.

As I could think of no safe answer, I answered not.

"What business could I have with you, sir," he said, "save business?"

A misstep. A volatile man, Carey, and though he did at first act in good fellowship, he was quick to return our speaking to the bounds of our divergent standings. I bowed.

"My lord, I fear my own love for your father did colour my judgment. I am here as your humble servant only, in such capacity as you may require and no other. I do beg pardon for my offence, asking that you know it stemmed only from an excess of affection."

Carey let out a soft snort. "I am told you are of the country, only marginally schooled, and yet your tongue can dance a jig about the truth as well as any of the over-read mandarins at court with whom daily congress is my unfortunate duty."

He paused a moment, a slight slackening in his expression that had me think I was to safe or at least safer ground.

"There is always time for business," he continued. " As a man much of this world, I understand that that time is always now. It is the memories of men that must wait their moment until some respite grants us leave to consider them. My father will always be in my mind, but my hands now must be about his work."

"As you will, my lord."

And his expression changed again, but this time to the blank slate of a clerk tending a store. "I am prepared to continue patronage of your company in the custom that my father has established. The Queen will soon, I am told, name me to continue my father's office as the Lord Chamberlain, and, as such, I will decide those players chosen to entertain at court and to otherwise distract her Majesty as she desires."

I bowed deeply. "I am most grateful, my lord."

"But in return I will require a service."

"My lord," I interrupted, "you should know I already have begun work on a play to be performed in your father's memory–"

Carey held up his hand. "Such plans as you may have to honour my father should proceed as you deem his honour merits. The service I require is of another nature." Carey paused for a moment, breathed deep, again sat in the chair, his face now masked with troubles.

"How closely did you know my father, Will?"

"Our company was well blessed by his favour, my lord, and on those occasions when we performed at court I had chance to speak with him. He was forthright in his opinion, kind in his manner, fair in our dealings, and I have always thought of him only well."

Carey nodded, facing away and looking out through the mullioned window into the evening, the edge of the distant sky turning the same red as the claret I had nearly finished.

"He was a soldier first, as am I," Carey said, "and not by temperament suited to court, some here finding his manner rough. He was better loved by those at arms than by the untried souls that stalk these halls to curry to the Queen's favour. Save for the Queen herself, by whom he was loved best of all."

"I should trust a soldier's opinion as to the measure of a man above all save the Queen's, my lord."

"He loved me well and I him," said Carey, "Does your father yet live?"

"By the grace of God, he does."

"And do you hold him dear?"

"I do, sir."

Carey nodded, his face turning back from the window to me.

"Then we have a bond not so common as it might be in a better world be. Few men know their fathers scarce at all, and fewer still with any affection. And yet all I have learned of worth, I learned at his hand."

"Then his loss must afflict you greatly, my lord."

Carey sat back in his chair, drew in a long breath, and let it out slowly in a sigh. "He lived three score years and ten, was an able soldier, held well those offices to which he was appointed, raised to manhood two sons, and goes to God as unstained, I think, as any man of his years and experience can pray to be. I should greet his passing with only peace." Carey raised his goblet and drank it dry. "Save for my dreams."

"Your dreams, my lord?"

"My dreams. Which are my curse and the purpose of your visit." Carey stood from his chair and resumed pacing the room, a troubled man who could find no peace when still and seemed intent to chase it. "You are aware, I am sure, that I did not until of late frequent your revels. It was my father who asked that I consider them, as he found them instructive. Such plays as you authored in particular. And I have noted that dreams figure in them often."

"I find dreams a useful device in a story, my lord."

Carey turned to face me. "In a story only?"

I paused to consider his question, sensing a growing risk in our conversation that seemed deeper on either side of any answer. "I think we know sometimes in sleeping truths we cannot yet know or bear in waking, my lord. That I do believe."

His face shifted again, now to the resolute stone that could mean either an uncertain man who would pretend certainty, or a certain man who wished he were not. "The truth I know in sleeping is that my father was murdered. Last night he came thrice to me in dreams, once each hour from that late moment in which I finally slept until dawn, and each dream the same. It is night and he is in the garden, which is curious, because he paid no concern to the garden – that was my mother's province and in later years they were not frequent in each other's company. He stands before me in the unfamiliar garden and tells me he cannot enjoy that peace that he has earned until stand punished those hands that stilled his heart, hands that had sworn they did love him. And he then holds out to me his right hand – a hand already red and poxed with corruption beyond what could be achieved in the short hours of his death."

Carey held my eyes for a long moment. "Then he charges me to his death avenge."

Carey paused, but I did not feel it was yet my place to speak.

"I will have those hands that stilled his heart found, Will. And I will have them punished."

Again, I waited to speak, beginning to divine his purpose and hoping he would say something further to prove my understanding false.

Carey stalked about the room, both tired and restless.

"My father wished I watch your plays for instruction, and what I have learned is this: we reveal ourselves through our words, our movements, in every passing moment. Both with intent and in secret we reveal ourselves, sometimes even to our detriment. This is one of your lessons."

He looked at me as if for confirmation.

"What plays I write are entertainments only and I have secreted in them no lessons. I do not pretend to scholarship."

By his clouded features, I could see this answer did not please him.

"Humility when true doth credit a man, but when false doth make him false," Carey said. "I find too much art in your efforts to believe you think them only as bangles for clowns. If I have learned lessons from your plays, then you have taught them. And thus you are at least part scholar, part teacher. *Igitur ex fructibus eorum cognoscetis eos.* And to have made this lesson so plain, to have authored such words and scenes by which such revelations are made so clear, and for these scenes to so close mimic life, you must be well able to see revealed in others those things that they would hold secret."

The danger to either side of his words was almost full plain now and my path across it exceedingly narrow.

"Any writer must observe the world close, my lord, and then steal from it such metal that can be wrought into that which he imagines. I claim no special gift beyond that."

Carey turned to face me direct, a new face now, a soldier's face, his most true face. His voice was sharp.

"I do believe you discern my purpose, and now attempt to withhold from me the only gift for which I have current need. Claim it or not, I ascribe it to you. So, lest you are prepared to call your patron a fool in his own house, you will admit to it."

I merely nodded. Carey turned away again, looking out the window into the nearly full dark.

"I believe my father murdered, but our law has no method by which to ferret out the killer. If I make the accusation, those in the household will be considered

– more or less vigorously depending on their station – and those in my father's familiar subject to some uninformed scrutiny. I have faith that, in short order, the charge having been made, some poor soul will be made to suffer for it, at Tyburn or at the Tower, according to his birth. But I have no faith that the truth will be served. If some man of standing should be chosen for the axe, it will be to fit some agenda that will be forwarded by his death. More likely, a servant will fall suspect, be subject to those gentle persuasions by which confessions are gained, and then be taken to the tree and hanged. And thus the charge will be answered, but the truth of my father's murder will be buried as deeply as his body."

Carey turned back to me. "I think you a man who knows truth when he sees it, and a man by long habit accustomed to observing those guiles by which we conceal it. So, you will learn the truth of my father's death. That is the service I require."

Now the danger was plain and my path across it gone. By what station did Carey imagine I would have standing to so much as speak to the Lord Chamberlain's family, his household, his circle at court? And should there truly be a murderer amongst that assemblage, how could I hope to protect myself from such machinations as they would have at their disposal to thwart my efforts and ensure my own bad end? And yet to decline Carey's request would mean the loss of his patronage, and, Carey's ill favour toward us being plain, we would likely not secure any new patron of standing, which would make our failure certain. Not only as a company, but we members too. Having been marked with noble disfavour, we would sink first in the ship of company, and then drown in the troubled seas of our individual ruin.

"My lord, I am true saddened at your father's passing and at the pain it must cause you, and doubly so for you to know it murder. Had I such powers by which I could unmask the assassin, I would do so, even without the promise of your patronage, as your father was a friend to me and to our company and is by us well loved. But I fear you see in me gifts I do not recognise in myself. Nor can I conceive of any ploy by which I could gain sufficient confidence or commerce with the Lord Chamberlain's circles by which to make even the most subtle inquiries."

Carey waved a dismissive hand, as though my objections were but a vapour and easily dissipated. "For ploys, I do not require your art, sir. I was born at court. Though I prefer a soldier's life, I have spent such time here as to speak ploy as a second tongue. My father's household and the court will be informed that I have commissioned the celebrated playwright William Shakespeare to draft a work in his memory, and that I request their forbearance in entertaining your questions as you gain insight into my father's celebrated history and character. Any that will not answer to you will answer to me. You have, already in this room, shown sufficient guile to use that pretended mission to serve my true one."

Carey turned away before I could answer, striding

to a table at the far end of the room and returning with a scroll tied with a ribbon and sealed with wax.

"Of course, such conversations would be easier were you a gentleman. The small rank of gentleman is held in only low value by most at court, but it will at least separate you from the vast sea of common on which we of higher station float. The College of Heralds has too long considered the matter of your father's claim to arms, and a gentleman he now is, which makes you a gentleman born. The College's fee has been paid, and you may consider that payment my real commission for your fictional play."

To have such knowledge of my family and to have discerned so easy that favour with which he could most likely move me, it was clear that Carey's mind was as sharp as his sword was reputed to be. Knowing he had looked so hard into me and into my family offered no comfort in these circumstances, but instead added to my dread.

He passed to me the scroll, the seal of the College facing up. I paused for only a moment before taking it, understanding that in its taking I accepted not only the station to which I had so long aspired but also whatever fresh hell I had by the lever of my own appetites given Carey the power to admit me.

"I thank you humbly, my lord. My father will be greatly pleased."

Carey nodded. "As to the matter of your company, it will take some days to have drafted the necessary licence and charters. And as I am currently distracted with my father's funeral and other matters of his estate, I imagine that we can conclude the business of the theatre at such time when we also conclude this other business now at hand. As for your father, Shakespeare, I have heard rumours that he is a man of questionable allegiance, at least in matters of faith. As no proof of these whisperings has yet been offered, I am happy to consider these charges falsely made by those who would exploit him with the legal blackmail made by whispering the name of God. A foul practice, and one with which too many entertain themselves, using the mask of faith to cover the sin of avarice. But as I have now through my own offices assisted in his status as gentleman, I would, for my own honour, have to act – and harshly – should I find I have aided a Papist in his seditions against the Queen."

He paused for a moment, still in his soldier's face, his eyes now a message that asked no question, required no answer and brooked no dispute.

He turned and strode from the room much like a soldier. His message was clear. Whether in thanks to his father, in the interests of the company, in service of my own greed, or in fear for those travails to which he could at his whim make me and my family subject, I was to be his good servant.

CHAPTER 3

I left Somerset House in the full dark. That morning, I'd had first to wash, as the previous night's excesses had come at dear expense to my hygiene, and then to cross from my rooms in Bishopsgate to the theatre in Shoreditch in order to be properly attired for my meeting with Carey. I had made way to the bridge and taken a boat to Somerset House so as to arrive at my appointment unlathered and still scented of such poor perfumes as I had at my employ. But the cost of a boat was beyond my usual custom and the uncertainties that I now considered gave rise to an impulse to husband what resources I could. I chose to walk the mile back to my rooms. It being night, I was glad I also had secured from our costume's store of arms a rapier, as being armed allowed me to feign such status as those common to Somerset House would hold. In the dark of the city, I valued that blade for its true purpose.

London was a balm to me and an excitement both. Many from my more pastoral roots found the city's tumult, chaos, and odour discomfiting and could not be soon enough away. While I would ready admit that the smells of the city far exceeded in both variety

and offence any I had encountered in Stratford,
the thrumming constant of its unbounded human
agency found in my soul a sympathetic chord so that
I too did thrum as though in harmony with the city's
own heart.

Stratford in the years since my birth had changed
scarce at all, so that even now when I would return
after long absence it was each time the same. But
London constantly leafed in every direction, both
out and up – new streets ivying across former fields,
old buildings suddenly sprouting added floors as
though their roots had gained new sustenance from
the energy emanating from the crush that ever more
crowded every lane and alley.

In Stratford, every face was known. And not the
face only, but also the facts and habits of each person,
so that you walked fettered by your own history
and that of your father and his and his, fenced from
birth within a pasture of expectations from whence
you might escape only at the cost of reputation and
livelihood. As my father was a glover, then I was a
glover's son and destined a glover to be.

But the tens and hundreds of thousands that
peopled the streets of London offered in their excess
a jungle of anonymity in which any man could
invent of himself a creature akin to his own longings.
And the soil of that jungle seemed enriched with a
kind of humus grown from the constant droppings
of ideas and the random interchange of the new and
the old, the proven with the previously unimagined,
so that daily some advance in science or art or even

just whimsy sprang forth in odd and wondrous flower. And then each flower drew some curious bee that would carry its essence to some other and some other and some other until the riotous blooming of ideas enchanted me, and gave hope that our lives and their ends might be other than links in a chain of bondage forged in the dull fires of custom, but might instead be fashioned by our own hands in the manner of our own dreaming.

London made me think that man had supplanted God as the prime agency of our human fortunes, not in the stink of pride, but with his blessing.

It was in such reverie that I made my way east along the river, deciding it too late to return my borrowed finery to the theatre. Instead I wanted only a meal and an ale from one of the taverns near my rooms, and then to write, the tensions of my meeting with Carey giving rise to that mental tumescence I could relieve only through the outflow of words. The ghost of a man's father, beseeching him in dream to avenge his murder – it was a perfect opening for a work that, on this dark walk, began gestating in my mind. I would set it in Danish lands, I think, their northern gloom more suited to this tragic tale's needs than the sunny and happier lands of the Italian states that often offered the brighter set for my comedies.

London was not just the cradle of the wondrous, however, but also the Stygian nursery of evils, both those familiar and their infinite and vile siblings. From across the river, I could hear the roar from one of the bear-baiting circles, where a noble beast would stand tethered as dogs were loosed to tear its flesh while it swatted and snapped at its tormentors, both bear and dog making unwilling wager of their lives while the crowd, in drunken bloodlust, wagered only their coins.

The infected horror of the crowd's roar offered full reminder that London's jungle offered its anonymous disguise to every appetite, wholesome or no, and that not just playwrights were drawn hence from our pastoral homes. Brigands, too, were drawn by the gravity of the city's multitudes, knowing its lanes offered more purses for their hands and throats for their blades. I took care with the passing of each alley and doorway. A man alone in the London night took chance with his purse and life, and a woman alone held her virtue cheap. So, I kept my guard, relaxing only upon reaching Bishopsgate and turning north the short way left to my door.

Relaxed too soon. From the dark maw of a court behind me and to my left, I heard the sudden scrape of feet moving with instant and urgent purpose. Alarmed, I turned quickly – my hand already reaching for the hilt of the rapier on my left side. I could see death's avaricious smile in the curved arc of a blade shining faint in the dim lamplight as it slashed at me. I have done much playing at fencing, the clash of swords being an aphrodisiac to any audience. On the stage, though, the steps of that dance are predetermined. Now, for the first time, I would step to its tune for mortal stakes.

It was the rush and savagery of my attacker's initial attempt that saved me, as I was able to duck under his blade so that his own impetus threw him past me. To my fortune, he caught his foot on an uneven cobble and staggered a few steps more before he could turn. I thought for a moment to seize on this happy accident and lunge after him, but that impulse owed to the same hot blood and recklessness that had cost my attacker his advantage. I chose instead deliberation and cunning, and so set my feet as I had been taught and levelled my blade.

My balance was sure, my mind marvellously emptied by the drug of this violent practice. I knew in that instant a rare moment of pure animal peace, the unsullied certainty of a creature wholly engaged in vital action. It was as if that moment had been dipped whole from the river of time and frozen to immortal ice so that the man I was within it was neither the man I had been before nor the one I would be hence. A moment in which the present was distilled so pure and my senses so open to it that even this street that had been my common path each morning and night was now seen new, the rough feel of the cobbles beneath my feet, the uneven orange dance of light from the tavern rippling the wall to my left into a kind of water, the sound of a dog barking near and the lower answer of a larger dog answering distant, a hint of black eternity poxed with stars in veiled teasing glimpses behind a scud of clouds. A moment invested with its own sacredness, a religion requiring a faith so entire that it admitted no doubt, no memory of past woe or old sin, no anticipation of future care or unborn worry, no contemplation of current want or need, but instead only the tip of my own blade, held steady before me and the tip of my opponent's blade and its glittering want some few feet distant. Those alone were this moment's gospel, its philosophy entire, and I was their devoted apostle. And I felt lithe and free and possible, unburdened for the first time since my distant-remembered youth from that chain of consciousness in which we bind ourselves with every new-learned fear and need.

My opponent had turned. The light was behind him and his face hidden in both shadow and a cowl. His weapon, too, levelled in stony certainty and naked malice. But then the door of the tavern opened to my right, spilling both light and two men into the church of our private sacrament. My opponent ran north, gone at once like a spectre into the bowels of night.

The men from the tavern paused on its lighted verge, seeing the fleeing man and my bared weapon.

"Shall we summon the bailiff?" asked one.

I shook my head. "A thief only, I'm sure," I said, "I am grateful for your timing, as I fear he had such business as he wished done in private and not performed in your audience."

"Then we wish you well, sir, and are glad to have offered our accidental service," said the second man, and they left toward the river.

And I stood alone on the filth-slicked cobbles, the sudden grace of combat dissolved, my breath coming in rushes, and my heart in that moment beating a tune so fierce and out of tune with the rhythm of the city it loved that I feared I would never feel London's embrace again.

With the familiar cloak of thought and memory again my burden and with care returned to me, I thought this: what thief chose an armed man as victim? Why choose a wolf in a city so filled with sheep? And was it only happenstance that he had lain in wait so close to my own door?

CHAPTER 4

I was late to the theatre the next day, as both my secret charge from Carey and the attack on my person had left me vexed and so unsettled in my constitution that I could neither write nor sleep. A candle and much paper was wasted in my attempt at the first, and not a little port wasted in my attempt at the next. Only in the blush of dawn did I at last meet the embrace of Morpheus – which was not gentle, but instead a fierce slumber poxed with dreams that so infected my thinking that my mind felt as a mouth that had consumed some corrupted thing. I was so sicklied o'er with the pale cast of thought that, in passing the court whence the swordsman had sprung the night previous, I gave it so wide a birth that I stepped in some filth dropped to the street from a window overlooking that court from the far side. I cursed my foolishness, knowing better than to walk so near the buildings, and there being nothing to fear in the court by the light of day save a drunk seated against the wall. He raised his head briefly at my passing, watching me with baleful eyes set astride a monstrous nose that had suffered greatly, I think, from some dire insult. It progressed from his face in such volume and varied direction as to appear a kind of growth.

The company was in mid-scene when I first reached the opening to the stage, and so I held back to the shadow to observe. Once known, I would be beset by inquiries concerning my meeting with Carey, and any further rehearsal would be of little value, all fixed instead on news and speculation. Burbage, at least, was of a better mood, and he, being more relaxed, put also Jenkins at his ease so that their scene read well and the production seemed ready.

At the scene's end, Burbage makes speech to Jenkins, and did so now with such soft art and subtle gesture that methinks the supplicative adoration that lit Jenkins's face was only half pretended. At their embrace I felt a stirring in my own heart of my remembered youth, when love still seemed a wonder and had not yet suffered from the poor ministrations to which I since have made it subject. When their embrace broke, there was an uncommon silence in the company, all recognizing that awkward spell we cast when we with only men perform those moments that do a woman's place require.

I stepped forth. "Did we at last shave Jenkins's ass, Burbage, that you can now speak to him so sweet? Or have you found in his manly wool a fond remembrance of those sheep with which you so oft make congress?'

The tension of the scene's soft words and long embrace were broken and the company roared in relief that I knew was less the product of my words than of their timing. Burbage turned, smiling, crossed the stage in his actor's graceful pace, and seized me by my shoulders.

"The prodigal scribe returns! And by his words I am afeared we now know his appetites and all must wonder, when he makes that soft talk with which he hath undone so many dresses, whether he means 'I love you,' or 'I love ewe'."

And again the company bellowed, and we were bathed in that good fellowship that is so oft only expressed in our barbs and taunts.

"But come," said Burbage, taking my arm and leading me to the edge of the stage, where we were seated and the company formed around. "What word from Carey?"

It felt unnatural to speak false to my fellows, so I hewed my words to be true in their facts if not in their spirit, for I was not at liberty to share Carey's mission. "He wishes to continue his father's place as our patron, and such matters as will make it official should conclude within August," I said, full knowing that such conclusion hinged on my unsure ability to put at ease his mind on the matter of his father's death, and that I was giving all present certain hope when instead they were in uncertain peril.

"Huzzah!" cried Burbage, springing from his seat to his feet with his special grace, so that he could take his stance, and his words became his performance – that being, I have learned, his only true speaking. For Burbage, all the world is a stage.

"Will, we did just this morning suffer the company of some members of the Admiral's Men. Alleyn, of course, two other players, and Henslowe – who continues to feed those dogs from his purse and, if we credit rumour, will have funds in another theatre in Bankside. They did sweetly false pretend condolence on our sponsor's death, but swaggered about the boards as though measuring them for their own use. And I answered that our good Will had already made congress with Carey, and that I knew no other – certainly not among their number – with the charm or wit by which to so certainly assure our fortunes."

Heminges, while seeming much comforted by the news of Carey's blessing, seemed also less certain that fortune shone as our sun alone. "They, too, have seen Carey," he said, "or they were on their way to. Or at least so they say."

"When?" I asked.

"From here they were to Somerset, by Carey's own invitation, if they be not false. And Henslowe has oft with his purse secured such blessings as he could not by merit."

This news troubled me, but I took pains to make it light, as I could see no gain from making unsure the minds of my fellows. "Carey is soon to be Lord Chamberlain and, by such office, will have truck with all the companies, even still remaining our good sponsor. That the Lord Admiral's Men should envision this invitation as some chance at a better patron than they now hold is no surprise – for they have never met a noble arse up which they would not stick their tongues so far that, should such lord sup soup, they do taste onions. Be at ease, sirs. Remember, Henslowe's purse may seem swollen to us, but it is a flea's sack compared to Carey's."

Which was greeted with general tittering of approval, although Heminges's face was still clouded.

"I do not know Carey, Will, but if he be a dog, then he may harbour fleas. They asked after you, too," he said.

"As they would," I said, "my being absent."

"It was the manner of their asking," Heminges said. "A chiding, as though they expected your absence and were trying to cloud us with thought of such ills as your absence could portend."

I bowed slightly to him. "I was late abed, having written much into the night. I am true sorry if my tardiness caused you worry."

He shook his head. "We all know your habits and your hours, so your tardiness offered no concerns. It was the slyness of their manner. Henslowe said that we did on you too much depend and asked Burbage if his steady diet of Shakespeare had not yet clumped his bowels, whether he would not prefer to ape words from some fresh quill."

"To which I answered," said Burbage, "that, should they find such words as worth this ape, it would be the first time in my remembering. Their dross is better suited to George Alleyn and his fellow monkeys, monkeys being smaller, while we apes require words fitting our stature."

"And did Alleyn receive this well?" I asked. Alleyn was the Admiral's Men's leading player and, while slight of stature, famous for his readiness to take insult and for his ease to temper.

"Not well," said Heminges, "though whether in offence to Burbage's words or to Henslowe's overture – by which he may have taken that Henslowe would prefer Burbage as his player – I do not now. Both, I should imagine."

I made a shrug. "Still, I hear only the usual sort of banter and nothing to give alarm."

"It was Henslowe's last words, Will, given over his shoulder as he and the other players dragged Alleyn to the street. He said he preferred several playwrights in his stable such that he could saddle whichever horse to which the public gave its current favour. And that, by having many, he did not have to love too well any that he must leave e'er long, Saying to that in these days no man should count on another's company far beyond the morrow, and that, with you even now absent, and at a time of such crisis as Carey's death presents, should we not wonder if we had packed too much of our fortune on the back of a single ass."

Heminges paused, looking a long moment into an unseen distance. Then he turned back to me. "There is villainy in that man, Will, and he gave me chill. It was his smile, as though he knew some ill that I yet did not."

And it gave me chill, too, to wonder by what magic Henslowe expected me away. He was a new sort of creature to which London gave rise: a man of no talents who himself could produce no product, no art, no service of want to his fellows, and yet did somehow attach his purse to others' endeavours. And in such fashion that his grew fat whilst theirs ended thin, as though by some perverse alchemy through which he did transmute by avarice alone the labours of others to his own gain. As he had no art, he also had no scruple.

Bankside, being across the river and yet convenient to both the bridge and the many boats that ferried there, was newly swollen with all manner of entertainments, which were now banned within the city proper. And if the now-deafening jingle of coin there exchanged was the new music of Henslowe's attentions, then those of us who lived by such entertainments should best take good care to mind Henslowe's dance.

CHAPTER 5

As I had thought, the Company was of no mood to return to rehearsal, our discussion of my audience with Carey and the portents of the Lord Admiral's Men's visit being too much of mind. The Company retired to one of the Shoreditch taverns in that human habit of turning what little news we have over continually in hopes of finding from some new angle a benefit we had not at first uncovered. But I was of no heart for this talk, knowing I must be false and my mind still infected with the pestilent mood of the previous evening's adventures and morning's unseen dreams. So, I took my leave and made toward the Royal Exchange on Threadneedle Street where I could distract myself with an even fouler task too long avoided.

In Stratford, the day was marked at each turn by only those faces I knew well, but in London, the unexpected meeting of any acquaintance is a curiosity. And so I found it passing strange to notice also on Threadneedle Street that man I had first seen that morning asleep against the wall in the courtyard near my rooms, his nose marking him for my remembrance. He paid me no mind as I purchased first my papers and then my inks, and he, too, did make a purchase, and could thus be only about his own business. Yet somehow his loiterings at this booth and that kept him always in my view, and me in his. I made note not only of his nose but also his size and bearing and manner of dress so that, should he seem too oft in my company, I could take proper care.

My purchases complete and this minor distraction addressed, I steeled myself finally to make to the end of the arcade and the fishmonger's stall, at which I had some hard business I would at last have done.

I am at heart unchurched, though I do bend my knee in whichever direction the Crown commands for my own safety's sake. Still, I am not unfaithed. I am each day reminded, if only by an unexpected flower, a happy fragrance, a gifted tankard, of the unearned and pervasive benevolence that girds us each against the pestilence of our banal condition. What beauties we enjoy we neither fashion nor earn, and yet they alone save us from the living damnation of our petty grubbing.

In that spirit I had, on a June day, like Saul, confronted a grace so bedazzling that I did, for a time, suppose a new faith. On that day, I also had made to Threadneedle Street to secure the supplies of my writerly habits when the girl in the fishmonger's stall at the edge of the Exchange called out in her sparkled voice so as to gain my attention and perhaps my commerce. In seeing her I felt as though suddenly gifted with some new sense, felt both with my heart and from lower down, such sense as to make the eyes and ears and nose and tongue and skin feel envy that they can only each in part experience what I could feel in total.

Her eyes shone with a blue innocence to make one imagine there be some other world painted in a palette beyond our imagining, these eyes only having escaped to our drab sphere to remind us there be gods. The gentle sweep of her shoulders and neck rose to support a face and head of such perfect proportion and aspect that the sight of them fell on my eyes like a smell and roused in me some appetite so unfamiliar that I did not at first think to call it lust. A cascade of hair – coloured both in saffron and in a blush of red echoing the flame she had already in me kindled – seemed spun by angelic spiders that could in their web secure the affections of all who looked on it. And twin swales coloured with both cream and light disappeared behind the cover of her rough dress like a temptation to madness, so that you would either have her or tear from your own body those now needless orbs you knew your eyes to be.

I am wifed but, being most times a bachelor in London whilst she is in far Stratford, I have treated the surly bounds of that churched alliance with the same elasticity to which they so oft have been stretched by even our most royal personages, and with the same diligence and honour with which our churchmen protect their pledged chastity. For I can envision no God who would from a poor scribe demand fealty beyond that of those kings and priests that he hath, in wisdom unbound by human frailty, chosen with his own hand. And while these august men have oft plucked the first buds from God's flowering, womanly harvest, I instead have dallied only with those flowers already fully and freely in bloom. It has been a mutual kindness we have bestowed upon the other, a corporal mercy by which we have shared in those delights so heavenly granted and, having done so, caged the more savage beasts of our less holy appetites that would loose themselves unbound on less willing flesh. And thus conscience does make lechers of us all.

And then I beheld the fishmonger's daughter and in that moment abandoned any pretence, any costume of thought, by which previously I had made polite my ravening lust. That she was scarcely beyond a child mattered not. That our first casual mutterings revealed her unschooled and naïve – an innocent who could be led, and trustingly, into a forest of words within which I could ease her loose from the tethers of her moral bearings and lead her to betray to me, solely for the amusement of my trivial wants, that which to her was most precious and the province, through the agency of a husband, only of God – this mattered not. For the flame of her beauty, like the magic fires of Sinai, consumed not itself, but burned away instead all that it was not. In my mind was left only my desire for her, any contrivance of decency charred to nothingness in the face of this seductive inferno. I knew only my longings and my own gifts. Having been told in countless beds that I

am comely of both face and form, that I have an easy
wit, and that I speak words that lay lightly on the
ear, I would now with these godly tools ply for Satan
that unplied flesh.

And so began my artful campaign. My first gentle
affirmations of her beauty. A brief touch; a lingering
touch; a first, chaste kiss. All the while I oiled her
fall with subtle reminders of how many imagined
sins she already had committed – until, still within
the bounds of any commandment, she felt herself so
foreign to the deserved love of God that she thought
herself already damned and surrendered completely
to me on a borrowed bed, gifting a mattress soiled
with the effluent of a thousand whores the sacrament
of her unspoiled blood as I plunged once more into
the breach.

I gorged on this ambrosial apple unsated, gaining
no sustenance. I was become a beast hollowed out
by unholy hungers, mad with ravening, debasing the
child through acts previously only imagined. After
this carnival of perversity, whatever ethereal light
had informed her features was instead transmuted
into dead ash – her eyes less animate than those
of the fishes she once had offered – and she was
become a mirror that held only horrors for me. In it I
somehow saw both this wilting thing that spread her
now rot-mottled pedals with torporous indifference
and that rare perfect flower that had first opened
unto me with trembling, fearful resistance. And I
now wept to think what I had done to a creature of
such beauty, and how she had for a time made me

think there be a heaven and that I might be worthy of it.

And in my shame, I visited our borrowed chambers no more, despite her messages of increasing desperation – each asking what offence she had given that did cause my absence and assuring me of her still tender affections, each reminding me of that grace she did somehow still possess and that I had lost forever.

And so, steeling myself finally, I visited her stall to make what apologies I could and try to convince her that what virtues she may think she had surrendered I had truly stolen. She was faultless in our tawdry enterprise, and it was my true hope that her aspect could regain such light and blessing as I had, in my wanton cruelty, put out.

But her stall at the end of the Exchange stood shuttered. When I inquired of the tanner at the stall next, I was told she had the day before thrown herself from the bridge, thus making to the river an offering of the only gift I had not yet taken.

And so I continued with my business. No doubt the revulsion I felt would in time recede, the proximate gravity of this vile exercise would shrink far enough away that it would no longer pull the tide of my guilt to consciousness. Thus would I live my days in such comforts as my poor memory allowed, forestalling that torment I suffered at this moment until such day as I shuffle off this mortal coil and am reacquainted with my true bride – who, with dead eyes, will joyfully lead me to her befouled mattress, where I shall be made to suffer full for my sins, and for all time.

And so I returned to my quarters, the light again failing as I turned up Bishopsgate, armed now only with my bundles and taking no heed of the gaping dark on all sides. Should I hear again that urgent rush and see that flash of steel, I thought simply to surrender my neck to the blade rather than my back to my mattress – being after my last sleep and this day's news much afraid to confront what dreams may come. But sleep I must, as tomorrow I was to report again to Somerset to begin my inquiries.

At my door, the landlord awaited bearing a message from Stratford. My son, Hamnet, was ill, and Anne wished I send home some funds for his care.

Thinking on Anne, I found myself overcome with fond remembrance of my youth, when first we met. I thought on the flowering of spirit her smile had then engendered. I knew now that such lovers as I had entertained in my years in London were just convenient vessels into which I had emptied my lust. In the fishmonger's daughter I had in sooth revisited the ghost of my own Anne's youth, and I wanted nothing more than to be again that besotted lad in his springtime, first meeting the wonders of both heart and flesh, not this jaded thing that now, even surrounded by the full promise of both, could no longer feel their warmth, neither on my flesh nor in my heart. I soft remembered that day when, when, betrothed but not yet wed, Anne gentle granted me her favours and I partook of that communion that pales the sacrament of any church into wanting sickness. Now, having broken faith with that communion, I in wanting sickness lived.

The death of the fishmonger's daughter pressed on my conscience, it being a murder in truth if not in consequence. In Stratford, a son I scarce knew, but in my fashion did love, lay ill, a son not many years younger than I had been when I did first taste his mother's love. I thought on that distant remembered boy and could but wonder how I had become the man I now am: celebrated by many, supposed by my fellows to be good, but in secret much fouled and, I feared, beyond any power of redemption.

CHAPTER 6

"Behold, Mother," said John Carey, the late Lord Chamberlain's second son, as they both entered that room to which I had been ushered upon presenting myself at Somerset for that day's appointment. "It is our dear brother's hired scribe, the newly minted gentleman. And in costume, no doubt so as to impress us with his reputation as a player as well, should George also need such services to portray Father in this glorious homage. Although, even given the late lord's not overly noble manner, I think I still find this Shakespeare's dress lacking."

I had again borrowed such costume as I could from the theatre's stores, but I could not even approximate in fashion the younger Carey's array, nor that of his mother. On their entrance, I made such courtesies as were required by our relative stations, but he crossed the room – seeming ignoring my obsequies – to a couch that bordered the large windows giving out onto the gardens beyond. Somerset House had first been the mansion of the late Duke of Somerset, but, upon his leaving his head on a scaffold at the Tower, had passed into possession of the Crown. It had been palace to Elizabeth in those years she was princess, before her ascendency, and its rich expanse now served home to some close members of her court, including the late Lord Chamberlain's family.

The younger Lord Carey sprawled onto the couch in an insouciant manner. "I'll not ask you to sit, Shakespeare, as I frankly find your errand tiresome and humour you only out of love to my good brother, who, as first born, has better reason than I to have loved our father well." Carey waved his hand in a foppish manner as to make the point that Somerset, having been his father's residence, would now be his brother's, and that he would continue here only at his brother's leave. "I would hope that standing might weary you, but I do suppose long hours making speech on stage will have trained you to tire our ears before we can hope to tire your legs."

"I do beg your leave for this intrusion, my lord," I said. "I, too, am here at some reluctance and only at your brother's charge. But having loved your father well for his long and good patronage of our company, I do hold your brother's commission to draft such work as will do him honour most dear and will approach it with my diligence. I shall impose for no minute longer than I have need."

"By your meandering speech, I suspect those minutes will number many, but I will relay to my brother your reluctance at his employ," Carey said. "So, the illustrious truths of our late lord. As even such trite entertainments as your kind do author must require a beginning, shall we start at his birth? It is rumoured my good father is the sire not of his own name but of no lesser person than the Good Henry, late king, making him not only the Queen's dear cousin, but in truth half her brother – and me, I fear, a distant nephew entitled by the misfortune of my later birth only to such scraps as might fall from such tables."

"My son forgets both himself and his manners," said Lady Carey, though not sharply, "though I am inclined to forgive his manners, as they are suspect even amongst our peers, and so I would not have him waste what good form he might manage in our current company. The late lord's name was Carey, as was his father's, and any thought otherwise is not your concern. Should you think to make some wit of it on stage or in rumour, as I do hold our reputation dear, I would devote my attentions to your misfortune."

"My mother, being Lady Carey, thinks much on the reputations that titles hold," the younger Carey added. "But for me, of Baron Carey, the name Baron held the more weight, but that, too, did pass to my brother. So, what reputation attaches to either Baron or Carey I count as his concern." He spread both arms wide in a kind of flourish. "I, being second born and no baron, am gratefully unburdened with such cares."

He had that sense of self and natural style that, were he of some other station, I would have offered to make him a player to our company – for in almost every work we require some evil foil to serve as counterweight to the hero of the play. These villains

are oft the favourites of the audience, as there is a
kind of freedom I think all do envy in giving oneself
over entirely to the pursuit of one's own appetites
and abandoning any pretence to social good or norm.
The younger Carey was hunger and greed entire and
nothing else, but wrapped well in style and costume.

I bowed. "I will author naught concerning the late
lord except that which will reflect on him honour,
my lady, as this is both my charge and my opinion."

"Then he shall in such play be only Baron Carey, if
not," she said, the last softly, "Earl."

Her son sat forward on the couch, his face a
malevolent mischief. "Oh, yes, you must include
that. When in his late illness my father was offered
by the good Queen to be made Earl, he did respond
that, as she had not seen fit to grant such honour in
life, he could not in right accept it in death. Evidently
he was desirous to gain whatever legend such selfless
act might lend to his dead honour rather than to gain
such lands, incomes, and benefits as it would lend to
the future comfort of his family. Is not this just the
sort of preening nobility that will best please both
my brother and your audience?"

"I shall make good note of the late lord's grace in
this instance, as it is admirable," I said.

"Oh, much admirable. For I, too, can now admire
from some distance such estates as I might have
enjoyed and the additional incomes with which
we could put paid to the claims of the various
bastard children who do seem to grow in the dark
shadow of my later father's appetites like summer

mushrooms. His estate now open to their claims, their own appetites are whetted by his imagined fortune, which, in truth, numbers scarce greater than his debts." He sank back into the cushions of his seating. "I suppose I should thank his appetites at least so far as concerning his lovely nurse, the sweet Mary in whom he took such comfort. I did inherit her after a fashion, but she proved a treat for the eyes only, and as I have stronger hungers in other parts, I turned her out in favour of a less comely but more available dish."

"And was the late lord loved well by his servants?"

The younger Carey coughed in scoff. "Are we now to measure a man by the love of his servants? Shall we ask the furniture, too, how well it enjoyed the press of his arse? I suppose better we should consider your love of him, as we have his patronage of players and other such leeches as he entertained to contain us in the poverty that does our humility ensure. Humility being godly, this was no doubt, was his righteous intent. To diminish his fortune so as to ensure our humility, for otherwise we would believe him such a careless steward that we suffer thus in accident "

"Such estate as there may be is the province of my elder son," Lady Carey interrupted, "so I do hope you will ignore speculation concerning it particulars coming from those ignorant of its contents. The late lord was much beloved of the Queen, even in his youth. In the late northern rising, where such Papists as did hope support from abroad rebelled against her rightful office, she placed him head of her armies, which he did command with much nerve and skill, securing her kingdom and her constant future favour, which was much expressed in his later appointments. Beyond which, I can think of little that would offer drama worth your ink." By which speech she meant, I think, my dismissal.

"If I may further beg your leave," I said, "you did say that the Queen offered him to be made Earl in his final illness, but I had thought his death sudden according to your elder son's remarks."

"He had these last weeks suffered what the doctors credited as some corruption of his lungs and seemed most near his death, at which time the Queen did offer and he did refuse. But he did for some few days rally, before that pestilence that had previous plagued him returned anew and fiercely, and claimed him in short hours," she said.

"In which hours his brave honour fled him," said the younger Carey, "Poxes about the mouth and hands robbed his speech, and he instead cried womanly tears as though his bedskirts were his daily and not his nightly attire. Would that the Queen had offered him Earl then, when he no voice to refuse."

A pox on his hands, I noted, as in the elder Carey's dreams.

CHAPTER 7

"I should think the world glad that your kind have the theatre for your craft, lest you put your minds in earnest to such dark ends as you so oft put them in fiction," the apothecary said, his tankard again empty and raised to signal for yet another fill. I had before taken his advice on matters of poison as I considered such agencies that my characters might use in their less-noble endeavours, and in the guise of such consultancy did again ask his company at a tavern of his frequent betwixt Somerset and Bishopsgate.

"I believe you glad there be a theatre, because what coin I earn at its art so oft doth fill your cup," I replied.

"You would begrudge a man the cost of his service?" he asked.

"Methinks I could better afford your actual wares than the ale needed to lubricate your tongue."

"Alas, mine is a solitary profession and I do spend long hours alone with my potions. And so my tongue doth rust from lack of custom and requires much balm before it can reclaim its art."

I laughed at the old man, who, though gaunt and

homely in his aspect such that one would imagine
his manner drear, was in fact good company.

"And I take it from your speech that your faculties
are recovered?"

His tankard replenished, he held up a finger, and
drew half of it in a long draught. "Just now. So, what
vile scheme can I help concoct?"

I leaned forward, the tavern loud and no ear
seeming turned to our speaking, but my wanting
still such privacy as could be possible. "I have a
character who did for some weeks suffer an ailment
of the lungs that greatly troubled his breathing such
that he was feared soon dead, but from which he
seeming recovered. Then the pestilence did sudden
return, marking his mouth and hands with pox,
stealing his voice, and causing such pain that for the
brief hours before his death, he cried as though a
woman. And I need know if this follow the course of
some known disease and his death be of nature, or
if it more closely mark some poison, and thus mean
him murdered."

The apothecary paused, his tankard half to his
mouth, and looked at me from beneath the tangle
of white hair that framed his brows. "And pray tell,
Will, how is it that you must ask me what ill has
befallen some character of your own creation? They
live and die at your hand and at your pleasure and
by what agency you decide."

In my thirst to divine the method of Lord Carey's
demise, I had poorly considered the logic of my
question, and did now need quick to offer some

dramatic device to explain my lapse, less the apothecary, who be no fool, ask further into my affairs. The master I now served was most jealous of my confidence.

"There's the rub. I wish in this play for the manner of this character's death to be mysterious – for he is a man of some station and with not few enemies – so that his fellows must puzzle the nature of his passing, unsure even if it be murder. And so I imagined such scene as I have described. I did think the loss of speech convenient so that, should some evil aim be true, and even if he knows its actor, he cannot speak the name. I have only yet started, and before proceeding further did want your good counsel so that the direction the story may pursue does not ring false in its nature."

The apothecary sat back and drew again from his tankard, the cup sounding near empty when set back again to table. But the apothecary was not yet holding it up for a fill as was his habit, and on his face those troubles that framed his first question seemed only half stilled by my response.

"And the pox, Will? What of that?"

I laughed and waved my hand as though the pox were a pittance and said, "Oh, the pox. That can go or stay as best fits, but the crowds do love some grotesque display, and their fear of plague is such that a good pox doth much discomfit them, and so I do like to use a pox as I can."

The apothecary shook his head with a soft laugh and drained what small drops remained in his cup, holding it up again to be filled. "The cruel nature of your wiles much amuses me, Will, on those occasions when I am blessed with the secrets of their devising."

The maid again filled his cup and took my coin. "So, to your case. For his initial distress to proceed over some weeks, methinks it be some natural sickness. For such poisons that are in common employ generally work in haste, although one skilled in the art could, I suppose, deliver doses so gradual in their malady that they would mimic the natural decay of illness. But they would need daily commerce with your victim. No – and here you can use your beloved pox to great effect – should this man have been near death with such ailment as did trouble the lungs and be only begun to recover, just little of those poisons that affect the lungs would of ease kill him. With only little art, any who wished him harm could grind one of the flowers common used as banes – Lakespur, Monk's Shade, some others – and by secreting the grindings in his supper achieve such end as you have described. His hands would blister short after having touched the poisoned food; and his mouth from its eating; his throat and tongue inflame as well, even to the point of stopping his speech; and even a strong man would weep, as, until such time as the agent did finally still his lungs, the feeling would be much like being burned away from the inside to the out."

And so the late Lord Chamberlain had been murdered, and the details of both sons' accounts, the elder from his dreams and the younger in his hateful recollection, seemed point to the same cause.

"These flowers? They are common to England?"

"Much common and favoured in many gardens. As so often with nature's most deadly treats, they are bright in their ornament and appealing to the eye, as though to seduce us into their acquaintance. I have oft wondered why God hath ordained it so, for it seems a cruel irony to have what would bring the eye such joy bring the body such harm."

My mind ran to Somerset House, the younger Carey sprawled on his couch, the windows behind him and the large and varied garden beyond.

My mind ran also to the man with the bulbous and disfigured nose who, while the apothecary and I talked, sat alone at the table nearest the door, and whose glance passed regular around the tavern and settled, it seemed, on all save me.

CHAPTER 8

The morning next, I made haste to the theatre with Jenkins, as Burbage had sent the boy to my rooms at a run to wake me in the still-early morning. Jenkins found me abed, as I had been late at my writing and making at least some little progress, those melancholies that had of late much vexed me somewhat abated after my meeting with the apothecary, I think by the thrill of the hunt. I dressed in haste in such clothes as lay handy, Jenkins being unsure of the mission but seeming certain that speed was more vital than costume.

At the theatre, Burbage was in argument with a man I could see only from behind. The man was outfitted in the plain and looser cut of dull brown much preferred by the Puritans. In their lust to deny any joy to mankind, they dressed to displease the eye in the costume of large turds. His head bore neither hat nor wig nor hair of any style or care, but instead that close and artless cropping that had them seem round of head. And then he turned, and I could see that it was our landlord, Miller. I knew he held some Puritan sympathies, but in the year since our last congress, he must have full succumbed to their sour and joyless catechism.

"Shakespeare," he said, his hands clasped behind him. I nodded in greeting. "Sir Miller."

He made disapproving examination of my person and dress. "It would seem we have drug thee from thy bed at such hour as most honest men have been long at their labours."

"As we oft do perform at evening, and as I must then sometimes write at night, I fear my hours do end later than is custom, and that I do rise later."

"Just as all else in your enterprise runs counter to God's natural order, so, too, do your hours."

"It's the lease, Will," Burbage blurted. "He says it is not to be extended."

Our lease on the theatre would expire at the end of July, this same month, and in fact in just a few days. Just some weeks previous Burbage had truck on the matter with Miller – Miller having said on that occasion that such matters would be addressed as to their current custom as time allowed, and Burbage returned feeling the matter settled as it had been each year previous and no longer of mind.

"You mean not to be extended again beyond the current year in question, or not at all?" I asked.

"I will have you and the instruments of your practice out before August," said Miller.

"Even having told me other when last we spoke?" said Burbage, his voice gaining edge and his face colour. "Is lying now admitted to the practice of your new faith?"

"I told you, sir, that matters would be addressed in due course. If you took from those words some meaning other than that their plain meanings carry, then perhaps too much of your conversation is constrained to those words written for you by others and your wits, through lack of practice, have lost what small ability they e'er had."

Burbage lunged toward Miller. Lunging myself, I took his arm, turned him aside, and bade him take leave that I might speak with Miller alone. While I had no doubt that the spirit of their previous business was clear as Burbage had relayed it, I also had no doubt that Miller did likely mislead him in such fashion that he could say he had spoke truly, for he had much practice with lawyers and that was their art. Having some gift with language myself, I fell less prey to their conniving, and did curse myself that I had sent Burbage to Miller on that first occasion.

Miller and I now alone, I asked his intent. "Methinks you are now so full embraced of your Puritan faith that our practice here gives you insult and you can longer bear to gain from our custom."

"I do take offence, sir, to your trivial entertainments, as they distract to oft unholy themes the attentions of eyes that should be focused only on God. They inflame the passions such that those present do then desire what God has proscribed. You do on stage have men truck with men and invite on us all such judgment as befell Sodom."

I smiled at him so as to seem in sympathy. "So far as men trucking with men, we do so to comply with the statutes her Majesty's ministers have seen fit to apply to our practice. I have no doubt the players would prefer admit to their number such women as who would this art pursue, as their lips and embrace would be far more welcome and more natural, and I would be much pleased should you chose to petition the Lord of Revels to so rule."

Miller coloured. "Do you think it would lessen my objections to see women, too, debased in your unnatural parliament of whores? To see them cleave, and in public, to any such your scripts require – not in marriage or even in affection, but solely to inflame the lust of those misguided sinners that seek in your theatre such grace as they ought find in a rightful church?"

"So, you say 'no'."

"So I say be gone from these quarters come month's end, and take the vile particulars of your hateful craft with you. Or what remains I will seize and sell, or more likely burn so that such pox as your kind carries be contained."

"So you say on account of God, or at least that God whose will you suppose to know. But the right of our presence to these quarters is a matter of law, not religion."

Miller held up a bound scroll, no doubt his copy of the same lease that could also be found in the desk in our stores. "This be law, and it grant you no right beyond the end of this month. And there is no new document of its kind that says other."

As I have a memory for words and had each year to sign this lease, being a shareholder in our company, and as it had ne'er been copied anew but instead only the old year each time crossed out and replaced with the next and any adjustment to our monies owed made note – as such scribes who did redraft such charters cost dear, and Miller amongst his other charms would cling tight to any coin in a way he would not to any woman – I was well familiar with its particulars.

"If that be law, then I would remind you that it also by law requires that, should your intent be not to renew, you inform us in such time as to allow us to remove ourselves in good order. The time required in my recall is two months, by which requirement, then, we will remove ourselves as you desire – not at the end of July, but instead at the end of September, by which time we can acquire new quarters."

Miller again waived the document at me as if a cudgel. "That requirement being void in such case as the tenant is arrears in his obligations, or should new matters arise by which I find the tenant to be a poor risk for payment."

"And yet we have every payment made at its time, not just this year but in each year prior. We have a full schedule of shows through the remainder of summer and well into fall, and then have charter for a series of entertainments at Court. And so I would know by what meaning of the word risk you find us so, you being so strict on meanings, as you have made clear to Burbage."

"Your company's name, even written clear hence," Miller waving the scroll yet again, "is The Lord Chamberlain's Men. It was his patronage that made your reputation and secured such court entertainments as you have enjoyed. It is by that name that you are known by those sinners you attract. And yet the Lord Chamberlain is dead. And so the major asset in your ledger is stricken, and none yet of public knowledge to take its place. Such shows as you may have scheduled will not a full year's rent produce, and such royal entertainments as you may imagine you will perform will need be confirmed by your dead patron's successor. And so I say risk, and clear, and have from my lawyers the same opinion."

"I would admit to your concerns had I not, even the day after the Lord Chamberlain's death, been summoned to Somerset by the new Baron Carey to receive the good assurance of his intent to continue as our patron, her Majesty having made known to him that he will assume his father's office."

"Those words in your speech of which I take most note being assurance and intent. Which, being words and not such charter as would either his patronage or office confirm, still lead me to say risk."

"But that be your opinion and no matter of law. Should you wish to court, then to court we shall go. And in those chambers you can make public your accusation that the new Baron Carey is a liar."

"I have heard only your words, Shakespeare, and not Carey's. So, if I call liar, I call it to you – and willingly, knowing full well the stink of Papistry the name Shakespeare emits. Even what faith you have, and I think well none, you will not admit to."

"And again opinions, and again I say court."

At which Miller made an oily smile. "To court I have been, or at least have been my lawyers. And they there voiced such concerns as I have here shared, adding also that, even should Baron Carey choose to be patron – and I am making entreaty to him to reconsider in the goodly name of God – my being well aware of the debts with which his household is burdened, I doubt that his personal support will be of such worth as had been his father's. This is coupled with a fair hope that the Crown will shortly less bless your endeavours, as her Majesty's continued embrace of such vile practices as are here pursued does cause great discomfort among the crown's good servants, the power of such good servants being in the ascendency. And so again I say risk, as did my lawyers in such argument as produced this."

From inside his coat he drew a smaller document, which he unfolded and laid upon the stage. A notice of our eviction, come month's end.

"And so you will out by month's end, or else be removed at force of arms. And I pray God will grant me forgiveness if I hope the latter, for it would be to his glory to see your debased company adorning the end of pikes." And with this Miller turned and waddled from the theatre, walking as a man whose troubled bowels would produce only water and so kept his cheeks always clenched as not to soil his trousers.

I immediate scrawled a note to Carey begging he grant me audience, saying that I had such news as best be shared in private and also that his name was being some abused in those commercial circles as in which we did have business. I gave the note to Jenkins and sent him to Somerset.

I did not think Carey would be much pleased with what little I had yet discovered concerning his father's death, though I could now prove, at least, that it be unnatural. But as I did, in fact, possess such gift as he imagined so far as my ability to discern much truth in the converse of others, I would talk with him more concerning his patronage. For to risk my neck – and I think in this instance that be not just common speech, but also probable fact – for his good favour at such time as I had thought the value of such favour high was one matter. But to do so for such favours as he could offer now and that may be, if both his brother and Miller spoke true of his father's debts, of little worth. And had Carey offered those favours in less than earnest, that was another matter still.

The London I had only two nights previous imagined as some vast jungle in which each could move anonymous and to his own benefit did of sudden seem the fenced confines of some farmer's wood. Each creature now seemed of every other's acquaintance – either in or owning of one another's debts; desiring or granting their favour; holding or being jealous of what little fodder the wood did provide. As each did some other consume for its sustenance, the world seemed sudden less an Eden and more a carnival of appetites in which each man could – and with little cause would – wish ill each other.

I wondered how in the chaos of such mad avarice I could ever ascribe sure to any one man the death of any other, or assume another's innocence when innocence seemed in such little supply.

CHAPTER 9

Jenkins returned before midday, having made considerable haste to Somerset and back, being, as the youngest of the Company, likely much wanting to make his name. He staggered into the theatre nearly stroked from the heat and handed to me a folded message sealed with Carey's signet, which I did quick secret within my garb.

"Were he a mare, I'd call him lame and add him to the pot," said Burbage, eying Jenkins as he walked unevenly from the wings. Burbage had been well into his drink since news of our eviction. And indeed Jenkins was much lathered as though a hard-rode horse.

"Were he a mare you would mount him sure, and not for riding," said Heminges, who too had arrived to join the mournful waking of our fortunes.

Burbage shrugged and nodded and said, "Mayhaps, but then to the pot." But the spark of levity that did so oft lift the spirits of the Company could find no kindle, and we stood quietly eying Jenkins, who sat in the dirt of the common audience ground, his legs sprawled before him and his back to the facing of the stage, panting as if a dog.

"If you good sirs are concluded of your sport, might I humbly trouble you for some water? I am afeared that I cannot at the moment rise to fetch it myself," Jenkins said.

Burbage snorted and handed down the bottle of sack he had but half concluded. "It would do my standing ill to fetch your water, boy, but I count it an admirable mercy that I do share with you such drink as I have at hand. This will heal thee well."

Jenkins took a long pull from the bottle, some distress on his face as he was not yet much practised with drink. But the urgency of his thirst overcame the objections of his tongue, and he then drank the bottle dry. Being not much used to drink, and his humours I think depleted by his exertions, he was almost immediate considerable drunk. Burbage took his chance to introduce the lad to a comic dance of the palsied, crowing fashion that made his former fellow Kemp much famous. We did in Jenkins's pratfalls and thunderous landings make much merriment until, in fear that he would soon be as well-bruised as he was well-fatigued, I took mercy, and led him back to our stores, giving him a jug of water, and put him to rest on a pile of fabrics.

Glum again, Burbage and Heminges sat with their legs adangle from the stage front.

"I hear the Swan needs some business," said Heminges.

Burbage nodded. "They will have some dates as chance allows, but not near so many as our slate demands."

"Would you each to Bankside and make rounds there of such venues as may suit our purposes? We can perhaps cobble together enough days – though we will be itinerant, I do fear."

"We can," said Burbage, taking to his feet, but without the elan that was his custom. He then offered his hand to Heminges and pulled him to stand also, the both of them wearied in their aspect. "And you, Will?"

"I will take our lease to a lawyer of my acquaintance in hopes that he may divine in it some relief that I could not – though, an eviction being already granted, I hold our chances slim."

"A slim chance now seeming still sweet," Burbage said. "The Lord Admiral's Men open a new play today. Will you join us to scout this once your business is complete?"

"Loathe as I am to fatten Henslowe's purse, yes," I said, "if I am not called to meet with Carey. But a penny only. With the groundlings at the front of the stage."

"Amidst the vomit and stench of our common fellows, with ale in hand, that we might from such close quarters attempt to vex Alleyn at his supposed art," Burbage said, some of his usual bombast regained. "I would have it no other."

I walked down Bishopsgate, just passing from Shoreditch into London proper when I was by my gut reminded that I had that day not yet broke fast. And so I turned into the tavern near my rooms, where I was common found. The hour being odd, I was alone, and the keeper joined me at the table when be brought me a stew and an ale.

"Will you move your rooms, Will, such to be closer to your new locations?"

And so word of our eviction had already spread. "Sour news does travel fast," I answered.

He seemed puzzled. "How sour?"

And I puzzled in return. "Our eviction, and on only short days' notice? How other than sour?"

He made a face as though not understanding, "I have for some weeks heard from vendors near with which I have business that the theatre and some surroundings are to be made clear for a new collection of shops – by rumour to rival those near the exchange at Threadneedle – so as to have the commerce of the expanded population."

"For some weeks?"

He nodded.

"And which vendors?"

"The brewer sure, I do remember that. The butcher."

"Passing odd, as we have only heard today," I said.

But I hurried to finish my stew and declined a second ale, even though I much desired it, so as to make haste to the lawyer. I now suspected that Miller's wish to be rid of us was no act of moral fervour nor out of concern to any risk, but instead part of a long plan to supplant us for the gain of his wealth. He had delayed his notice only to do us harm from spite, the Lord Chamberlain's death – which evidently some had long anticipated – being just his excuse. I sensed in that motive such grass from which a lawyer might make hay.

Some yards further toward the river, I passed a butcher's door. Thinking it most likely be the same butcher from which the tavern keeper had heard news of Miller's intent, I turned in. I there found a man surprising small, but with arms below the elbow much pronounced, who stood behind his counter chopping at a mutton.

"My pardon, sir," I called, and he turned, having not at first heard me over the concentration of his endeavours.

"Good day," he responded.

"And to you. I will not trouble you long. I am a glover new to London – having been approached as a possible tenant for such exchange as to be built near, and soon – and did hear that you, too, may have been so approached and did hope to hear your thinking."

The butcher set down his blade and wiped some gore off his hands on the apron that draped his legs.

"I was asked," he said, "and did agree – though much reluctant, as I own this building free, having it from my father's estate and keeping my house upstairs. But they have approached most every keeper of an establishment of any custom in these lanes. Any tenant near has already found either their leases sold to new landlords or such building as they are in bought entire, so that they will move to this new district, be it their will or no. For those few of us who remain, we are afeared that such custom which frequents these streets now will all be to these new shops, and if we move not hence, then some other who competes for our trade will. And so we will move to avoid our ruin."

"It seems there is much that good Sir Miller did not share with me in our original discussions. But me starting my business new, having been apprenticed at my father's shop in distant Stratford, perhaps he considered it of no concern. It seems he was plainer in his truck with you."

The butcher shook his head. "It was not Miller in my case, as I do not know any such, but a lawyer who doth speak for some other investors in this scheme – my new lease being not with any sole man, but with their company. In which company, they did strongly hint, are persons of nobility. That last said, I think, though, not so much to convince as to coerce."

"I thank you, sir, for your honest congress. I wonder if I would have been better served to remain a country lad, where life doth seem less complex."

"It is a new world to me and much strange, always of lawyers and shares and lenders and charters of such dense construction that we no longer understand our own affairs. Always instead we seem to find some other mouth feeding at a teat we had thought our own, and feeding a man grown much fat from no enterprise of my understanding."

"This company, how is it called?

"The Somerset Company, sir. Supposedly only my new landlord, but increasingly, I fear, my new master."

Somerset. There was a name to my familiar. And I remembered the message Jenkins had brought from Carey, my having forgotten it during Jenkins's drunken revels. Having left the butcher's company, I opened it and read it as I walked.

Shakespeare –
I shall meet you on tomorrow at dusk where the new Cathedral rises at the point nearest Newgate, as for us to have too common congress in public knowledge would strike my company here as odd.
Carey

Such now my life, conducted increasingly in the dark and in secret and with such fellows as could with ease do me ill and whose true affections I could not know. This London I had previously imagined a cradle of hopeful wonder seemed now to be sprung thick with peril and perfidy.

CHAPTER 10

"You seem prospered since my last visit," I said to Webb, a lawyer with whom I had occasional business. He once did take his payment in verse, as he was then courting a lady of considerable fortune and of such tender heart that she could be well-moved by my blandishments. My words won her heart and for Webb did her hand secure, so that on some occasions since I have again made payment with poetry, as she does oft wonder why a man who gained her favours with such sweet words has since lost his honeyed tongue.

The rooms in which he kept his office now were near the courts where he plied his trade, and were more richly appointed than were those spare rooms he once did keep not far from Bishopsgate.

He turned up his hands and smiled. "The benefits of a wealthy wife. She not only would have me ensconced as befitting our station, but her society often has need of my trade. It seems that wealth attracts law the way a dog attracts fleas. And, Will, her society pays with coin, not words."

"As my words did help win your wife and thus your wealth, I should think you value them dear," I said.

"Much dear, my friend. Much dear. But I assume it be wealth that brings you hence today, as you have in ready supply such words as I imagine you need."

I gave to him both our lease and the notice of eviction, and recounted my conversation with Miller. Upon quick review, he made a sour face. "Methinks your Miller has some good friend in the courts to have a decision that is so clear to your detriment and so little to his gain made so quick, this business of risk being too much the realm of opinion and too little that of fact. But, as it has been rendered and as you have so little time before its enforcement, you have little choice but to comply. You could challenge, but even if your challenge proved successful, such success would like come after you already have been made to leave your theatre. So, a challenge seems not worth its cost, unless you make suit to claim some damage, which would be an uncertain business."

"Which was my thinking, too, until I chanced to learn from a butcher that this matter of the theatre seems likely for Miller only fodder for some fatter calf."

Webb raised his eyebrows in question. "Then perhaps I should hear the meat of what matter as your butcher shared." I relayed what I had learned regarding the new-planned mall of shops in Shoreditch.

Webb rose from his seat and pulled out a large drawer from which he produced a sizable map of London and its immediate environs, his face lost in thought. "I hear in this meat much mischief, and suspect too much appetite for it be Miller's alone." He flattened the map on the table between us, marking with his fingers the scenes of our discussions. "Here is your theatre. Where is this butcher?"

I pointed to the place on Bishopsgate, south from the theatre toward the river, and also to the tavern at which I first heard news of the exchange.

"And the butcher thought the offer he received was common to all business near?"

"He did," I said.

"And so the district of shops most near the city border would be emptied and their commerce moved into Shoreditch, which would be outside the control of the City Corporation and instead fall to that authority that does Shoreditch's rolls maintain. And so those coffers currently enriched of its taxes would be emptied and other coffers currently empty would be filled."

"I hear that taxes collected in any parish oft mysteriously shrink before they reach the Treasury," I said.

"Oh, there be much corruption in lands, Will. In their taxes and in their transfer, the law providing an ever-denser thicket of words in which we lawyers find definitions of sufficiently varied shade so as to make of them what our clients will – at least to such extent as their purse gives us cause. If you think the more law the more justice, you think wrong, for each law comes twinned with its own mischief. Give me law enough and I can make a hen a cow and have you pay beef prices for your eggs, and pay again for the privilege of collecting them."

"Miller's corruption is my only current concern. Such larger sins as you and your ilk may commit, I shall leave to your own conscience and penance, as I have sufficient of my own to consider."

Webb slumped back in his chair for a moment. "I find Miller's role odd, for I know that he has some few holdings, but little more than you yourself · have amassed near Stratford – though, his being in London, have probably been advantaged by the late inflation. The scheme your butcher has relayed is a fatted calf out of reach of his purse."

"The butcher does not know him, and has dealt only with other lawyers who have spoken for this Somerset Company."

Webb nodded. "Miller could hold shares in this Somerset Company, but I think then, too, he would have relied on the company's lawyers for his commerce. For if that company's shareholders prefer to conduct their business behind a veil of law, they have reason to stay masked. And they are also likely wont to ensure each step of their adventure be executed such that it could not later be assailed by some lawyer who could find fault in their approach. No, if Miller is of their number, I think his fellow shareholders would be much aggrieved to find that he would endanger their enterprise through such folly as his truck with you suggests – for if I can find any document or testimony that he is either of such company or in league with their efforts, then it has clear been his long intent that you be gone from your holdings so they be free for his other exercise. And then also tis clear that he did owe you notice. And then, such notice having been owed before the late Carey's death, it being further clear that his claim of risk is a ruse, making his delay simple fraud, and of a most vile kind as meant sole to do you harm without even any real gain to him."

"If he is not of this Somerset Company, then what?"

Webb again leaned over the map. "The plot on which your theatre sits is direct on the main route about which this entire enterprise would centre, and is most close to London proper, from whence most of the custom this scheme of shops hopes to attract would come. That makes the property of your theatre vital to their enterprise. I suspect that Miller would have you gone so that no lease encumbers the property and it may be sold free to this Somerset Company, likely at a dear price."

"Meaning he has long planned the sale and did clear owe us notice."

"Indeed." Webb took the map from the table and returned it to its drawer. "Leave the lease and notice with me, Will, and I will think on this further and see what news of this scheme I can learn. An enterprise of this scope is, in law, like a herd of beasts – it will have left droppings of documents thick on the ground. I think it likely we can compel Miller to grant you what time you require to manage your removal, and probably convince him that you should have such time without the cost of the rents that you would have ready paid had he been other than an ass."

"Make what haste you can, as we have only little days and I have little purse. I know how the cost of your service swells with the time you find for it."

Webb stood and gave a short bow, as though to an audience. "As I have but my time to sell, and as such reflections that such time allows oft add to the value of my advice, haste profits neither my art nor my purse. But I should have word for you soon."

"And will perhaps save us some on our rent."

Webb smiled again. "I think what you will save in rent I likely will charge in service, so that you are not, in whole, affected ill while I do still profit, and only dear Miller will find himself at loss."

"I suppose it is too much to hope that your wife be in some melancholy and require a new verse to lift her heart?"

Miller drew from another drawer in his desk a wood case, which he turned toward me and opened. Inside was a necklace adorned in gold and richly jewelled. "Just this past month, I had business with a merchant house in the Bourse at Threadneedle that required my travel to their competitors in Antwerp, which business I concluded to their good. Much of the fee I invested in this, which I will give her next week to mark the date of our marriage. It will, I think, my wife's favour secure for some long months. Jewels are to the eyes as words are to the ear, my friend."

"Remember, all that glisters is not gold."

"True," said Webb. "In this instance, much that

glisters is emeralds and pearls and other bangles that make gold seem cheap by compare. But they do all glister and will for a time blind my wife's eyes to any need for poetry."

CHAPTER 11

I was late with Webb, so the Lord Admiral's Men's performance was near to starting by the time I made Bankside. Many booths and tents marked the vendors of food, drink, and varied sundries that flocked about any performance like gulls, all clamouring for a snack of coin from the crowds gathered. I made to the theatre straight, paying my penny and pushing with much effort and accepting many insults as I made through the throng crammed in the yard to the front of the stage. In any theatre, this was the reserve for those poor groundlings who would, standing in the muck, the play enjoy; such comfort as a seat in the surrounding arcades might provide being beyond their means. The crowd was thick and my passage through it would harvest come morning, but I made my way to the stage front. As his word, Burbage had claimed the prime spot, he and Heminges fending off those who tried encroach until I could press to their left and gain their company at the front edge of the stage just as the play was begun.

"How with the lawyer, Will?" Burbage asked.

"I think well, but soon events will tell." His

manner was weighted in the way of one who had heard sad news since I was last in his company.

"And what now?" I asked, at which Heminges reached across to pass a small pamphlet, atop which clear I could read mine own name.

Do your coins make rich
Wm. Shakespeare
Satan's Good Servant?

As Clear you already do despise the good grace of God by choice to frequent such vile entertainments as do here transpire, I rightly fear any further charge doth fall upon such ears as are already sealed up against any appeal to grace, but do pray that once you know the debased nature of its human agents, you may in their foul deeds recognise the evils buttressed by your coin, and the lusts and appetites that cloud your vision will fall away and you will see clear to frequent these iniquities no more and beg God his forgiveness and return to his fold.

Wm. Shakespeare, much eminent amongst the merchants of filth that are the diseased fare of these venues, though lawful married, hath oft lain with those fallen women who can endure his favours, but in his latest adventure hath made such brazen insult to God's command as to shock the conscience of even his fellow players who before celebrated his depravity, a shock so dire that they have to me relayed the details of his sordid conduct.

In recent weeks, having made acquaintance of a fair child who did her father's booth tend at the Royal Exchange in Threadneedle, he seduced her to his foul purposes, much to her despair. She, being a goodly child and not the wanton harlot of his usual custom, having yielded to his cunning blandishments, lost sight of God's grace and leapt from the bridge unto her death.

We did to both Sheriff and Bailiff appeal that he be made to answer before law for such offense, but as the child, now dead, can offer no testimony, and such witness who to our keeping has entrusted this tale is of the theatre also and of insufficient character to speak in her stead, so it falls to our poor office to at least share to you this tale so you at least know those devils whose mouths you feed and may, perchance, redeem your ways.

A Puritan Friend

I felt my shame hot on my face, and could scarce look up at my fellows. I was double shamed that, having the past day been much distracted both with Carey's charge and with the Company's business, I had, after the harsh night I first passed upon learning of those events related in the pamphlet, since suffered for it only little. Then, triple shamed to know that what distress I felt now was for myself as I weighed the cost of having the insult I had done to my own honour wide known – distress any good man would feel for that child alone. What shame I would now in public bear was my earned wage, while the despair that pressed that girl to the river's depths was an unearned gift I had fastened around her neck like a millstone.

"I will not call it false," I said.

And Burbage shrugged and reached his arm around my shoulder and pulled me to him close, saying into my ear to be heard over the clamour of the crowd that now did greet the players as they took the stage, "I call thee my good friend, Will. And I do say good, knowing full such ills as we may each commit, sure knowing full my own, and sure that you do suffer for those sins you know to be such, and do require no scold from me but instead only my love."

Heminges, too, did reach to squeeze my arm in assent to Burbage's word. And my eyes burned with tears for my deeds, regret for my reputation, and love for these friends with whom I was unjustly blessed, whilst all about, our common fellows rollicked at the comedy on stage. For these short hours they would take leave of the concerns of their mean estate, the pamphlets they had been handed crushed into the muck at their feet.

After play's end, whilst we waited for the crowd to disperse, Alleyn called down from the stage, saying "Will, it seems your spear does shake, quivering likely in weariness from its frequent employ. In this at least, sir, I must admit you my better, for whilst the ladies offer me some little love, I have not the surfeit of their adoring from which you profit." And he gave a deep bow, his gibe seemingly meant in good humour.

Burbage then having to add, "They do thee little love, there being so little," then grabbing his codpiece, "and so little," Alleyn succumbed to his tempers and rushed at Burbage, and was restrained by his fellows and dragged back across the stage, such being the common method of his exit whenever he and Burbage met.

As we made our way back to the bridge, I was accosted by those of my acquaintance who had seen the pamphlet, but more in good spirit than in ill, as such broadsides as this pamphlet had been regular fired at varied persons in our professions by the swelling Puritan ranks who did find in us so much offence. And so, whether those I knew felt the charge true or no, they did ignore it or else used it in sport.

I suspected that such common eyes as these were not this instrument's true audience, but that it was true meant for the loftier vision of those nobles by whose patronage the business of theatre maintained its precarious balance. In this pamphlet, in the late attack on my person, and in our eviction there seemed some broader scheme to do our company ill.

I parted company with my fellows, them to a tavern and me to my room, as I had no appetite for merriment. I knew also that I owed these fellows who had again proved their loyalties the tardy duty of truth.

CHAPTER 12

I was early to the theatre next morning, for my bed held no rest. Through the night, I full confronted again those demons I had well earned, inventing what arguments I could to make less certain my own guilt. But I could see plain through each attempt the stark fact that the girl was dead – dead at her own hand, and thus, by the teachings of Catholic and Protestant both, beyond hope of redemption. I puzzled considerable on how I, as the agent of all evil in her regard, could still hope forgiveness if she be beyond the grasp of mercy. In my last excuse, I told myself that I could say true in my heart that I never did intend her ill, but how could I claim I intended her good or ill when I had tended her not at all? Having been bewitched by her beauty I credited her hardly human, but instead simply a vessel to use for my own pleasure. Even now I sought comfort in such words as bewitched, as though to excuse through the agency of some magic that choice I made in full conscience. She was as full precious as are we each, and was now as full gone as we each will be, but well before her time and absent what chance at hope or wonder or love or the comfort of a husband or the blessing of a child as she may have been due. And I could by no word or thought or action make it other.

The cast of such thinking must have been plain on my arrival.

"Will," said Burbage, "think no more on that pamphlet, for there can be no good end to such pondering. Make what confession you must – even to some priest, if that be your need – and then be so humble as to know yourself human, as are we each, even in our failings. You used that child ill, true, but you can no more own her latter sin than she can own yours. To attempt to hold, as does God, all such evils men by our own hands create instead of surrendering them to his fair mercies, that invites madness."

I was choked for a short moment at his kindness, and new aggrieved that I had not been true with him and my other fellows as to the nature of my affairs these past days. I drew Burbage and Heminges aside so as to right at least the sin of my secrecy.

Heminges's face stayed flat and beyond my intuiting while I made bare Carey's secret charge and that same night's attack, my discussions with his family and the apothecary, the swollen-nosed shadow that I still did from time to time encounter, and such news as I had from Webb concerning Miller's ploy. But Burbage's face showed red, and his jaw clenched as though in labour to still itself. When I finished my discourse, he clouted me on the shoulder – and not in jest but with such unfriendly intent that I near fell.

"I would have stuck thy face if we did not need it pretty for our next play," he said. "If you have forgot we are your friends, and have much proven so, then did you too forget that we are a company, and you but one shareholder? It is not your place to make this league with Carey not only absent our assent but even our knowing."

I could only nod. "This I do know, and I am both shamed and sorry to have done so."

"You make too much a habit of shame of late, methinks," said Heminges, his words cutting the deeper for being said with more measure and some sadness.

"So, our standing as the Lord Chamberlain's Men depends now not on our common art, but instead on this uncommon mission?" Burbage said, his anger still plain but, as was his nature, quick abating.

"He did not say so plain," I said, "but made it ample clear that my response to his request be either yes or yes, if I held his patronage dear. I do hope you know I value your company above our company, and do hold you friends and dear, and have been much troubled to have held this news alone. It was, in fact, your fair love to me this evening past, and at such hour when I so little deserved it but did so much require it, that made me know I could be false to you no more. And I do now, must humble, beg both your forgiveness and your console."

Heminges made a long sigh, seemed as though to speak, then not, and then finally did. "Will, I can this forgive, if only because you have been true to us in such time as you could still have been false and clear out of the misgivings of your own heart. But be warned that I will not forgive such insult again, for if

we cannot have confidence in the fellowship of our
own company, and our own company, then where
can we place it?"

"And I," said Burbage. "And enough. But on to
console. What plan do you make?"

"I am to meet Carey tonight, on pretence to share
with him what news I have regarding his father's
poisoning – for I am now confident it was such – and
to gain his leave to question those attendants to his
household that were witness at his father's death.
But also, under guise of such abuse as his name has
taken, both from Miller and from his own brother,
to see clear his actual standing and to learn if he is
bequeathed more in debts than in fortune, and thus
learn what value his patronage may still hold."

"As would be good to know," said Heminges, "that
we might balance the cost of our risk against the
reward of our service."

"Just so," I said. "Let me also ask you this and
you tell me if my thinking be too vain. Inside only
few days, I have alone confronted an unsuccessful
killer and a successful pamphleteer, and we have in
company been subject to the loss of our quarters. Do
we count such events separate or should we in their
sum consider the threat of a larger conspiracy to see
our company failed?"

"If we count them separate and they be one, then
we aid through our own foolishness what plot we
may confront," said Burbage. "If we hold them one,
and they in fact prove separate, then we lose nothing
but some worry."

"To which end," said Heminges, "I already have a thought." He spread a copy of the pamphlet on the stage. "What do you see in its printing?"

"Much truth," I said, "and my own shame."

Heminges made a face as if I were a child that had too longed whined at some hurt. "Whether to Carey's end or to this possible conspiracy, what we need now, Will, is the gift of your considerable wits and not your public penance. And so I would ask that you indulge your own sorrows in private and do us the favour of attending full to those dangers we face."

I could not contradict his console. Such ills as the company now faced they did partly at the cost of my own failings, and so I could best serve it now with my attention and not with my penance. And then, thinking more close on his words, I understood his point.

"By what do I see, you mean: what do I see in its type and not in its meaning," I said.

Heminges nodded. "We have truck enough with printers to know that you can oft discern the press of some document solely from those imperfections of form its letters hold, or from some curious habit of spacing, or from much else. So, I ask what we see in this that might tell us its printer so that we might there gentle inquire as to its author."

Burbage wagged a finger in assent. "And, as we have considerable custom with printers, what press we might find has likely previous benefitted from our purse and does hope to again, and so will count our goodwill more heavy than that of a one-time pamphleteer."

We laid out printed copies of our own plays and various handbills we had commissioned, noting which had been made on what press, and balanced their clues against those the pamphlet held – principal being a gap in the larger W at the start of my name, and also, in a faint fading of the type from the left to the right, sign that the pressure of this press was not full even.

"Dear God," said Burbage, holding the page of a handbill promoting a recent production that showed both same errors plain. "That pamphlet is from Jaggard's press, sure."

CHAPTER 13

Jaggard was printer, bookseller and a full member of the Stationer's Guild, so our Company had regular truck with all his concerns. Being that he also was a man of not little ambition and by reputation would ready do that most to his own benefit – although none would actually call him false – we did hope he would betray this smaller customer so as to retain our favour.

"My good sirs," Jaggard said, guiding us from the clamorous confines of his print shop to the room next, where he stored some materials, "and even 'gentleman', as I am told the esteemed Shakespeare may now rightly be addressed. That you all three seek my congress leads me to hope you have some large need?"

"A large need concerning a small matter," said Burbage, and he slapped the pamphlet down stern on the table.

Jaggard snorted a short laugh. "I've seen it of course, but pay it no heed. Pamphleteers by reputation are as like to call a cow a crow, and then still try sell its milk."

"As I am in this both cow and crow, I would know who takes such interest, whether in my milk or in my feathers," I said, "for I would be neither milked nor plucked."

Jaggard shrugged. "Some Puritan much aggrieved at your art and no more, and of what consequence? Any man of reputation these days may find himself target. This is proof of your standing and of no more. And so, were I you, I would celebrate it if I did not choose to ignore it. Anything that makes your name, even if with some whiff of scandal, likely more fills your audience."

"Then I would know its author's name that I may thank him to his face."

At which Jaggard's face grimmed. "And how from me?"

At which Burbage lost patience and held up that handbill which mimicked the pamphlet in its imperfections.

"Do you think us such fools that, having had much printed, we would learn nothing of your art? That learning having also swollen your own purse?" Burbage said. "In any printing, there are small faults unique to the press of each house. And such matching faults do plain appear both here," Burbage pushed the handbill into Jaggard's chest, "and here," pushing now the pamphlet with his other hand. "As we know you to have printed the former, then we know you, too, have printed this unkind assault on our friend and, I might add, your good patron."

Jaggard now lay both documents to table and pretended a close examining. "I could see where eyes only some little schooled would see it so."

"Then you say on your honour this comes not from your press?" I asked.

"On my honour? I cannot say sure, as such a small job could easy pass from its ordering to its execution in the hands of my son or some other without my console, it being simple in its requirements. We are, after all, in the business of print and do not make habit to decline such commerce as might present itself."

"So, comes some Puritan from the street, one who has not previous made your employ, and asks printed this charge against a regular patron of long standing, and for only what few pennies this job might be worth, and in your mind his commerce is as good as mine?" I asked.

"Sir, you misunderstand me. I say only that it be possible that such job could transpire and I have no knowledge of it – some of the shop being skilled at their craft but not much read or knowing of our business, so that to them it seemed only some paper and some ink."

"Even so, such job being only of recent minting, you could quick discern its author by asking those in your employee, you saying you had no hand it is commission yourself," Burbage said, now standing so close to Jaggard as to limit his comfort.

Jaggard backed nearer the door. "I do wish I had known of this job at such time as it was offered, as I would have declined it. But having taken it on, and its author wishing to be anonymous, to reveal him would offend my honour. You, being men of honour, must see this sure."

"A short minute past, you implied this to be not of your press, then perhaps of it, and now of it sure but your honour binds you to hold secret its author," I said, "you having first said it was our short schooling in your art that even made us think this from your press to begin with. What apt pupils we must be to have so quick discerned the truth both of the pamphlet's printing and of your honour."

Jaggard, now much flustered, shook his head. "Sir, you have advantage of me in matters of wit – that I ready admit – and by that art you now make me seem to say such as I did not mean."

"Then let me phrase this simple so as not to tax what wits you hold," I answered. "You claim no knowledge of the offending pamphlet being printed in your shop, but also refuse to learn if it be so. Further, if you did know its author, you would tell us not, as your honour – which does seem to come and go at your convenience – would have you hold that secret dearer than the value of our future commerce?"

"I can only say that you were meant no insult at my hands and that I do true regret any that was unknowing done. I will say no other, as the more I say, the double more you seem to hear."

"Then we will take leave so that you can reflect on your honour in private," I said, "while we reflect on what future need we may have of it. Or of your commerce."

Jaggard importuned us stay as we left – sure, he said, that, being men of honour all, we could reach such settlement as offended none. But we left him to his blathering.

"Honour or no, I cannot credit that Jaggard would protect some small chick at the risk of offending such a hen as us that doth oft lay such rich eggs," Heminges said.

"He would not," Burbage said.

"Which means we have some other hen in our hen house," I said. "If not some fox, and our Puritan Friend, then, whether hen or fox, is likely neither Puritan nor friend."

CHAPTER 14

A fiery curve like some slice of hell escaped fresh to heaven bent along the western horizon, striped in fading bands by the smoke of some thousand cook fires arising weak against its brilliance – the thin smoke magnifying by comparison the brilliance of that sight it first seemed to diminish. This proof of the vanity of any paltry human enterprise lent a sinister aspect to the gloaming hour as I made my way around the expanse of St Paul's. With each passing day, it seemed the ancient building grew ever more decayed, as if the lightning bolt which rent its spire asunder some five and thirty years previous had been the catalyst for the hands of time to clench the cathedral and squeeze the life from it.

As I had only before been to the cathedral grounds in day, I was used to them crowded, filled with business more secular than ecclesiastical. The grounds now emptied, in this failing and reddened light a litter of papers and other discard gave a small stir in what little breeze the evening offered. Their fluttering was reminder to me of the constant commerce in both souls and shekels that did here daily transpire. I imagined the whip arm of Christ had long since wearied in his attempt to make the temple clean, and the darkening melancholy of this emptied desolation dripped to the scene as though from his own holy despair.

To be alone in the expanse in which the Cathedral was set, and atop the city's tallest hill, left me feeling naked and open to the eyes of God. In the usual press of London, I oft felt as though just one blade of grass in some large field, such that my efforts and my offenses did so easy blend with my neighbour's that they seemed of diluted consequence. But I now felt as exposed as Adam, like a bared throat that awaited whatever pleasures cruel fate wished to offer. I was much unnerved. So much so that, when I heard feet ring on the cobbles near and saw that it was Carey I felt much affection toward him in my relief, even though just an hour previous I was sore distressed thinking how I might discharge this evening's business to other than my own detriment.

Carey was dressed the same as he had been at our last meeting. His clothing was of fine material and manufacturer but of little ornament or excess, only now with a broad belt and sash from which hung a scabbard holding a broad sword with a thick hilt and handle – it suiting his manner to wear a soldier's weapon and not the rapiers that were common to his class.

"Is our congress now so common that I no longer deserve the compliment of some finer dress?" he asked, his comment balancing both his humour and his disapproval. My time had run short, and I was dressed only as I could manage from my own closet.

"In truth, I had attired for our previous discourse and that with your family out of the stores of our company, my own clothes being at best such as you see now. But as you seemed to wish this truck be held quiet, I dressed such that, should I encounter some that I know, they would not find my costume of note and thus my business, also, note not."

Carey waved his hand as though to bat a fly. "So, what news?"

"From your brother's recollection, and knowledge gained from an apothecary, I can, I think, confirm the agent of your father's death. Were you at Somerset the night he died?" I asked.

"I was not, but arrived the morning next."

"Did you note upon his person any mark of violence or such other as did strike you odd?" I did not want to ask about the poxing of the hands or mouth direct, as this might colour Carey's recollection, but instead wanted to hear plain his remembering.

"Of violence, no, though he was then already dressed as should befit his station and powdered and perfumed as is the habit. He was much reddened about the mouth, but I thought that likely of his illness."

I relayed his brother's account of his father's final hours, though not in the same unkind spirit in which I had heard it, and then also what the apothecary had said of banes, their effects, and their common place in many gardens.

"So, you are saying poison?"

"Yes, my lord. It seems certain. And it confirms your own dream, in which you saw poxed both his mouth and his hands."

"His hands were gloved when I saw him that morning next, but his mouth was unnatural red."

"If you think it wise, I would like to meet with such of your servants as were attending him in his last days. For those poisons as his symptoms would suggest would sure have been introduced through his supper."

Carey nodded. "So, you think some servant wished my father ill?'

"Whether some servant wished him ill, or was the agent of some other who wished him ill, or was perhaps just witness to such act, I cannot know. But as kitchens and suppers are their province, I do hope they have some knowing, even if they know not its portent."

"Then I will have them know you wish their thoughts on my father as their good master for your work, and you can decide best how to frame your inquires to tease out the truth." He paused, scanning for a moment the surrounding city, many lights now showing in its pooling darkness and the sounds and alarms that seemed somehow more common to the night making their faint echo. "In your message, you mentioned some abuse of my name. What of this?"

"Know first, please, that I am the messenger only, and such as I have heard is not my opinion, but only–"

He held up a hand. "Do you think me such a fool that I cannot tell message from messenger? Speak clear and waste not my time with your apologies."

"Your brother made claim that such debts as your father held equalled the estate he bequeathed, though as your brother seemed some soured at his status, I thought perhaps his opinion coloured by his contempt. But my landlord, too, in a recent matter made the same claim, which made such claim seem common thinking."

"And how are my debts of your concern?" Which sounded both question and challenge.

"Twofold, my lord. As such debts as you may have inherited were first your father's, and as the fires of greed do oft burn brightest in foul mischief, I do consider that such debts could be motive in his murder. And second, as you have asked me talk plain, I must for my company's sake consider your patronage, and such effects as your debts may hold for us, for good or ill."

Carey's face set hard, and he paused a long moment. "I have secured you in this current service for such insights as you have in your writing clear shown, but do not suppose your gifts as accountant are required. As to your company, do you suppose that my father did ever, or would I, pay for your service from our own purse? Such favour as you hold through my office, whether the weight of its name or selection to perform at Court, come at no cost to me, and payments for those performances are from the Queen's household, not my pocket. But gold is true oft earned in blood, so I shall consider my father's accounts, and should I find such that

points to mischief, then I will have your counsel."
He drew a breath as though controlling his temper.
"Who, pray tell, is this landlord who makes so free
with my name?"

"Miller, my lord, who owns our theatre but seeks
our eviction current. He is Puritan, and much
dismayed of our arts."

Carey nodded. "I have had word from this Miller,
his signature among some Puritan others on a letter
praying that I withdraw support for your troupe so
as to please the honour of God. I did not plan them
answer, as their stations and opinions seemed both
beneath my concern. But now I think I may warn
him that his liberty with my reputation may cause
him harm before any such that his God may have
in store for him." Carey then reached into the top
of one glove and pulled from within a folded paper,
which he opened. A copy of the pamphlet from
Jaggard's press.

"On the matter of reputations," he said, "I was also
was recent made an anonymous present of this."

I could feel my face colour and such that I feared
even in this dark it be plain. "My lord, I–"

He again held up a hand. "I ask no explanation,
as such appetites as men entertain do oft find
satisfaction in strange beds, and so to judge some
man for such acts made public that I myself have
frequent done in private satisfies no definition of
justice. But the fact of reputation, that does matter.
And so I will scold you stern to be sure in future
to shake thy spear only in such fashion as not to

gain such fame for that performance as you have from those of more public display." He waved the pamphlet as though removing from it some stench, and then let it fall to join that trivial litter of human vanities that flowered across the Cathedral grounds. "The harm this does you is not to sever that thread from which my favours hang, but only to saw it half. One scandal is an accident, but a second would prove a habit from which I would be excused."

I made a short bow. "I thank you and will hold your counsel close."

"Do you suppose that pamphlet, too, came from this Miller? For I may add that to the curriculum on which I shall have him schooled. As your company bears my name, such public insult to it accrues some to me."

"To be true, I did at first think it so. But I have had cause now to wonder other." I explained the events of the past days in their varied machinations, including such matters of land as I understood. "I see in this confluence of misfortune not so much poor luck, but rather some plan that means the company ill, or at least my person."

Carey seemed unsettled, which I took in some surprise, not supposing that my fortunes weighed heavy in his list of cares. Companies of players were thick on the ground, and should one fall, and he still wish to serve patron, he could easy find some other.

"This matter of lands you mention. This company with which you think Miller be in league is named Somerset?"

"It is, my lord."

"And so some would borrow the name of my house to lend their scheme weight, unless those shareholders be also in residence there."

"So it seems."

"Shoreditch, you said? This is the centre of their plan?"

"As far as I can know. Our attorney will inquire further and seeks such records as may confirm the fact of things."

"My father gained some land holdings in Shoreditch years back in the settlement of an old matter. As they are not of his baronial estates, I did not account them much – the baronial estates coming to me by primogeniture and such other interests as he did hold bequeathed to my brother for his maintenance. That a company of such name should involve properties of that district and at such timing gives me pause."

I thought to my meeting with Carey's brother, at the scorn he plain had shown for his father's name and at this new knowledge that he now owned properties in Shoreditch by virtue of the late Baron's death. But I was unsure how best to say my thoughts to Carey. As I had at every moment in Carey's company, I felt like a drunk man making his way on frozen ice, taking each step with certain care and afraid at each of some bad fall.

"My lord, I must relay that, in my converse with your brother, he did not in his manner hold your father in the same affection as do you."

"To speak plain, you mean my brother was in turns petulant, offensive, and graceless, but no doubt fine attired and presenting his insult with some considerable style."

"I would not impugn his honour to phrase it so, my lord."

"You cannot impugn what he does not hold. Were he in some desert parched and water offered, if water be honour, he would drown in its drinking, having no custom in its management."

I made no answer, Carey's opinion being plain and me seeing nothing to be gained in agreeing to such insult to his family. Carey sighed long, and then continued.

"We are at some change in time, where lawyers are as much feared as men at arms and the Bourse makes such moneyed mischief by means of companies and shares that those lands and estates in which wealth were once measured do oft become instead the instrument of some other's gain. And nobles, who did once hold their title and honour dear and made their allegiance to the Crown only, now oft make bedfellows with such common grubbers as these. Even our good Queen must make a fashion of obeisance to such usurers who do her nation's debts support. And all manner of such craft and art as did before hold even a common man in standing, be his trade in wool or iron of those foods on which even our lives do hinge, these now all find the products of art have become abstract commodities, the paper owning of which somehow extracts all wealth. Now he who makes such real objects as on which these new fortunes are founded is left to beg scraps from these same sorcerers who toil not, nor spin, and yet are afforded fortunes that Solomon might envy. They be our new lords who reach their station not through fair service and loyal obedience but instead through such sleight of hand that leaves all wondering how some other did end up holding their purse, with some lawyer standing near to call it fair."

"I do admit," I said, "that I am oft much confused by the ease at which those who seem to contribute least do seem to profit most."

"My father's death seems more surrounded in mischief than I had imagined," Carey said. "The servants will be at your disposal immediate, so do not tarry in their examination. And I shall consider such debts or properties as may seem party to this evil. Meet me in two days' time at this same place and hour, and we shall see what the sum of our learnings be."

Carey turned, waiting for neither answer nor assent, clear used to his instructions being met with strict comply.

I was again alone, the distress that had preceded Carey's arrival back full and compounded now by the full dark of the cathedral district, the church itself being not much lighted and the space about it yawning black like a hungering void.

I made my way in care toward the light and the sounds of those lanes closest, knowing that what true dangers I might face lurked more likely there, but feeling in this current darkness an oppression of spirit that would answer to no reason. It was instead like the fear of the dark I had felt as a child, most oft when I would make way from the rooms where I was schooled past the charnel house that stored the bones of the dead.

I turned the corner of the cathedral, barking my foot once hard on some stone – which did for a short moment distract my fears toward more real pains – when some piece of the dark seemed to move of its own accord and not as a piece of the whole. And then I heard the soft padding of feet taking care of their sound, and that piece of dark moved plain and toward me direct and with seeming purpose.

I turned and ran, my own feet slapping loud, and could now hear those behind me slapping equal loud. As I had not that day dressed from our company's costume, I also did not carry any sword, but only the short dagger that was my usual – and that used usually only to carve at food, not at spectres formed seeming whole from the bowels of night.

I stumbled brief on some unevenness, thus losing pace. Those feet behind me held speed to draw closer, and then I heard clear the metal song of a sword drawn from its scabbard. Ahead, and near the wall, I saw stored some stones and timbers that awaited use in the cathedral's finishing, and I ran hence, hoping to find a tool for my defence. Grabbing from the top of one pile a rock near the size of my hand, I turned and hurled it at my assailant. It struck him on the shoulder, but not of that arm which held his sword – in whose blade seemed focused all the little light there present, so that the sword seemed in its gleaming invested of some foul purpose of its own devising.

The blow from the rock slowed the spectre's headlong rush, his feet now making a more purposeful stalking, the blade held easy in his right hand as though from long practice. I grabbed a length of pole that I found handy, it being longer by some two feet than my own height, and turned with it, my hands braced wide to control its length, so that I stood like a pikeman. I hoped that, if this was the same assailant I had previous encountered, he would again prove reluctant to join with a prepared foe.

But if it were the same opponent, he had more appetite for his work this night, and he continued near. I swung my staff at him with all the force that I could manage, but its length and weight blunted my effort. The spectre raised his left arm, accepting the blow against his ribs. Then he clamped his arm down solid on my weapon and grabbed it with his left hand, and I could feel in the pole's sudden and complete immobility a strength well past my own. But as I had two arms to control the staff and he but one, I thought I might wrest the pole free or pull him from his balance. So, I braced my feet and swung with my entire effort. He simply danced his feet in the direction of my attempt, taking in that moment the chance to advance his grip on the pole closer to me, his sword now more raised, as though, with the moment of its satisfaction more near, it was now more aroused.

His hand crept up another length and he swiped with his sword, measuring the distance remaining, which was uncomfortable slight. I was overcome – not with fear as I would have thought, but instead with despair, my end seeming plain at hand. Past death's boundary at the end of what short moments I was still allotted, I could sense no comfort or promise or even threat of suffering. Instead I sensed just a blank expanse that in its absolute negation made seem those visions of hell as I had heard of previous pleasant by compare. And I thought sudden of the fishmonger's daughter and knew her there to be my waiting companion, though in such vastness we would have no congress, but would each drift alone. And so, sudden wearied and absent any hope, I resolved to release the pole, accept the blade, and prayed that in the void at least I would be absent any consciousness, and that the vision of this vile and draining horror would be washed away with my own blood.

Instead it was my opponent who released the pole, turning sudden to raise his blade against some threat I had in my reverie missed. It was Carey close behind him!

Carey's blade descended hard onto that of my enemy. Some last sudden angle in Carey's effort drove the offending blade not only down but also to one side. Carey then drew his blade up and flicked it across, the tip of it cutting into my assailant's left arm.

The spectre seemed only some little dissuaded by this injury, though, keeping his blade level with his right arm, his feet making an artful shuffle, and his sword circling with some subtle motions, as though to invite Carey to attack. Carey held his blade high above his head, as if an axe, and the assailant, sensing some opportunity, lunged forward.

Carey turned a little to his side and brought his sword down with much savagery but also craft, so that again the foe's blade was directed down and away, and Carey did again draw his own back across the attacker's person – this time cutting across the top of his chest. Carey pressed his advantage, bringing his blade down again in the same fashion – this time knocking the enemy's blade aside so that Carey's next blow bit unimpeded into that hollow where the neck met the shoulder. His blade continued down far into my assailant's chest, crushing through flesh and bone, the foe's death coming sudden and complete.

I was stunned at this conflict's speed and nature. Such swordplay as we have in our plays is always of long and artful dance and ending with a thrust that leaves the afflicted poetic in his final agonies, allowing good occasion for some quip or speech to either ennoble or amuse our audience through his death.

What I had witnessed was no wound of my acquaintance, but instead a sundering through which death did speak complete in a tongue of blood and organ and shattered bone and with an eloquence by which the grave gave full flower to the validity of its argument.

Carey turned to me. "You had no thought to offer your help?"

"I… I'm thankful you seemed to have no need of it."

He snorted. "He seemed some little practised with a sword, but more of that gentle prancing as the city's fencing tutors suggest for duelling, where the parties make dance in the name of honour and oft call such little honour as they hold satisfied as soon as the other suffers some small scratch. I have learned my art at war and would have it done quick and to my advantage and with only such little style as necessary to show my foe's guts to the sun."

"Or the moon," I said.

He pulled the cloak from the corpse and used it to clean the blood from his blade before he returned it to his scabbard.

And I looked down into the face of the bulbous-nosed man who had been my common companion these few days last. The exact injury to his nose was now more plain and strange – as though somehow the organ had been exploded outward from the inside and then left poorly to heal.

"I would make your introduction to that man who has served my shadow since our first meeting," I said, "but I fear your ministrations do leave him mute."

"He can make his conversation with Satan, then," Carey said, "but I will remember his homely face to my father's fellows, as I should think that nose would be easy recalled."

I looked down at my late shadow, flayed so that he seemed forked, with his head to the left and his arm and shoulder to the right, that yawning grin of violence glistening between in this dull lighting.

Even though his intent had been that I now be on such journey as he current suffered, I was still much suffused in that rank despair that I had felt in that moment when I thought myself perched on the brink of such abyss as in which he now plummeted endless, there being no bottom to it nor top nor side. What sense I had previous of death had been of theory only, for while I have seen many dead and even some by violence, I had never before seen death so fully attired in its finery. I knew each minute forward I would feel that same cloak upon my own shoulders – so that no matter how cheered and graceful the raiment of any given day, it would be dulled by my knowing that it was a transitory grace beyond which waited this monstrous nothingness. I was now already part claimed by death, and feared that did somehow make me its servant.

CHAPTER 15

I stood before my own door in Stratford in the failing light, much wearied from hard travel, having made in one day a trip that should take two. But in my new familiarity with death I did know it too well to think I had beat it hence, for in the unnatural calm of my household I could feel death's residence.

I had returned to my rooms from St Paul's to word my son was now dire ill, my wife requesting I make home with all haste. But death doth travel with what speed it pleases, and in such time as took her message to reach London and me to reach Stratford, it likely had already borne my son to that destination that now too much coloured my thinking. So I stood, fearful of my own doors, the varied melancholies of my recent experience such that my shames and my fears and knowledge of my petty avarices and banal secrets eroded the pretended honour by which I once entered this house as its worthy master. Seeming to sense that I had come this long distance but could of my own power come no further, the door opened, my Anne standing there, her face some aged from our last meeting and me knowing her heart likely aged more.

"Our Hamnet is dead," she said.

And only then was I able to take those final steps that brought me to the threshold to take her in my arms, but she was stiff and unyielding in my embrace and quick to break it. We made into the house, where my daughters were quiet but their embrace truer. And so I held them long, some shamed that I did need from these children to draw such comfort that I should, as their father, have offered instead.

"I received your message only this evening past and made such speed as I could," I said to my wife. But even in my own hearing of these empty words I knew I had near a week previous heard Hamnet ill, and had thought on it only little since.

"He held life hard until just this morning," she answered, "and oft asked after you. In your absence and the growing stature of your name – at least in compare to such simple folk as do still here abide – you had become some godlike in his eyes, and he did believe you held some power that would his ills reverse if he could outrun death until your arrival. And so I think you did in your neglect at least some prolong his life, and for that I do thank you. Now, I have much wifely duty before his funeral and do beg your leave."

She left to the kitchen, and I sat a long hour with my daughters, making a little talk of no consequence about such local matters as they could at their age understand. I knew well my son's own body lay somewhere in these rooms, but I feared yet to look upon it, and feared also the company of my own wife. And so I did stick with these smaller women, who were of such age that they could not all my sins remember or even yet understand.

In our chambers later, I shared news with Anne concerning the College of Heralds and the granting of our armorial bearings, thinking her knowing our son had died a gentleman – and that we could thus array his procession with his Coat of Arms – might some little lighten her grieving.

"If such vain display doth please you, then by all means we shall have it," she said, "as it is his right as your son. Your son. Though I did bear him and suckle him. Your son. Though I have these several years hence both fathered and mothered him. Your son. Though I did these last days comfort him and wipe the pestilence of fever from his brow and clean his filth as he was too weak to use the pot and try make light his fears in the press of death – and did listen to him in his last breath ask instead for you. Your son. And so, yes, such glories as you have won our name in your distant strivings, by all means, let us make them public so that all may know how well you loved Hamnet and that all may know him your son."

Her face was bleached with scorn. "But your father will be pleased. And he has been most kind to us, and for that small mercy at least I do true thank you."

I felt a burn of anger that I knew was kindled more by the truth of her words than by the hurt of her saying them.

"I had thought this such time as a husband and wife might find in each other comfort," I answered. "And instead you give me venom."

She turned to the chest nearest her, taking from it a paper that she threw on our bed. The pamphlet. "Such venom as this, which I only yesterday did receive so as to lighten those final hours in which I watched your son die?"

I knew sure she could see in my face the truth of it, and I stood mouth agape, trying to imagine what words could make safe passage and finding none.

"The great Shakespeare, whose quill pens such speech as to make men laugh or cry or quail or swell with pride, all as he likes it, stands dumb in the face of a simple woman? You, who have such words as to make young girls surrender first their virtue and then their lives, have none to answer this commoner, made in her abandonment no longer even wife but just maid and nurse?"

"Anne, I–"

She spun, shaking her head. "No, sir, please. Pray you silence some small while longer so I can still clear have my say. For, once you gain you speech, it will sure flow such that I can hold mine own thoughts clear no more, but instead will be such clouded in your arguments as to doubt all I know be true. And then I must also hate myself as I do now so rightly hate you."

She paced by our bed a moment, her lips moving but no words issuing forth, as though keeping her own congress. But then she again did turn and speak.

"Though I be some years your senior, I know you have long thought me a fool for my poor schooling, and weak, as my standing as woman would require, and so you thought I could neither know nor bear the truths of this world. But lest you think this so, I tell you now true that I understand well men's lusts and their weaknesses and never did imagine that you could live so long apart and not of occasion seek some satisfaction. I knew this true at some hurt, but did never speak it, nor withhold from you my wifely duty during any time when you sojourned here, nor even, again in truth, let it much diminish my own affection for you, which was true. And being a woman and thus, in truth, stronger, so was I true, true to you."

She was quiet again, again pacing, her silent speech with herself continuing as though in rehearsal. And then she stopped again, facing away this time.

"And I do know what marriage means. It is not in common a matter of heart but a matter of office and dowry, such that in usual a wife may share a name and bed and progeny and still be in her husband's mind much like his cow or barn – perhaps more valuable than the former, cows being oft short lived, but likely in value held lighter than the barn, as it will the next cow contain, and the next. And while a man may make some blandishment in courting, it is akin to those words used in a shop to gain some advantage in price, the negotiation in which a man persuades a woman to be wife and thus give herself up entire to his ownership. A woman does know her place."

She turned toward me, her face now awash in tears that I had not heard in her speaking, as though she had become such in custom of weeping that she did it now without sign or notice, but instead like breathing. As though grief were now not some transient affliction, but instead a true part of her being.

"But, Will, you did make me believe it other. Against my own heart and mind, me being even in our courting of sufficient age to know the nature of the wifely office, you did with such constant sweetness and such jewelled words have me think myself special, and thus us special, and thus love special. So special that I did grant my nakedness and favours and heart and soul unto you even before our marriage, thinking in your care their keeping safe, when I should have held some back as my own, should have kept some small corner of me and thus have had those defences that other women hold to make the insult of their husbands' poor faith less dear. Instead I am unarmed and unarmoured and feel the truth in each cut of this," now pointing down at the pamphlet, "total and to the bone."

And she turned and paced again into another rehearsal, my heart already bleeding from her deft performance. But I dared not speak, knowing I owed her silent attention to all she had want to say. I had in recent days my own soul examined, chiselling away at that false statue of self that was my previous imagining, to find instead this much lesser and flawed figure with which I must now reconcile. In her words I felt not a chisel, but instead a hammer that showed me not just flawed but reduced complete to some worthless gravel. She continued.

"When I gave myself to you complete and in secret and as yet unwed, you were simply son to a glover, though with much wit, and so I did imagine you would a witty glover be, and me a glover's wife. And that fitted me fine, Will, as a glove to my hand. But you found this new ambition, and as I know that a man will to his ambitions cleave as he will to no woman, I let you go – and not with any hesitation but instead my blessing, even knowing what cost our separation would sure exact. And while I never supposed you would be complete faithful, you did well maintain the comfort of our household and increase its wealth, did when at home treat me with such tenderness as you did in youth. And so I supposed that you did care for me in such best fashion as you could manage, and felt I could expect no more from any husband."

She snatched the pamphlet up again from the bed. "But in these particulars I do not read a man seeking convenient solace from such place as he might in private find it, but instead in public pursuit of some younger thing – some better thing than that of his having or experience. I read a man caring more for his lust than for his reputation. Or mine. Or, then, for me."

She let the pamphlet fall to the floor. "But your son is dead, and while I know now you have no true heart for me, I do believe you had some for him. And so now, in your pain for him, you seek comfort from me, none other being available." She pulled her gown over her head and stood before me naked, her hands to her sides, those tears that still streamed running from her eyes running down her face to her neck to her breasts to her belly, her breasts now sagged, her belly showing the cost of her children and her age, and her thatch now showing some grey. "I do true understand my wifely office, sir, and cannot in law withhold it. But I do warn you that comfort is a matter of heart and not of flesh. And as I have no heart left for you, I have also no comfort. I am sure this aging sack of skin doth much pale in compare to such virginal pleasures as you have late received. But take of it what you will. Just know that you do take. For nothing is offered."

And she stood still and naked before me, her speech clear finished and in both form and content better than any with which I could answer.

"I will not insult you further, Anne, with any claim that what you read me false," I said.

"I am most gracious thankful for your kind favour, my lord," she answered.

"Nor will I try to excuse the matter, having thought on it much and suffered for it dear these few days hence."

"The girl, then, being much fortuned to be dead and thus beyond such agonies as no doubt you have borne – unless such rules of Hell as we have been told be true. But even then her suffering sure would be no equal to such that your fine mind must be able to invent for itself."

"Anne, I do not wish to argue the matter with you, for I have no good words to make my wrong be right or even seem so. I will have you know, though, that the beauty I beheld in that poor girl that I full admit I did poorly use was a mirror of your own and of that fair affection we did taste so sweet in our youth. And so, while you may true blame my lust, it was a memory of such lust as you did inspire, your favour having been to my taste so sweet that my heart had hungered for it all the years of my absence. And so I sought in this girl a surrogate for our own love, not just such trivial satisfaction as might some pent need relieve, but instead that intimate congress that I have, only with you, ever known. And I was a fool to think I might find it in any arms other, which I did realise almost immediate. Then I did take that girl's favours no more, at which she knew that she could not have my love as some other did already hold it entire, and it was in despair of this that she chose her end."

For a short moment, the fierceness that had so informed Anne's features softened such that I imagined my words had found some purchase. But then her aspect changed to a sadness that did trouble my heart even more. For to have earned Anne's hate did hurt me dear, but to know myself also to be the instrument of this grief did cut much deeper.

"I finally understand the truth of you, Will. I had imagined you words' true master, but in truth you are their slave. Such lies as you just uttered, you believe be true, as any idea you can frame in words claims equal credit for you with every other. So, if you can by some trick of poetry say night be bright and morning in its mourning be dark, you are so joyed with your agile wit and the music of those words that you hold them true – even as you burn a candle to write them, night in fact being night and no other.

"And so, all these years when I did hold you true as I had never sensed you false, it was only that you could not feel yourself false, your own pride being such that you imagined any phrase of your creation must so please God, your hand being such akin to his own, that it could hold no lie. And so your deceptions were much complete, you having first so complete deceived yourself.

"Oh, Will, you have stopped my hate and made it now full grief, for I had believed myself betrayed. And betrayal, being the retraction of such love as once was offered, does hatred make. But I now know that such love was not in truth ever offered, but I was even in those sweet remembered days of youth just one figment of your imagining, and no more real or false than are those characters with which you have peopled the varied stages of your life. For in your mind, all life is but a stage, and we poor players do there strut and fret our hour upon it at the mercy of your imaginings."

She stooped, retrieved her gown, and dressed herself. Then she shook her head at me slow as though at a child she had learned was not in fact wilful but failed at its lessons as it had no gift for them.

"Will, I pray you forgive my harshness, for I no longer have strength for it and must save such strength as I do yet still hold to bear my shame."

And I, too, now to tears. "I hope your judgment wrong, but current have no answer for it. But I will tell you this plain and in words tricked with no poetry. You have no shame to bear, as any evil either current or past is mine alone, you only ever having been true to me and gentle, and in your office as either wife or mother always a faithful servant of your duties."

She smiled slight, as though expecting my ignorance. "As if my shame was yours to forgive. As if, had I made you cuckold, you could walk proud through town, my having said you hold no shame. As if your daughters could say to their tormentors to hold their tongues, you having called their barbs dull."

I looked down at the floor, upon that pamphlet the injuries of which I had counted, until this night, only slight. "So, this has not been received by you alone?"

"You must at least feel true grief for your son to not have felt some eyes upon you on your arrival, as I have felt them burn deep each time I even pass a window."

"Surely our friends must pay this little account, such Puritan antics being in London quite common and, their vile intent familiar, their contents also being much discounted. This will quick pass, what scandal it offers melting like some spring snow, and the public's eye drawn to the scandal next and the scandal next."

"Have you been gone from Stratford so long as to forget its climate? The snow of scandal does not fall here so oft as it does in London. And so, such weather as this being unnatural to these climes, it will be the conversation for some years."

I considered this careful. "Anne, I do in my heart and in your sight bear full all guilt in this that I have earned, and shall too wilful bear such public shame and scorn as to it attaches if that be your will. But if it will your own burden relieve, and that of our daughters, then I do have such art of persuasion to have all believe these charges false. For even here most must know this sort of mischief common in London, and oft directed at those of my art."

Anne sat on the bed, looking much wearied, her tears finally stopped and all feeling fled her face, which now lay flat and barren.

"And so you make me share your shame. Knowing that in affection for my daughters, I will not have them bear this and so must assent to your lies and, in my assent, be party to them, admitting that first wilful chink to my honour. And so I say, yes. Go. Be false to our neighbours and with my blessing."

I nodded. "Any lie I tell accrues to my honour, not yours."

She smiled weakly. "For that lie at least, I thank you. But the hour is late. I am much tired, and we must come morning bury our son. I ask you, let me sleep, and alone, as my sorrow will sufficient fill this bed."

Alone in that room, normal used for guests, I sat long awake, finally giving up hope of sleep. I did fancy for some time that I could end the seeming endless grief my life had late become, my dagger near and my heart feeling that would welcome the company of the blade.

And I thought it queer how that despair I first had felt just one night past when I was sure my death was at hand, which at the time did seem so oppressive and so fearful, could now seem so seductive. How knowing what horrors did, at the end, await us all made the thought of having to bear those horrors over long years so harsh that the idea of surrendering to them immediate appealed – if only in hoping, in that surrender, I might escape my consciousness, which was the only avenue by which fears could reach me. It seemed that, by surrendering to death I could instead defeat it, that thought seeming so sweet that I long held my dagger against my breast and even now cannot say what swayed the balance that this story is writ now in this ink instead of ending then in my blood.

I knew, too, in this vain exercise, the truth of my wife's words. My mind could make true any thought I did think, and then make it false, and then make it both. Whether from cowardice or hope or stubbornness or just simple sloth, I would not take arms against my sea of troubles and by opposing end them, for I did not have courage enough for even that.

CHAPTER 16

A hole, in its essence, is an absence. A space in which something expected is missing. A grave doth make this plain.

I stood beside my wife, strangely comfortable in her company after the evening just past. That honest assessment of our current stations now allowed us each to stand as who we were, with all pretending stripped away, and to watch as the coffin bearing our only son was lowered slow into that absence so as to remind us what expected thing we would miss this day, and the next, and in the month hence, and in the year. And also to remind me what I had missed previous, having most of Hamnet's life been his father in name only and not in presence.

He had made good progress in his schooling so that in my more recent visits he took joy to converse with me in such Latin as he had acquired – me thinking by his gift with it that his Latin soon would exceed my own – and I had started to share with him some of those books that I had first enjoyed when I was near his age. In this scholarly congress I had made a bond with him that I never did manage when he was a boy, me being more comfortable with the girls when they were younger – supposing, I think, what expectations we hold for girls being slighter, they seem more near complete in some way, as they will not be schooled and can learn early at their mother's knee such skills as will be their province. And so they become their fathers' darlings until those strange years in which they acquire their womanhood and cross that boundary which places them permanent beyond our manly understanding.

But in our sons we hope to fashion our own immortality, to shape men through whose loins we will be pleased to pass our name. So, in our expectations of them, in our striving to cure in them those faults we see in ourselves, we do never hold them in that pure and simple affection that we afford our daughters. For a daughter can be a joy only, unanchored by the weight of our name's eternity that does so weigh on a son.

My father stood across the expanse of the grave, some straighter on account of the quick-made standard bearing our name's new coat of arms. His petty opponents in the press of mourners would know that no such mark of station would adorn their graves or those of their children and, I hoped, suspect that my success in London, which did somehow grant me the status to secure these bearings, could also be used, if they continued in their unwelcome suits against my father's interests, as a weapon. But I could see also in my father's face the knowledge that his name would now end in this hole, his grandson gone before his son. And so gone with Hamnet were those grand hopes men do hold that for some long future the name they watered and grew and shared will pass generation to generation, in ascending glory, and that they thus might live eternal. Now, instead, in this hole, my father could see not just that hard promise of his own mortality – for if such boy as this, all his years hale and fair, could be so sudden gone, then the claim of time on my father's aged and wearied bones must be that much more sure and close. No, he could see also the already fading name of Shakespeare, it having only my few remaining years to gain what glory it may, and then be gone.

The service at the grave, as had been that in the church, was short and plain, in keeping with the spirit of the Crown's ordained religion, which despised the pomp and ornament of its Catholic ancestor. I thought this folly. Death is stark enough, and it seemed to me such religions as we might fashion in our human imaginings concerning a God beyond our hope to know should at least contribute to our own comfort. The absence of the grave could be made to feel less yawning, its inexorable gravity less fearful awesome, if we did fill the air around it with those rites and songs and costumes and incenses that made a Catholic gathering better theatre. For what was religion, really, except such human theatre through which we tried to please a distant audience whose tastes we little understood.

And then that last moment, the coffin lowered, the earth shovelled o'er it, the service done, there being no ritual further to prolong the idea of a son who, in truth, had been gone complete before I ever had returned home. In that moment, the hole of his grave did swell and consume my whole person and thinking, all my distracting reveries swept aside. Again I was party to that dizzying emptiness that short days previous I had never imagined but that did now seem so present, this bridge of life across which we tread, seeming so fragile and subject to such easy injury that by what magic we did at all ever suspend ourselves above that underlying void was beyond my understanding. And the temptation, again, to hurl myself instead into that hole – to become part of that absence, to never again be party to life's incessant worry and striving, to instead in death make such true communion with my son as I never had in life – that urge was on me strong, and its disease in me so clear that even Anne, on noticing it, took some pity and lead me by my arm from the pull of the grave that I could not, at that moment, escape on my own.

We retired to our home, where by custom we feasted our neighbours and pretended again that each hole, each grave was unique, that it held the death of this man or that, and that it was not the portal through which we saw death entire. Pretended again that what we saw as a hole was not in fact a window through which shone the dark truth of eternity, the ever-night which awaits us each at our own sunset. Pretended again that it was the frenzied fabric of life that we vainly wove around the hole of the grave, and not the grave itself, that mattered.

Death is the real stuff of this world and the next, and it is only our vanity that makes us suppose other.

The morning next, I rose early to make my return to London, finding no more comfort in Stratford. I knew I would likely never again return here as to a home, but instead as an unwelcome landlord. My father, in the habit of the old – knowing, I suppose, he would soon have what fill of oblivion he may require – rose early to horde the portion of wakefulness his life still offered. And so, while I had meant to steal away unnoticed, having taken my leave of family the night past and my visit having left me foul in my temper, he met me in my leaving.

"Will, I must say true that I do fear for thee."

"Life is a fearful business, Father, but I suspect myself no more prey to its insults than another. And so how do you fear?"

"For your soul, Will. I do not inquire into your marriage bed, as it is not my affair. But I have seen the pamphlet that I know did greatly concern your Anne, and did overhear those artful remarks by which thee hast deflected its charges away from the honour of our name. Were I a better father and stern, I would have thee swear to me the honesty of your objections. But I will instead pretend to their truthfulness and thus make myself in conscience party to that lie that I will in consciousness pretend I do not know."

"As you ask no question, I will offer no answer."

He sighed, and sank into a chair. "I will admit I

am made shallow happy by the favour thou hast secured us – the recent arms, the increasing comfort of this house. But, Will, it is our godliness only that will serve us beyond this life; and we have recent reminder that this life is uncertain and, even in its longest, measured short against eternity. In those ways I could serve example as a good Christian, I have. But I do wonder whether thou hast even any little care toward God's opinion, or toward his church, and so I do fear that the grave, which I do true believe holds thy son in the warm embrace of God's favour, will hold thee other. And as you are my son and as I do love thee, this grieves me."

Though I think myself a respectful son, and while my usual temperament toward any authority is cautious – as the prideful satisfaction of rebellion carries in its own commission the risk of its punishment – the experiences of the days just recent past and the sense of death now as my constant companion had rubbed my heart raw and easy prompted to anger.

"Our godliness, sir? How godly? In your example? To cling some, but in private, to one religion, while trying also to pay sufficient service to another so as to preserve such station that you did all but squander in your vain attempt to serve two masters? As you are not martyr, you have failed in the former. As you are still hypocrite but poor at the art, you have failed in the latter. And as your failing did invite those attentions that have also eroded such human estates to which you did aspire, then you also have failed us all. No, then I am not godly, as I will ready admit that

I will kneel to whatever object of worship the Crown may choose to present, it being in my philosophy as valid as any former or as any later and as likely that whatever god may bear witness to our affairs is either the same amused or the same offended by either effort.

"Or perhaps you mean more full godly, as was Mary, our late Queen, who in her thirst to satisfy your god's honour did send so many to burn or hang or otherwise suffer dear solely for the service of their conscience. Or godly perhaps as our new Puritan brothers? So certain in their imagining of God's will that they piss on those few pleasures he doth grant us and think that in abusing his gifts they serve his glory? No, sir. I claim myself in no way godly. I know my own sins, and I do suffer them complete, but I have met no man yet not fully poxed with sin. Even could I make my own sins pure, I would not be godly – for it would seem to require I choose one god or another by which to define it, and then grow some appetite for cruelty, as any god of my choosing would need that I abuse any man who follows some other.

"My sins are of my appetites, and my selfishness and my faithless holding of others hearts, and as such are vile enough. But to be godly would require that I do purposeful evil and then pretend it good. That I constantly seek chance to stand judge of my fellows and then do them grievous ill in service of an imagined master. In the shadow of such sins that I already have so careless committed I am sufficient darkened. I have no stomach for more, and so will not be godly."

And I left, closing the door hard behind me, sorry already for my harsh words to a man whose path in life was marked by more charity and care to his fellows than I could claim, and whose hypocrisies were those only of one trying to serve both flesh and conscience in a world that made one pay dear for either attempt. And so I could now add to my swelling ledger the sin of dishonouring a father who had faithfully executed that office toward me as well as his conscience and human limitations allowed. Who had served me far better than I could claim to have served my own son. Who had, in fact, served father to my own son more than had I, a son who had died alone denied the only blessing he had ever sought from me, my company.

CHAPTER 17

"It is a scheme of some considerable imaging," said Webb, having various maps and documents already displayed on my arrival. I was grateful to have word he had news, as my absence seemed to be trying Carey's patience, and it would ease my circumstances to have some sop for his growling appetite.

"The members of the Somerset Company include Carey's younger brother," Webb continued, "and while he holds the second largest stake, he is by some distance the least notable shareholder. Cecil, the Baron Burleigh, who is the Queen's good friend and counsellor, holds the largest stake, with some shares held by other members of the Privy Council and leading members in the Worshipful Company of Mercers. And since the Mercers control the Bourse, at which shares of the Company would be traded, their involvement is most convenient.

"I will have you know the Company's members have gone to some pains to protect their secrecy. Their shares are held by other companies, the shares of which are held by yet other companies, so that to tease out the actual ownership of Somerset did much try my art and did, in some instances, require passing coin to those with access to records that are beyond my view. And even so, I can call this account only my best reckoning and not for certain true."

"When men wish their congress secret it is oft in shame of their motives," I said.

Webb nodded. "Just so. Now, of note, if you consider this ledger, you will see that all members of the Company gained their shares by purchase, save Carey the younger. His stake was secured in exchange for title to his considerable holdings in Shoreditch, which he gained at his father's death."

"And had he not inherited such properties, then he could not have joined the Company?"

"Had he not inherited such properties, there likely would be no Company," Webb said. "Let me explain further. The younger Carey's properties went into the company as payment for his shares, but are not held by the company. Rather, the company exchanged those properties for cash, and then broke those properties into various parcels that were distributed out to the shareholders as a kind of dividend – to all shareholders save Carey, as, he, having contributed the properties, could not expect also to benefit from their conversion."

"This seems odd," I said. "Is not the purpose of this company to consolidate mercantile properties in Shoreditch, the company being in essence a land venture? Why buy and hold titles to some properties within the Company, but then take such trouble to not hold others?"

Webb nodded. "That struck me odd, too. Put aside the matter of Carey's lands for a moment, and let

us consider again the Company's holdings. Your
butcher's account is largely accurate. Since early
June, various agents have been buying leases or
properties as he described so as to control almost
all trade in Shoreditch and in that area of London
nearest. And, while those leases and properties did
all eventual end up in the Company, they were not
bought by the Company, but instead by numerous
other agents who would buy them first and then
sell them immediate into Somerset's holdings – but
at some profit. Somerset's attorneys then would
approach the affected tenants to secure them for this
new venture."

"But why use other agents to purchase these
properties when this only served to increase their
eventual cost for the Company?" I asked.

"For one, so that each transaction would seem
individual and not reveal the interest of the Company
in the entire district. Were I advising a client and I
were to learn that a single company had designs on all
properties in some area, then I would tell my client to
hold hard for a dear price. By using multiple agents,
they avoid landholders gaining this knowledge. But
I think this only a minor concern. By this model,
these properties purchased, all in one area, are now
seen in public records to have sold once to one party,
and then again to a seeming second party, and each
time at a higher price. This already is creating a stir
among those with the wealth to speculate in lands."

"The appetites of greed being thus whetted, such
buyers will pay yet a higher price, believing they are

privy to some new trend, and that they will sell these holdings at some price yet higher still."

Webb again nodded. "Speculations are the current fever of the newly moneyed, as they see lands and goods and companies not as objects of some intrinsic value but simply as conduits through which to attract wealth. You have bought some lands around Stratford. How did you think on these lands before you made purchase?"

I shrugged. "Their usual yield in crops and income in leases, so as to know what gain they may produce in compare to what price I will pay."

"And you think how such lands, once in your ownership, will profit your estate. But," Webb held up a finger, "for these speculators, such issues mean naught, for the value of the land itself is the only crop. Which crop they fertilise with the avarice of others so that it grows tall in men's minds. They then sell this imagined bounty to some other, who then must make this crop seem somehow taller still."

"But such trend can only hold so long as profitable sales continue."

Heaton held up a sheet that detailed the inventory of properties that the players to this scheme had amassed. "Somerset already has sold back lands it has purchased from its agents to other agents, again at a higher price – the scent of such actions already having pricked the noses of our new class of moneyed speculators, who now are so hungry for this perceived feast that they little question its cost. But, most peculiar, while Somerset offers this ravening crowd the varied morsels of those small properties within its company, its shareholders – who, through their truck with the younger Carey, now hold many larger lands surrounding the Company's holdings – do not offer such larger parcels for sale. More peculiar still is the current traffic in Somerset's shares. Aside from the younger Carey – whose ownership in Somerset is held plain in his own name – the Company's more shadowy shareholders hold their claim behind the veil of other interests in other companies, which interests are now also being sold through the Bourse, and for staggering amounts. "

From the gleam in Webb's eye, I could see he had some larger and final mischief to reveal, but one he thought he might already have made clear. And so I pondered his map and ledgers a moment and then offered my guess.

"The younger Carey has been played the fool," I said. "Through the inducement to be member of their august company, he was tricked into handing over to his fellows those properties that he would have held as his own, those properties being much larger in area than those contained now within the Company itself. He was sold this same vision of some new district of stores and the Company's monopoly on that district's commerce, which vision now is also being whispered about as reason for profits in land in Shoreditch. But his fellow shareholders are selling the lands within its corporation to drive speculation in properties in the district, while holding the larger lands gained from Carey to sell at the last, highest price. Meanwhile, they also are selling their shares, so in the end, they will have profited twice from the same fictions, while Carey will be left landless and with shares in a company that is then worth nothing."

"Less than nothing," Webb said, "for while Carey has contributed his own wealth to the enterprise, the other shareholders have paid for their interest with debts secured by and held in the name of this network of companies through which they make ownership. This debt is transferred, along with their shares, to the new owners while Carey's fellows slink off, like rats from the sinking ship of commerce."

We paused for a moment, and a matter that had some puzzled me was now clear.

"And thus the name," I said.

"Pardon?" asked Heaton.

"To call the company Somerset – I did wonder after this, for it seemed likely to draw attention to this enterprise that those of its creation might wish to avoid. But this will end in scandal, with many investors feeling ill used. The only person they will find at which to aim their wrath will be the younger Carey, the name of his house serving to confirm his place as head of this scheme. But as he, too, will be much harmed, it will not seem he conducted purposeful mischief, but instead did wager too much in a game he too little understood. For him to claim other would mean to indict persons with the power and station to do him considerable ill, and on whose continued favour he will now be even more dependent, what few assets he was left for his own maintenance having been squandered. And, from your telling, I would suppose any proof to any claims against any other members of the Somerset Company would be much fogged in this maze of companies and loans and interests you have described, so that only the guilty, who built such maze, can find their way clear, any else having been sucked into its labyrinth to wander to no end."

Webb sat back in his chair and smiled. "You should have been a lawyer Will, as you have the talents in conspiracy that it oft requires."

"Invention of conspiracies is vital, too, to my own art," I replied. "But mine are played out on stages, not in lives. I fear I do not have the appetite for the real dish."

Webb packed away the varied maps and documents that illustrated the scheme, leaving on the table only my company's lease for the theatre. On seeing it, I made a wry smile.

"I suppose it is a weakness of my craft," I said, "that I did become so engrossed in your tale as to forget that business which first brought me here."

"On that, I do not yet have news, but I am to meet with Miller today. Methinks the mischief to which he has, unknowing, attached himself being so grave and the parties to it of such weight, it shall make it easy to settle matters to your liking."

I left Webb's office and headed for Somerset, where I had further business.

Shouldering my way through the thronged lanes, I

thought on the difference in experience for Carey, and his station, and most others, for Somerset sat direct on the Thames, its walled lawns and gardens covering the long distance between the wings of the house and the river, and its stables and carriage houses behind. Stepping from its doors Carey would join either the artful peace of its gardens or the privacy of his coach, while I, stepping from even Webb's rooms in this fine district of the city, found every sense assaulted immediate – the stench of the chamber pots emptied to the cobbles and the waste of the horses; the constant clatter of their hooves and the rumble of cart wheels along the stones; the babble of voices all in near shout to be heard at even close distance; a twilight of shade even at midday as the timbered stories added atop every building oft o'erleaned the streets to gain some few more feet of space. While men had through all history sought one another's company so that even rustic tribes would make villages, in our pastoral heritage we allowed some space that a man could take a moment in contemplation, could enjoy some ease away from the press of his fellows. But London allowed no solitude, only a forced intimacy that seemed at times a kind of violence. It was the friction of that constant commerce that sparked the birth of many wonders, true, but one that also seemed to give rise to our plagues, to flame into violence, and even to drive some to madness.

I had much madness to consider. The late Lord Chamberlain had first fallen ill in May, and his condition had such declined by June that his death did seemed certain – and it was in June, it seemed, this Somerset Company scheme was hatched, accelerating upward as the late Carey's health tended down. His seeming recovery, while news dear to those who loved him, would much injure the purse of this Somerset Company's players, the younger Carey's inheritance being key to their plot. This seemed motive enough for murder, plain. But by whose hand? That of the Baron's son, or some other? And how to know the truth of that?

CHAPTER 18

"He was a fair master," a chambermaid answered. It was as long an answer as I had managed from any of the late Lord Chamberlain's attendants in near an hour. I suppose the habit of discussing any noble person of their care with any stranger, even at the direct behest of their current master, seemed fraught with much danger and little chance for reward.

"I tell you all in sooth that you can speak plain and without fear. The late Baron's son has commissioned that I write a clear remembrance of his father. And as every character has many sides, I would have known your honest thoughts and will thank you for them true, but share them exact to none. What source might serve for any line of my work will be for my mind alone."

"As she said, fair," said the cook, "though stern as well if you failed in your offices. But he made your office known and made even occasional thanks when you performed it, which is more than I expect from some others in this house."

"What can you tell me of his final illness?" I asked. "As a man is much revealed in how he bears his sufferings."

"With grace, sir," said the chambermaid, "most of those long weeks. As he oft reminded, he was a soldier first, and as I did have care of his person, I did see some fearsome scars from his time at that art. He once said that such insult as sickness offered paled much compared to those he had suffered from human hands."

"You said most of those long weeks?"

"Save that last night, sir," she replied, "when his illness returned much fierce and I think he did suffer greatly, though I think he bore that as well as could be wished."

"And you alone attended him then?"

"I tended to my station, which was to clean his person, clothing, and bed."

"You alone and no other?"

And she took fear, I think, in this question's repetition. "Mary was my help, but being new to the household and still in her learning was help only. She would bring his meals and carry what I instructed to the laundries. The late Lord did enjoy her company, as she is young, and comely, and had better manners than us most."

Seeing no maid young and comely present, I asked after her. "And where might I find this Mary that I may have her thoughts, too?"

Some looks were exchanged amongst the staff that, in their discomfort, told me much, especially in company of her answer. "The younger Lord Carey, sir – John, not George – did take her immediate into his employ at his father's death," the chambermaid answered.

"To attend his person," the cook added with sufficient shading to make her suspicion plain.

"Our house scribe," said John Carey at my admittance, "who I do hold, in credit to your late publicity, in higher regard than I had previous. For I oft must use the weight of my name and office to despoil reluctant virgins and leave them despairing, and yet you sink your spear where you will on the strength of your words alone. If you can offer some instruction in this art, I think it will profit you more than those simple antics on which you current waste your talents."

I bowed, seeming to accept his jibe in good humour, though the edge of the words was spoke more cruel than would have been the words alone.

"I beg pardon for this additional intrusion, my lord," I said, "but your brother has asked that I have the thoughts of your father's staff, and I am told that Mary, who was late and only brief in your father's service, is now in yours. In fact, I believe you may have mentioned her on our first meeting."

"Ah, the fair Mary, a tasty morsel I did oft encounter in my father's room and of that blushing and blooming ripening that I hear tell you, too, do much enjoy. Yes, when my father did finally pass, I moved quick to secure her, and her service. But even that first morning, when I had so looked forward to having her help me dress – I much enjoy the first reaction when a new girl learns I am free with my nakedness – I noticed that her hands were sorely poxed. I was much pained to have her discharged from the household, as I could not risk that she was in fact less virginal than she appeared and that her pox might infect not only her hands, but also, well, such other parts of her person of which I would make use."

And so the girl who, by the chambermaid's account, brought the late Lord Chamberlain his last meal, in which likely was secreted the poison that killed him, displayed such pox as handling that poison could cause.

"Discharged, sir? Have you any thought where she might be found?"

He waved his hand dismissively. "Selling what only goods as she has to those who might take less caution of their health, I should think," he said. "But should a man of your talents find her, you can no doubt talk your way into those sweet chambers that would cost most others dear, if you fear not her pox."

"Norton, I think," answered the cook, when I asked after Mary's surname and any other particulars they might offer. "From her speaking, I would guess her from Yorkshire."

"Where would she go in London, being now put out of Somerset?" I asked.

"On such rare days as we had liberty, she would visit her father, who lives somewhere near. Close to the river, I think she said."

"Did you notice any injury to her hand in her last day?"

"Aye," answered the chambermaid. "Just that last day. She was puzzled to have what seemed a burn, having not burned herself. I wondered if it might be due the medicines for our late Lord."

"Medicines?"

She nodded. "In his illness, there were many doctors hence – some from the Queen's own service, the late Lord being a cousin of hers and much favoured. Oft they would provide some powder or potion to be added to his meals. Just that last night, another in the robe and cap of their practice was in the kitchen providing Mary yet another powder. I think I surprised her when I entered, and she spilled the powder on the table, sweeping it quick into her hand and then dusting it onto our Lord's supper."

"How was this doctor called?"

"He offered no name to me, nor I should think to her, as in habit they would brusque present their wares and instructions and take their leave, chambermaids and cooks being of little account. I did wonder what skills as a physician he might have, though, as he had clear at least once failed himself, and dire, too."

"Failed himself how?" I asked.

"His face. His nose must once have been most grievous injured and tended poor to have healed so hideous."

CHAPTER 19

Baron Carey, wishing still to meet clear of the eyes and ears of Somerset, joined me a few streets east, and we walked along the Thames.

"I see you now carry a blade," he said, noting the rapier I had relieved from our company's stores the morning I left for Stratford. It was now my constant companion. "May I see it?"

I drew the sword and handed it to Carey. He made a brief inspection of it and passed it back. I placed it back in its scabbard, and he reached over and took my right arm near the wrist, squeezing up toward the elbow.

"I would recommend something heavier, but fear you wield as much as your stature can bear. I hope at least that its presence will serve deterrent, but recommend, should you again face threat, that you make better use of your legs than your arms."

"Always my first instinct, my lord."

We passed a short distance in silence and in the smell of the river in the summer sun – that of fish and of filth, of fair water and foul waste, the Thames being the fat vein on which the city fed and that sewer into which it emptied, a standing symbol of man's penchant to despoil that on which he most depends.

"I was sorry to hear of your son," he said.

"And I that his sorry passing delayed my office," I replied.

He made a soft grunt of excuse. "I am impatient by nature, but I pray you know my sorrow true. Such words beyond that seem too many or too few, and I have no gift for them anyway." A pause. "So, what news?"

I told to him the scheme of lands and shares I had heard from Webb, my telling oft interrupted by his temper – his brother, by the tale's end, being dead many times over and by imaginative and unpleasant means. Some other parties to this scheme, too, were much abused. He took some minutes to reclaim himself, until his breath came steadier.

"These vultures took scent of my father's death and then schemed to abuse the carrion of his estate for their foul purpose," he said. "The prospect of his recovery making their plot void, I fear some had a hand in its membership then murdered him, or perhaps all hands, in conspiracy."

"It is a company of some weight, and to make charge of conspiracy on this alone would be a tricky business," I said. "Especially since involvement of any beyond your brother may be most difficult to prove."

Carey nodded. "It shames me to think it, but my brother alone is of such character that he would do this deed himself, just for his own benefit, and likely even take some joy in it. I can, at least, make this entire enterprise known, and put out the fires of greed they have lit beneath their boiling cauldron of speculation, leaving them all to suffer with the cold soup of their losses."

"You may wish to wait, my lord, as we still have some chance to trace this matter back to its true author. Did any in your circle know of the hideous-nosed man?"

Carey shook his head. "I made broad inquiry, but none recalled him, and he would be easy recalled. Though it now seems, perhaps, that any who did know of him would have good cause to say other."

"More cause than you know, my lord." I told him what I had learned from his servants, of the man's ploy as doctor, I feared this news might rouse another bought of Carey's tempers, but he seemed instead only saddened.

"I remember Mary, as she was most kind to my father in his illness and he did much favour her company. My brother again in play, wanting to make her servant to his lusts and then having her discharged on account of some pox? An easy tale to credit given both his character and his appetites, but could it be he suspects your true mission and would have her beyond your questioning?"

"Perhaps, my Lord, but current past my knowing."

He shook his head slow. "I shall ask audience of the Queen and relay to her such as we know. I will not have this scheme continue and these vultures profit by my father's murder just so that I have chance to exercise my wrath."

"As you will, my lord, but would it be wise to wait some few days? This Somerset scheme is only at its beginning and it will not yield its players their profits for some weeks, so we need make no rush to still it. But once the parties to this scheme see it known, they will make quick to cover what signs they may. Current, we know of their scheme, but they do not know we know. Their ignorance ought be our weapon."

"But how to wield it?" asked Carey

"You can ask after our deformed assailant more close in the acquaintance of those we know involved, but not to them direct, and perhaps hear of such man in service to one or another of the conspirators. And having Mary's name and some hint of her father's lodgings, and her being of some remarkable beauty, I should think she will be not to hard found. I can seek her out and have her testimony in this matter."

Carey made a kind of laugh, as though in observance of some irony.

"How is it now my timid playwright has such an appetite for this work? For on my first offering it to you, you took some pains to avoid it. I would have thought you happy to have it done."

And I had to reflect a minute, it not having occurred to me that, in my encouraging Carey, I was extending this charge that I did so fear when he, in suggesting to make straight to the Queen, had offered it over.

"It may be a weakness of my art, my lord. Having such a story begun, I must know its end."

"Then I shall count myself blessed by the service of

your curiosity," Carey said. "And I shall make those inquiries you recommend."

He turned back toward Somerset and I continued on toward Bishopsgate, knowing I had in my last answer to him been false. It was not curiosity that now compelled me, but rather the sense that my conscience – which I had long considered to be well or at least sufficiently formed – had in late days been shown to me much wanting in its constitution, leaving me so distressed in my own company that I could not keep it much longer were I not amended.

I cannot know what lies beyond this life, and I do increasingly fear nothing but the thinking that my son's eyes might be now upon me – and not clouded in childish worship, but instead invested with such vision as to know the truth of me whole – that weighed heavy. I would at least this office perform, full and in good conscience, if only for my own selfishness. For I could bear no longer such thoughts and melancholies that current oppressed me of my own account. It seems a man must serve something, thus our human appetite for gods, as they give us compass. And perhaps I had at last found one worthy of my worship.

Truth seemed as fair a god as any.

CHAPTER 20

I arrived back at the theatre just as the afternoon performance had concluded, the crowd streaming out and seeming in good humour. My fellows, still in their costumes and paint, made me much welcome with both their usual insults and their honest sympathies, my having had no occasion to see them prior to departing for Stratford, nor since; my day being spent first with Webb, then at Somerset and then with Carey. It much buoyed my soul to be back in their company.

Jenkins, still in his womanly garb, curtsied and gestured toward my sword. "I see my fair charms hath made thy steel firm, good sir."

Burbage overspoke the general laughter. "I would suffer you not to endure such little injury as that narrow blade might inflict, my lady, when you should instead be penetrated by my broader sword." And more laughter, but then Burbage to me, "Pray tell me, though, Will, that your rapier be mere ornament for your dealings with Carey, and not carried in true need?"

And so I related such events as had transpired since I had made their company last, all being much aghast to hear how near death I had passed at St Paul's, and much intrigued with the news as I had from Webb and of Somerset House.

"After St Paul's, we can at least consider Carey's favour true," Burbage said, "him taking such risk on your behalf."

"Having beheld this contest," I said, "I think Carey at little risk in any matter settled with swords."

"We would be advised," said Heminges, "to remember our lord's martial talents before we next perform for him. For should he make stern critique, it seems as like to cost us our heads as his patronage."

Burbage produced a bottle of the sack he so favoured, and the bottle made the rounds of the Company. I was surprised to see Jenkins, who had only recent made the bottle's acquaintance, drink from it so lusty.

"In drinking, at least, I see Jenkins is your good pupil," I said to Burbage.

"Such good pupil that we must either increase his wage that he may pay for his drink, or increase mine that I can continue to supply him, as he current does much abuse my charity."

"Take care, boy, that drink does not become your master," I said to Jenkins.

"I have served worse," he replied.

"And so he is Burbage's good pupil," said Heminges.

"I do not call drink my master, sir," said Burbage in pretend umbrage.

"Perhaps your scourge?" asked Heminges,

"Oh, scourge, to be sure," replied Burbage.

"We need another bottle," said Jenkins, as, omitted in the conversation, he had taken chance to finish the first.

Burbage smacked Jenkins sound behind the head and laughed. "Then fetch it, boy, for you know well where it is stored."

As Jenkins made his unsteady way across the stage, Burbage spoke to me.

"What news as to our lease?"

"Webb is to meet Miller today, and is optimistic for our interests. I should have word tomorrow."

"Since we know at best our respite will be limited, we have continued our search," Heminges said, "and have found a baiting ring in Bankside for sale that can be had cheap, as it is in sorry repair. But its foundations are solid and well suited in size and shape to our needs."

"And we could buy it outright, Will," said Burbage, "so as to avoid in future such mischief as our lease has caused us. Its current owner is in some distress and we could have this place right quick."

"This seems a wise course," I answered. "But what of any temporary stage, should we have need?"

At this, their faces soured. "Henslowe is at some mischief, Will. At every venue where we inquire, he already has claimed every date available. As his troupe already has a stage, I can't think why he would empty his purse so, save to do us ill by leaving us no stage."

"To plot to do us such ill, he would first need know our ills," I said.

"And know them before us," Burbage said. "At the Rose, at least, he bought their open dates some weeks ago."

That night for the first time in my remembering, I made sleep easy – wearied, I suppose, by the week's travels and trials and the day's long business. However, I awoke not to dawn but in full dark and from the grasp of a dream. In my sleeping, I relived the attack – not that which Carey had so conclusively thwarted, but that first attempt – and relived it complete, in every detail. The scrape of feet behind me, the sight of the blade passing above me as I spun and turned beneath it, my foe's awkward steps past me, that pregnant moment where we both stood, blades extended. But in my dream, he did not turn and flee into the darkness, but instead reached up and lowered the cowl that had hid his features from me complete. I watched, expecting to see that ruined nose with which I was now over-familiar. But instead the space that would hold a face yawned full black and empty, as complete a hole as had been my son's grave. The hole seemed to spread, as if it gave off dark the way a candle gave off light. And I somehow knew that this dark did not obscure what it covered, but instead consumed it. This time it was I who turned and ran. And while there was no sound, my every sense tingles with the knowledge that the consuming dark was at my heels, gaining, ever gaining. It was then that I awoke.

It is not much my habit to dream over much, but what dreams I have, at least those that rise above that simple litter of sleep, the half-remembered detritus of nightly musings, oft seem to hold for me some portent, some knowing, that I had in my conscious thinking ignored. I puzzled hard at this consuming darkness that in dreaming had taken the place of my expected assailant, but could take no meaning from it beyond my own peril, which I did now suspect was only little diminished by the death of that single foe felled by Carey's blade. For a moment I was sore tempted to return to Carey and accept his offer to explain what mischief we present knew to the Queen and leave its disposition to her good offices. But if truth be my god, I could little expect its service to pass without sacrifice. For every god of my acquaintance thirsts hard for human suffering to sate its holy appetites.

I returned uneasy to my slumber, wishing for my late youth where, with unstuffed brain, golden sleep did reign.

CHAPTER 21

"And what brings such a fine gentleman, like yourself, to these parts this good morning?"

My sleep troubled, I had risen early and made to those districts nearest the river where the chambermaid thought Mary Norton's father lived. The woman asking after my presence was less than my own years by some margin, but those years as she had lived had marked her dear. Her teeth were most evident in their absence, her eyes much dulled, the skin of her face sallow beneath its rouge and powder. The tops of her breasts, pressed up for display by her tightened corset, had a slackened aspect, like sacks of flour half emptied.

I bowed with some theatre. "Why to make the acquaintance of the city's good people, milady, so as to gain their console on a matter of some consequence."

She laughed, seeming honest amused, and her features, to be true, were some improved by what I suspected was for her an uncommon moment of mirth.

"You have a mouth on you, you have," she said. "As have I, and I can put it to such use as I promise you will well enjoy for two pence. Which I am sure you would not deny me, you already having had my acquaintance for free."

"I will pay your two pence glad," I said, holding out the coins, "if I can have use of your mouth in conversation for some minutes instead."

She eyed me with some suspicion, but then pursed her lips and took the coins. "I will take your offer, sir, if we might sit for our talk. I spend my waking hours on either my feet, my knees, or my back, so to take some leisure on my arse instead during my working day is a small luxury."

And so we sat on a wall along the river's bank, and her face softened as she lifted it to the morning sun, a quiet moment spent in some joy known private to her alone.

"I thank you, sir, for pretending at least to think I deserve your courtesy. I was not always thus and am not now by choice. But a child's hungry mouth consumes what it will and made snack of my dignity long ago."

"Madam," I said, "I have no such claim to virtue by which to stand judge of another. But I am surprised that you work your trade this side of the river, having thought our increasingly Puritan city fathers would have all entertainments off to Bankside or Shoreditch or the other liberties."

She snorted. "Entertainments? Dear God, at least have the mercy not to compare me to the bear baiters and actors. What little reputation I might still have I would keep."

"Actors, madam? Having known them long and you only little, I know already not to make such claim, for you are too much a lady to keep their company."

"And Bankside, sir? Where I would need compete with ladies less long in my trade and more fair in their charms and for clients more used to their custom? Here I am oft alone to serve those Puritans who are much shamed to find that their human needs do oft o'ermount their spiritual zeal, so that, in their shame, they do conclude their business quick and pay for it most dear, thinking it some rare evil and not some common urge."

"And so you are as wise in business as you are rich in beauty," I said.

"And you, sir, are a kind liar, and are wasting your two pence, for you have already lasted longer in conversation than a Puritan does in lust."

"Then I will ask you plain. I am looking for a young girl, in years short of twenty, dark haired and of some considerable beauty, who did until recent work in service at Somerset House, known by name as Mary Norton. I am told she lived close near the water in this district, with her father."

My companion drew a breath and blew it out, pursing her cheeks in the doing. "I did know a Norton, a John," she said, "who had a room near, and who, I remember, until recent, had a daughter such as you described – and well short of twenty. He died in winter. A Yorkshireman I think, by his accent."

Yorkshire, as the chambermaid had mentioned.

"Have you seen the daughter since?"

"No, sir."

"What more do you know of him? What work did he do?"

"Most common, he begged alms. He had but one hand, the other supposed lost at war in his youth."

For two pence more, she agreed to show me the building where he had lived, and I marked its place that I might return later and ask after Mary in those locales where she would be best known. Pressing a final two pence on the woman in thanks for her service, I wondered more at the nature of the city and our place in it. For me, it had been the stage on which I had acted a new self, only imagined in my youth in Stratford but here made real in service of the city's appetites. And as London had been the fount of my fortune, I had pretended it such for all. But every sense made plain the city's ills as clear as its glories. The sight of the poor begging alms – dirty, poxed, and of too much bone and too little flesh. The smell of the squalor that did affect all but that I noticed much stronger in this district of estates meaner than my custom, as people here lived in such close congress that the stench that accompanies any human enterprise was oppressive thick. The sounds in this district, too, fell harsher on the ear. The calls from the keepers of such shops as this area's custom could support being in tone more desperate than those coming from the finer shops nearer my rooms, for a shopkeeper strives for the coin that brings that same day's bread far more urgent than he does to add just another to an already fattened purse. Children's cries, too. Some crying only in that innocent insistence of infancy, their cries being their only tongue. But the deprivations of this quarter schooled even its babes and made their cries more fluent so that I could hear plain tales of hunger, of illness, of despair spoken only in wails and tears, for they were conditions which the young knew full well in experience long before they could speak their names.

As I made my way from this district toward that of the courts and my appointment with Webb, I knew suddenly that this city I had thought a kind of jungle was indeed such. But I knew, too, that its rich foliage had its roots sunk deep into the soil of those tens of thousands of poor. The city, sucking from them their natures and humours to sprout this vainglorious display, but returning to them nothing except the brown and discarded leaves from which the poor must hard derive their sustenance. For they know any excess will almost immediate be claimed by the roots of those finer flowers that they serve but in whose glories they will never share. And on that dark forest floor, a woman whose soul had no less claim to grace than my own would sell her virtue cheap in private unto those who would revile her in public. And yet she willing accepted their dishonest congress if only in hope that one mouth, a mouth that likely already cried full fluent in the despair that somehow dimmed even the sun in these narrow lanes, at least would live and perhaps one day climb this tangled foliage sufficient high to bloom.

Meanwhile, we creatures that lived in those higher branches considered our debts and fortunes in congress with one another, ignoring complete that larger debt. For our lofty perch was owed to those soiled thousands that did faithful support its roots, even while those same roots did use them so foul. I realised sudden and in shame that what we call charity is only a late and partial payment to parties we have much abused and who have no hope in law to make claim, as the law is a creation of us finer creatures and bent at every turn to our purposes. We use it to harsh hold the poor to their stations and us to ours. Then, as we shit our waste to the forest floor, we call it charity and congratulate ourselves on our generous exercise of God's mercies.

CHAPTER 22

"As to your lease, we can reach what accommodation we will with Miller," said Webb. I was seated again in his rooms. "But that accommodation will only last some few days."

"We shall need more than a few days," I answered.

"This matter seems mischief to its core," Webb said, "for the more I uncover the more I find beneath. I met with Miller, explained what of this Shoreditch scheme I knew, and hinted at what I did not. It was clear in his reacting that he knew only little of the larger plan, and not at all of the persons involved. It being also clear that, as we surmised, the matter of your lease was not one of conscience but rather of commerce, and that his delay was simply a small cruelty to satisfy his distaste, which seems to be as much for your person as for your art. The plain fact, Will, is he does not like you."

While I had been in my dealings with Miller perhaps sharp in tongue, as I find his manner near as offensive as his philosophy, I was surprised to hear that he focused his animus on me direct. "Why so hard for me?" I asked.

"You are, for him, the embodiment of all he despises. An actor and playwright both, and thus you author and display the evils he imagines. But it upsets him, too, that you have risen to a status near equal to his own from what he sees as common roots, for this does dispute that Calvinist thinking that Puritans much embrace – the faith that men are born each to their station, that station reflecting the favour in which God holds them. For you to have reached this status, and by means of such art as he views sinful, means that either his religion is false or your means are Satanic. Few thoughts push a man harder toward evil than an argument against his religion."

I could only agree. "A man will in the name of God do ready such ills that he would never consider of his own accord. And I do true believe that many hear God's voice in what are in fact the whisperings of the darker chambers of their own hearts, so as to excuse such evils that they cannot admit are sprung whole from the cauldron of their own appetites."

Webb patted his desk with his hand. "The matter of Miller's conscience aside, it is commerce that drives his hand. My having made plain what cause for damage we could bring against him, his delay in notice being clear fraud, he did ready agree that you may remain in the theatre for so long as he is its master. But those days are short numbered, as he has agreed to sell, and such sale scheduled to conclude just one week hence."

"Giving us eight more days than we had, but not nearly so many as we need. What of the property's new owner? If we assume the theatre sold as part of these conniving speculations, then the new owner sure has no true purpose for it, save to sell it soon again. Would they not, then, welcome such rents as we could compel Miller to pay so that we can remain in residence sufficient long to make an orderly retreat?"

"An inquiry I already made. And I was much surprised to have it so quick rebuffed, until I learned who the new owner would be. Henslowe. And not owner of the theatre alone. It seems he is one of those agents the Somerset Company employs in its purchases. He has bought three other parcels in Shoreditch, having already sold two at profit, and is entertaining offers on the third. "

"What of the threat of disclosure? If Henslowe is in league with Somerset, then he knows the stature of its players and what ills might befall him should their plot be thwarted through cause of his actions."

"I tried that tack, but he replied that any knife we hold to his throat we hold equal to our own – or even more so, as the disclosure would come by our hands, not his."

"And yet he holds the theatre instead of selling it."

"Of those properties he holds," Webb said, "it is the largest and will thus fetch the dearest price. So, by holding it some weeks longer as this scheme unfolds, he can not only enrich himself but also impoverish your company by denying you access to its stage, which some new owner would sure lease to you most ready. And thus by one mischief he can cause another."

This new knowledge of Henslowe's hand even tighter around my throat bubbled so angry in me that I could not stay seated, but instead rose and paced in Heaton's room. An idea was forming that I would have whole before speaking it – so that, when Webb tried again to speak, I rose a hand to still his tongue.

Finally I answered him.

"I learned yesterday that Henslowe had, some weeks ago, made payments to block every stage in Bankside from our use, and so I already knew that he had knowledge of our misfortune in advance. But by this we now know that he not only had knowledge of it, he was in truth its architect, as he schemed first to drive us from our own stage and then to keep us from any other."

"This would seem true," Webb said.

"Answer me this. Some weeks or months hence, when the Somerset Company's final properties have been sold and so the false infection of this speculative fever stayed, what then becomes of Shoreditch?"

Heaton sat back for a moment, tapping a finger against his chin. "Those leases that will concentrate much commerce within its boundaries already in force to support the fiction giving fire to this speculation, Shoreditch will be new home to more shops than current. As the Somerset Company will have sold all those properties out of its inventory as part of their scheme, these parcels will be held by varied owners, all of whom will have paid dear. So, those owners will strive hard to increase the area's commerce in hopes that prices might one day equal those they paid and justify such rents as will allow them to afford those mortgages they may have secured to buy them."

"So, this mall of shops that was created as a myth will become a fact?"

"It will. And, in truth, for those owners patient, it may well in time be a worthy investment. Not the sort of investment that the Somerset Company would prefer, though. For why breed your cow and take the risk and trouble to raise a calf when you can instead steal your neighbour's herd and sell it whole?"

"But, Shoreditch, being outside the city's walls, and thus its laws, and thus at liberty, we can expect that this now more-thriving district will see much traffic in those entertainments that are to the liberties confined?"

Heaton's finger stopped tapping his chin, and instead pointed at me straight. "And be the ideal site for a theatre. Especially one bought not at the height of any speculative frenzy but instead at its start, and, thus, owned free by its company."

I slumped once more into my chair, the energy derived from discerning Henslowe's plot exhausted by having realised its end. "And so I find myself already mated in a game I had not known begun."

"Take heart, Will," said Webb. "The solution to any ill is found only after its diagnosis. Give me some time to reflect on this matter, now that we know it more whole, and I may well find unbarred some door that Henslowe has forgotten."

"And if no?"

"Why, then we make a new one."

It was short past noon only, but I was considerable wearied by the morning's adventures and by the night's interrupted slumber. And so, instead of returning toward the river to inquire further after Mary, I decided to return to my rooms. I needed to reflect on my company's dangers, for the plot that was now shown as a direct attack at me held more currency at the moment then that which had felled my dead patron.

In walking to Bishopsgate, I saw the city now not as a jungle, but instead as an abstraction. Its buildings and lands were props only, their meaning most clear in a web of deeds and ownerships and shares and mortgages at whose centre new and malevolent spiders did pluck and spin such strings as did hold or loose our lives at their pleasure. And I wondered how we had become enslaved to such mysteries. For we had taken that simple world of God's giving – which in its fruits did all our needs meet and under whose sun we had once stood all equal – and made in our society a machine of such complex devising and unclear purpose that some were careless ground within its wheels while others were ascended to true dizzying heights. The cause of either fortune or calamity now seemed so random and arbitrary that, while we imagined we worked each to our own benefit, we did oft instead simply toil – perhaps to our ill or perhaps to no end at all. Our labours left us wearied, but a weariness gave birth to no dreams by

which to divine any purpose to either our sleep or
our waking.

That afternoon, for the first time since drawn by
Carey into this strange service, I took stage with
my fellows for our company's performance. I was
much comforted to have lines that required only
my remembering, to have my steps and actions
foretold, and that my agency caused no harm but
instead merriment. We were performing a comedy
of considerable antic confusion in which some of us
men were dressed as women, who were in fact men,
who for purposes of the story were pretending to be
women. And so I spent some hours lost in the easy
practice of my art, lit with laughter, and dear glad of
my circumstances if only for those brief instants. For
such rare blessings as life offers cannot be saved or
hoarded but must be ate complete in their moment,
and we must find in that meal sufficient mercy to
sustain us until we find its kind again.

CHAPTER 23

"Norton? None that I recall, sir, though I have truck with many each day and might never know their names."

I was speaking with a baker only a few doors from that building where I was yesterday told that Mary Norton's father lived. It was my fifth inquiry of the morning, and in each case I received similar answer. If the lady yesterday had steered me true, and I did believe she had, then this Norton lived quiet and was of little note to his neighbours.

"He had but one hand," I added, "having lost the other, I am told, at war in his youth. He would beg alms, I hear."

At this, the baker stole a short glance to his wife, who stood to his left, moving just his eyes as though he had thought better of the effort before he could move his head. Her features made a small shiver of quiet alarm that I also saw before she made her face a mask.

"I can't speak for your district, sir," the baker continued, "though judging from your dress and manner, it be finer than this, but there are many hereabouts some insulted by life: many lame, many ill."

Clear, he knew something, but clear also he wished not to say it, and seeming from fear. Not a little ashamed, I decided to prey hard on that fear.

"I'll be plain, sir. I inquire in service to the Baron Hunsdon, son of the late Lord Chamberlain and soon to assume that post, and on a matter of some concern to his household. I will remember well those helpful to my mission."

The man's face froze harder still, in that aspect one takes when afraid of what one's features might reveal, so that, in trying to reveal none, one reveals much. His lips moved twice, as though to speak, but he said nothing. Finally, as is so often the case when times call for both courage and guile, it was the wife who spoke – women by their station oft being hard used since birth and thus better knowing the delicate steps to that dance by which they might make an escape.

"Sir, we know not your business and pray you not tell us, as we are of simple estate, and the attentions of even a gentleman such as you, much less those of a baron, even if well meant, will like as not fall hard on our household. If Norton be the cripple who did of late live in that room just short up this lane, then yes, he would sometimes beg of us what scrap of bread we could in our limited capacity for charity offer. And we would offer it glad when we could. As to his begging alms, that would not be in these lanes, as he would be a fool to beg from beggars, but more like near to St Paul's. I should think those near there would know him best."

My shame felt hotter still, as I could see the man feeling some belittled that his wife had had to make such speech in his stead as he could not manage in his own fear. They did clear feel at threat, though. I could not tell whether it was just the alarm of coming to the attention of persons who could with ease, and with intent or not, cause them ruin, or whether it was because of some specific knowledge that they had not shared. But in any seduction, it is that first small surrender that matters, the first yes. In admitting that she knew Norton, if only in her attempt to send me off to St Paul's and away from this shop, the baker's wife had said that "yes" and opened the small crevice into their lives that I would now lever wide.

"Madam," and I turned also to her husband, "and good sir. My inquiries are most discrete in nature, and the Baron need know only such that I learn, and not its sources. And as he, through my agency, is most grateful for any service, I ask again if this is your full knowing concerning Norton." On the counter in front of the man I placed half a crown, which I supposed was near to his profits for a week. "As I am just, I fault no man for what he knows, as knowledge does oft come to us unbidden, even such knowing as might weigh upon us in its particulars, for we cannot always know its import at its gaining." The baker took the coin and secreted it into the pouch in his apron.

"But," I continued, "knowledge kept secret once such knowledge clear ought be shared, for that, I do count men liable."

In taking the coin, the man had now admitted to greed as his wife had admitted to fear, and so, their honour already exposed as flawed, the man finally spoke plain.

"I would have you know first, sir," the baker said, "that in all matters I am the Queen's good servant, and if the Queen say pray as thus and not as that, then I do so pray. For in truth such as us do not seem to suffer over much from God's good favour whether we ask it in Latin or in plainsong, my sense being that God will judge us final by our hearts alone and not on the manner of our praying."

"I call that wise thinking," I replied, "as it is the same as my own."

"All do not agree," he continued.

"Norton?"

"Sir, even with your threats and bribes, however polite made, I will not speak false against a man, even one dead. I can say only that there are some number in this quarter who feel that religion is the province of God, not of the Crown, and that no crown has right to say that what was once right should now be wrong, especially when such change seemed mostly for the crown's convenience."

"And again I ask, Norton?"

"And again I say I cannot speak false. Only that I do know there have been some priests at times in the area, ministering to those who would hold their own religion, and that some have said that Norton counted in that congregation. But as I do not consider a man's soul my province, I ask no man his allegiance where God is concerned."

"You say, then, that there are some Catholics in this district?"

"Some, yes, and in every district, I would think," the wife speaking, again, "if a man could see as clearly another's heart as he does his face."

"But perhaps more in this district than in some other?"

"Sir," the baker said, "for the rich, should a king say your religion will now be this and not that, much is lost in this world should they say other. But for the poor, their only hope for treasure lies beyond the grave, and if they hold their faith true, then to change for the Crown's blessing would cost them all they might have gained in eternity, and for nothing in this life. And so they do cling harder to the old faith, having nothing else to cling to."

"And in that clinging, reject the Queen's authority?"

The baker shook his head. "No, sir, for they understand what is owed Caesar and what is owed God, perhaps better than those whose vision is cluttered up with gold and lands and goods. And so they are the Queen's faithful servants in all save the keeping of their souls."

I let a silence build, for as a quiet builds, some will rush to fill it. But the baker and his wife spoke no further.

"He had a daughter, Mary, I am told," I said. "What of her?"

"I do remember seeing him in the company of a girl on some occasions," the baker said.

"He would remember," the wife added, "the girl

being most comely and just of that age where she might turn a man's thoughts as well as his eyes," although she said it in sport, and not in temper.

"As if any could turn my eyes from you, my love," the man added in equal sport, the affection between these two being plain, and also their attempt to make me party to it, and so make me inclined to think on them well, and not to their harm. And so I did.

"Also, I am told he had a son," the wife added, "but somewhat older than the daughter, and so of working age and not likely to still share his father's quarters, being so sparse as they were."

We talked further, but I had what knowledge they could share, having for my half crown learned only that the district harboured sufficient Catholic sympathies that it had the occasional service of a priest, which would be a dangerous business for the priest, at least. I noted, too, the baker's ready defence of those Catholics that still clung to their church, and, as I did not in him sense such tongue as could find words easy in the moment, knew he had thought on this matter long to have such defence so ready. And so I suspected, too, that the baker and his wife counted themselves Catholic, but I could call that evil no more than I could call my own parents evil for trying to serve both God and Caesar, and for having suffered dear in both attempts, and for no purposeful offence to either.

"I thank you for your honest congress," I said on leaving. I stopped in the door and turned back. "This building where Norton kept his room. Would you know its landlord?"

"A Puritan named Miller," said the baker.

I left his shop to continue my questioning, unsure what Miller's place here might mean. As the owning and leasing of properties was Miller's only business, that he should own and lease them in this district was no shock. And yet, in this web of lands and titles and shares, it seemed I could not touch any thread of it and not feel some other tighten around my own throat while distant and unknown eyes waited until I was well secured and their hunger had need of me.

CHAPTER 24

"The prodigal scribe returns, and none too soon," Burbage called as I entered the theatre, much surprised to find Webb in his company.

"Today's performance does not start for some hours, sir," I said to Webb. "I should think you could easy afford a cushioned seat, and would not need arrive so early to secure a favourable spot with the groundlings."

"As fond as I am of your revels, it is this other drama in which you find yourself so deep embroiled that brings me hence," Webb answered. "As my news is sufficient earnest and the time you have to act on it short, I thought it best to come direct."

"If it is news favourable to our fortune, it is most welcome, as such has been in short supply," Heminges said.

"As your esteemed Shakespeare can tell you," Webb answered, "one of the ancient practitioners of his art said *audentis fortuna juvet.*"

"I am neither scholar nor Papist," said Heminges, "so I will thank you to spare the Latin and speak to me plain."

"Fortune favours the bold," I said, "or so Virgil claimed."

"I may not know the Latin," Burbage said, "but I know the truth of it. Bold, we are the men to be. But bold how?"

Heaton seated himself on the edge of the stage, Burbage and Heminges to his flanks and I stood to his front to receive his news.

"In the matter of your lease, I can find no escape from this mischief that Henslowe has authored, as you must in fact vacate in just a few short days under term of the lease, and in only a few days more if you wait for the sale to Henslowe. The rub is in what you take with you if you leave before such sale concludes."

"What rub in this, sir?" Burbage asked. "Our stores and talents are ours in any case. What would you have us take?"

"Why the theatre itself, my good sirs. Every board and nail of it."

As we watched rapt, Webb unrolled our copy of the lease on the stage floor, pointing to the section in question. "Over the many years in which you have been tenant, both your company and Miller have contributed to the construction of the theatre. But as it did not exist in the original lease, the land then being vacant, the disposition of the structure is not addressed in the document, save some language concerning improvements that could be as easy construed in your favour as in Miller's. In his careless pursuit of every penny, Miller never had the lease redrafted to reflect his stake in the structure. I have discussed such with our favourite Puritan, and as

Miller is now some afraid of what reward you could receive should you claim fraud, he already has agreed not to contest ownership of the building, should you have it gone before his sale to Henslowe concludes – provided, in return, you promise to pursue no cause against him in the matter of his notice. And as Miller is now acting, if not in concert with you at least not against you, he also allowed me to review the documents concerning his sale to Henslowe, in which Henslowe clear presumes the theatre and the land are one in ownership but in which nowhere is this stated plain."

We stared at Webb silent for a moment. Then I said, "You are saying the lease makes the theatre ours, provided we can remove it before the sale concludes?"

Heaton held up a cautioning finger. "I am saying, as a lawyer, I can interpret it so. Should Miller to law, his lawyer could easily interpret it other."

"But," I said, "Miller will not contest."

Heaton again raised his finger. "Henslowe could well contest, but his agreement is with Miller, and so his action would have to be against Miller. In my conversations with the good Puritan, it is possible that I let slip some details regarding the Somerset Company, its designs, and Henslowe's role in them. And by such discussion Miller may wrongly have concluded that Henslowe would have no interest in the building itself, but simply in the quick sale of the land. So, Miller may have presumed that, by giving you leave to remove the theatre, he can avoid one ill and that, by having the land vacant and undisputed for his sale to Henslowe, he can avoid the other. In the coming few days, your concern is Miller's claim and not Henslowe's. The question, then, is this: can you have the theatre gone from here and reconstructed at the site in Bankside in those few days?"

All of us looked to Burbage, whose family had some interests in lands and whose father's interest had first constructed the theatre. Burbage had always handled any matters of construction on our behalf. He stood now, with his hands on his hips, surveying the tiered stands that surround the grounds and stage.

"The timbers are heavy, but the framing is simple," he said, "and we already know the foundation of the property at Bankside can suite this shape. It is more an exercise in labour and transport than it is in any builder's art. We can have the hands of our own company free and of those actors who are common our hirelings cheap, and then pay those few skilled craftsmen we need for the leading roles and to direct our efforts. It will cost us dear in sore muscles and blistered hands, but, yes. This can be done."

"What of the Bankside property?" I asked.

"I took liberty of meeting with its owner," Webb answered, "who is in considerable haste to have what cash for it as he can, as he is current in some distress and has also heard tell of fortunes to be made in Shoreditch. If you agree to pay a small rent until the sale is made, he will give you leave to begin your construction immediate."

I shook my head at this unlikely prospect, having thought just the morning last our company full stymied by Henslowe's ploy. "You did say, sir," I said to Webb, "that you might find some door by which to escape our troubles, or create some other, and you seem to have done both. For we can foil both Henslowe's mischief toward us and his plans for his own company in the same action. That is," turning now to my fellows and raising my voice to that I used for the stage, "if we be bold enough to court fortune's favour."

Which was greeted with a general tumult of affirmation. Even Jenkins, who had joined our congress late, was game.

"I was never bold before," he said, raising another bottle of Burbage's sack, "but drink does make me so!"

"I shall make us a start," said Burbage, firm in his voice. He leapt from the stage, joining me on the ground to its front. Then, squatting down, he put his hands under the edge of the board that framed the front of our stage and, pressing up with his legs, pried it up. The board at first groaned in protest and moved slow, but then gave way entire and came full loose to fall flat on the stage. "Jenkins, make haste to fetch hence all those actors of our employ. Heminges, you scour the taverns for any owners of the company not here present. Will, conclude with Webb such paper matters as needs be, and then hasten back, for it is your back we need today and not your wit. I will find us tools and a few men schooled in their use."

Burbage turned and smiled broad at us all, in his element as foreman to this task. He was a man powerful in body, with a natural grace for that body's use, and with a charisma that he oft could summon so that men did follow him ready. "I do count us bold, and fortunate to be in this company. And should fortune balk to answer at this door the good lawyer has found for us, then we shall kick it in and teach the harlot her position as our servant. Over the next days, when your back aches and your muscles protest, I ask only that you think on Henslowe, emptying his purse to keep us from Bankside's stages while we sell our trade in that district's newest and finest venue, the..." Burbage paused. "Why, we have no name for it. Will? Words are your province."

"The Globe," I answered. "For we will there bring the wonders of the world to London, and in this gilded orb our own fortunes claim."

Burbage snatched the bottle from Jenkins and held it high. "Gentlemen! The Globe!" And he drank deep, passing the bottle to us each, and us each drinking deep – save for Jenkins, for when the bottle returned to him, it was near dry.

"I shall have to fetch another," he said, "not wanting to dishonour our enterprise with this small portion."

We laughed, tied hard in that sacred bond of a brotherhood set to some hard task and at dear odds. We scattered to the jobs set to us, hurrying to destroy the theatre we had for some good years called home. Never was a band happier at its work.

CHAPTER 25

The next morning, I scarce beat the sun's first light to the theatre, but there did find Burbage, Heminges, Jenkins, and some of our hired actors already at their labours.

"Will," called Burbage in feigned surprise, "I thought you made this hour's acquaintance only on your way to bed, and never out of it."

"Recent events have made me strange in my habits," I replied. "Stranger still is that I must beg your leave, as I am to church."

"To church, sir?" Burbage answered. "Does your sloth drive you even there to avoid such true work as to which we real men do already lend our backs? I can think of many acts on which the church much frowns that are common in your custom, but I do not count keeping holy the Sabbath among them."

"But, as it is the Sabbath, we must all tend to our spiritual duties," I said. "Mine, in this case, owed to Carey. If I am to find this Mary Norton, I fear I must use God as the snare."

"Then be to your holy office, sir, for your service to Carey weighs as heavy on our fortunes as does mine to this pile of wood. Your wits will be your tool and my strength will be mine, and so we will each work with that tool by which we are best served."

"But I will first to our costumes," I said, "for it seems such company as Carey's service requires I keep is always either above or below my station, my own garb being in turns either too fine or too foul."

"And today?"

"Too fine, for today I shall be of London's poor."

Burbage face turned some to concern. "London's poor, by their station, not being allowed to carry arms."

I nodded. "And so today I must make do with my dagger only. But as it is Sabbath and daylight, I shall have to trust myself to those mercies granted all conducting their commerce plain in God's sight."

"You make light, Will, but I remind you that you were recent accosted at St Paul's – which, night or day, should be plain enough in God's view – and he choose a spectator's role, unless you count Carey his angel."

"Come, sir," I said, clapping a hand to his back and sounding braver in my tone than I felt in my spirit. "Are we not bold men, and thus in fortune's favour?"

Burbage nodded, him too now choosing that bluff courage with which we mask our concerns. "We are that. And with you in costume, then your mission becomes theatre. And as you are unsurpassed in theatre's arts, you will best any foe."

Burbage returned to his labours and I to our store of costumes. But as I attired myself in such beggar's garb as would suit this morning's adventures, I knew that my costume did not make London a stage and would serve poor armour against any actor bearing both real malice and real steel.

I returned to the district near the river. From the baker and his wife, I knew the district was much peopled with Catholics, and they had as much as named John Norton a faithful one. As he was by all accounts well loved by his daughter, then the Papists might claim Mary among their number, too. Having observed my parents' habits these many years and knowing how they would on any Sabbath when a priest was near take pains to secretly make their sacrament, I assumed that the baker and his wife, who I thought Catholic sure, would do likewise if some priest did serve in this district. And so I watched their door from an alley a little distance south. I had not waited long before I saw them leave, but not together. Instead the wife left first, walking the few doors to the building where John Norton had lived and entering, not through the main door but instead into the cellar. Perhaps a minute later, another man rounded the far corner of the building, entering also into the cellar. Now the baker left his door, scurrying quick up the street and into the same cellar, along with some ten others in the minutes I watched. When some time had passed and no others appeared, I walked up the street and made a circuit of the building, finding no other door from which this congregation might exit. From a small window to the rear I could hear faint the congregation respond entire in what, in those few words I could discern, sounded Latin.

In a little more than a hour, the door again opened and, one by one, those present made their way out, though never in company. The baker's wife was second to leave, the baker some persons later. When none had left for some minutes, I was about to leave my station at the alley's mouth, thinking I might press the baker and his wife harder, now having my certain knowledge as to their faith with which I could compel them to be more true. Then the door opened a last time and a girl stepped out. Her black hair streamed beneath her head piece. She was fair in form and aspect and of a slight and budding build. I immediate recalled the fishmonger's daughter who I late so sorely used and felt some little sickened that my lust could flicker still through my shame. I knew this girl must be Mary Norton. She stood in the door, in conversation with some other whom I could see only in shape behind her, he being more into the dark. Then Mary left, turning north, the door closing behind. Staying a distance back, I followed, hoping to mark those quarters where she now lived.

She made her way quick through the narrow lanes. Being a young woman alone, even on a Sabbath morning, was, I was certain, an uncomfortable business. She continued north farther than I had suspected she would, the nature of the district increasing in station as she left the stench of the river behind. The shops grew finer, then finer still, such that soon the costume I had picked so I would seem part of that meaner area where she had late prayed now marked my person instead of hiding it. I was thankful that, it being Sabbath, these finer shops were all shuttered closed, and the streets were light in traffic. Still, I made ready obeisance to all I passed, bowing and doffing my poor cap, trying to mimic as best I could the manner of some minion about a master's business.

At last at the side of a mercer's shop she opened a door such as would lead to the quarters above that housed its keepers. I made note of its sign and street so as to return tomorrow, when the shops would be open and I would be dressed in the neighbourhood's habit. Then I turned for Shoreditch and the theatre – only to find my way blocked by two Puritan gentlemen I had passed only some short moments previous.

"The girl does make a sight, but not one meant for such eyes as yours," said the man to my right. Though he was Puritan sure by the nature of his dress, you could tell him one who could not squelch entire his vanities, for his dress while plain was careful tailored and of rich fabric. And a gentleman too, by virtue of the sword on which he rested his right hand.

I snatched off my cap and made a short bow. "I beg pardon, sir?"

"I've no doubt you make common habit of begging," said the second man, dressed in similar station to the first and similarly armed. "Which on its own does breach the Queen's peace and might require a bailiff. But it is your fouler intentions we current question."

"Fouler intentions, sir?"

The first man scoffed a snort, than rapped me hard across the face with the back of his gloved hand. "To think you might play at wits with me offers clear insult, and no man insults me without answer. Count yourself blessed that you are not allowed a sword, or I would have it out that I might rinse my honour clean with your blood. The girl to which you had such clear intentions, you poxed sack of filth."

"Girl, sir?"

Which he answered again with the back of his hand, my nose now running blood.

"That child whose passage you have marked with such interest. And if you answer again with your unschooled attempts at cleverness, I will next respond with my blade."

I looked down, feigning shame but not having to feign fear, wringing my cap in my hands. "I did see the girl, sir, and will admit to admiring her, but I had no ill intent, save what sins of thinking I might make in my heart."

I now felt the glove of the second man hard across my face. "I call your thinking on her insult enough to her honour," he said.

I had to tamp down the spark of anger that flared at this treatment, finding the flame not squelched but instead triple hot as the single flame of anger kindled now its twins in shame and humiliation. But having chosen my role, I had to keep to it.

"And I do ready apologise, good sirs, as I am wifed and do dishonour both her good name and God, and even on this day, it being Sabbath. I am weak in my will, sirs, but do say true that I sin only in my mind, though that that be sin enough to God's eyes."

This answer held them for a short moment, they having hoped to strike some spark of outrage by which to justify my further abuse. They now thought hard after some new tack.

"By what business are you even present here? It being Sabbath and the shops being closed. Or do you common wonder in such quarters as you cannot afford, so as to lust after both the flesh and the goods? Perhaps it is theft on your mind, and not rape. What are we to presume but mischief? I think we should have you to the bailiff."

"Pray you, sir, hold," I answered. "It is Sabbath, true, but a man that I do sometimes serve on errands has sent me hence to the stationers not far distant, Master Jaggard's shop, as my master had ordered done some handbills that he would have passed tomorrow early. Having not been able to fetch them previous, he has sent me to have them now, him telling me that he and Master Jaggard have sufficient commerce that the printer will suffer him this service, even it being the Sabbath."

The first man wrinkled his nose. "And who is this master that would make so light of God's day?"

"Why, Master Henslowe, sir. He finances the Admirals' Men? The theatre company?"

At which he slapped me twice across the face, using the back of his hand and then the front. "You can pass that on to your master, if you be man enough. I had wondered at your stench, thinking it remarkable for even a man of your standing. I should have noted the odour of the theatre at its bottom." He turned to his companion. "We waste our time here. The girl is safe indoors."

The second man gave me a parting blow. "I have marked your face, and should I see it again you will count this meeting gentle. Should your errands for your corrupt master bring you this way in future, divert your route so as not to foul our street with the miasma of your wake."

In reply to this final insult, I simply bowed again, thanking these gentle sirs for their understanding and mercy, knowing I had had but a taste of that diet which many in this city did eat daily. I wondered at the strength of the constitutions that could stomach this treatment as their regular fare, and what diseases of mind or spirit its sustenance must engender.

The two men continued on their way, and I now diverted toward Jaggard's shop, thinking it best to maintain my false mission so long as I might remain in their seeing. This route took me directly past that mercer's shop above which Mary Norton now stayed. I noted that the goods displayed in its window were not woollens of English manufacture, but were instead silks and such fineries as must have been had from abroad. These fineries being thus scarcer, they were all the more in favour with noble and royal patrons, they being among the few that might afford them. And I saw, for just a moment, the rustle of a curtain in the upper window that o'erlooked the scene of my recent humiliation.

Upon returning back to the theatre, I was much shocked at our company's progress. The stage was gone entire, the stands now reduced to bare timbers only, and even those being part down. The boards of each section sat in stacks sorted and numbered so that each could be quick returned to its place at our new site.

Burbage strode toward me, his clothes and person streaked in dirt and sweat, shouting across the yard, "Will, you lazy ass. Methinks you did tarry some in your–" And then stopped short, seeing the blood that streaked my shirtfront, the swelling about my nose, and the bruising beginning to show about my eyes. "My God, sir. I beg pardon. For it seems you, too, have suffered in your labours."

"My pride more than my person," I said, and I relayed my tale.

Burbage shook his head, looking away for a moment, his jaw clenched. But then he smiled. "And yet you thought to put what stink you might on both Henslowe's and Jaggard's names?"

"In truth, we were not many streets from Jaggard's shop. And as I suppose he does still much hope to regain our favour, I said his name in case I was taken hence in either their company or a bailiff's, thinking he might support my claim in his own interest. But Henslowe? Yes, I spoke him from spite alone. And in that speaking, it did occur to me that Henslowe was the author of the pamphlet that late did cause me such grief, for he would easy have with Jaggard such weight of business that could explain Jaggard's company in his mischief. Not that such matters now, Henslowe's other mischiefs being clear known and of heavier consequence. But it speaks true to the depth of his conspiring."

Burbage shook his head in recognition of this new insult. "I am true sorry for this abuse you suffered in your pretend role as Henslowe's messenger, and can only hope that some ill will befall him in result of your clever use of his name." He paused, drawing from inside his shirt a paper folded and sealed in wax with what I now recognised as Carey's signet. "On the subject of messengers, it seems some can be about their master's affairs without fear of insults, Sabbath or no, as Carey's man delivered this for you not an hour past." The paper was much soaked in Burbage's sweat so that I held it by its corner, shaking it some to at least a little dry the page.

"Have you read it, and should I take your musk as your edit?"

"Read? No. Think on my sweet perfume only as true proof of my affections."

I smiled, broke the seal, opened the letter, and read its brief contents. My face must have fallen as clear as my heart, for Burbage asked, immediate. "What foul news now?"

"Carey will send a coach for my company on Tuesday evening, as we are off to visit Topcliffe," I said.

At which name not only Burbage but also those within earshot fell silent. Burbage now looked hard into my eyes, his mouth some agape.

"Richard Topcliffe? The Queen's inquisitor and priest hunter?"

"The same."

"Make with your time as you like, Will, and consider your duties in these petty labours forgiven. I would sooner have my part in this affair than yours. For just to hear the name Topcliffe shrivels my sack such that I should sooner play Jenkins's roles."

I nodded. "The same for me. And so I will stay in hopes that these honest labours might occupy me sufficient that I will forget tomorrow's evils until tomorrow, for I fear it would do me ill to have the leisure to reflect on them alone."

I would be safe enough with Topcliffe in Carey's company, Carey being current in the Queen's good favour. But Topcliffe had practised his unholy arts at torture often enough on such as the Queen had once loved, her favours being tossed by the currents of history and thus fickle in their objects. Topcliffe's reputation was that he better loved his art at pain than the information it produced, and so he was always in search of some unfortunate for whom he could invent such cause that made the man subject to his unkind ministrations. I had already those enemies I knew, and could sense lurking others I knew not. The city's Puritan fathers despised me for my art. In comparison to the masters of the Somerset Company I was but a flea, but one they might, for whatever itching I could cause, have squashed. Now Carey would bring me direct to Topcliffe's attention and make me numbered among those few that

Topcliffe would know by name instead of being only one in the anonymous throng. Being known, and also current being at odds with men of sufficient standing to whisper my name into Topcliffe's ear and direct his attentions in my direction, I feared my next invitation to his presence could be both more fearsome and less gently delivered.

I considered for a moment the observation of the baker's wife, and her reluctance to be party to any above her station out of fear of how heavy their attentions might fall upon her household. Now I realised that she was, in this, wiser than I. For it had been my ambition since the day I made London to rise ever higher, in both accomplishment and acquaintance, thinking only on such view as the lofty heights toward which I strove might offer and never on the safety of that perch, or the distance it left to fall. Not for the first time in the days recent past I thought with some envy on the simpler life I had spurned in Stratford and the quieter charms I might have known. But I quick put that thinking to side, for my station was what I had made it and I could not by imagining make it any other.

As I had now sworn to serve truth, or at least to know it, I had also to admit that my ambitions were true part of me. For both their good and their ill, they were my nature. Had I remained in Stratford to play the simple glover and march circles in that rut to which I had been born, I might on this one day be happier there than here. But in almost every other day prior I would have hated my station and my work and my fellows and my family – such hatred being really sole for myself for having denied my own longings out of fear of their risks.

Whether Catholic or Protestant, our religions call constant on our humility and call it sin for a man to want greatness. But I think these moral fetters are the design of our priests and nobles, not of God. By locking us to our lesser labours in the shackles of humility and calling it sin to want them broken for greater things, our worldly masters both protect their station and ensure the unquestioning labours of those that make easy their comforts.

I say, if God did true make us in his own image, then it be our duty to strive to be as near to him as we can manage. Yes, near to him in good, and in that I oft have failed. But near to him also in glory. For he would not have a world of his making stuffed full with men and yet unadorned by such wonders as men's hands and minds might make. He would, I think, prefer instead the full and chaotic flower of our varied and marvellous efforts. For this world is his stage and he would have acted on it the best theatre we can manage, if only for his own amusement.

Should my ambitions end in my agony, whether in private at such hands as Topcliffe's or in public on some scaffold, I know my own cowardice well enough to imagine I would, in that moment, curse my strivings and wish I had settled for a simple life in mean estate. But I knew now too that such final regret would be a blasphemy coerced by pain and not achieved by reason. And so I would arm myself with my own glories, for I consider myself any man's equal in wit, and I would embrace full what challenges lay before me.

If that be pride, and if that pride be sin, then I curse any god that calls it so.

CHAPTER 26

We toiled long that night, past the sun's setting. At dark, the theatre's reduction became so near complete that we were like hounds on the scent and could not be satisfied until it were done. We had down the final beams by torchlight.

Come morning, all was ready for transport to Bankside, such papers giving us right to commence construction having been fresh delivered by Webb, along with the signed agreement from Miller giving us claim to the theatre's materials, and those teamsters Burbage had hired standing ready at an early hour.

Burbage made to Bankside to oversee our actions there, while I remained in Shoreditch tending to the loading, having from Burbage a list of those materials needed first, and then second, and so on. The day's work had gone smooth, the theatre's timbers and woods some two-thirds carted away, when Henslowe appeared with Miller in tow.

Miller looked much discomfited.

We had just loaded a cart when Henslowe strode up to the horse foremost, grabbing its halter and calling across its back to me.

"Shakespeare, I will have you jailed and hanged, for this is theft plain, and of goods to which I have claim. I have bailiffs on their way."

I whispered to Jenkins to fetch Webb immediate. And as he ran off, I went to meet Henslowe at the cart, speaking not to him but to the teamster.

"Why do you tarry?"

"That gentleman has hold of my horse, sir."

"And does he pay your wage or do I?"

"You do, sir."

"Then be off. Use your whip if you must, on the horse or the ass that holds it. And when you reach Burbage, bring him hence."

The teamster snapped his whip once, to the flank of the horse on which Henslowe had hold but near enough to Henslowe that he released his grip and the cart was away. With the impediment between us gone, Henslowe advanced on me, sputtering in his rage, waving his arm back at Miller.

"I have bought this property in good faith, and from this honest man here, only to learn this very morning that your... your... *company*," which he tried in tone to make into some curse, "has torn down my property in the night and now tries to spirit it away. Not believing that even you could be so audacious, I fetched Miller and made hence and am here stunned to see this offence be true."

"Tries to spirit it away, sir? Tries? It would seem at current we have more than half succeeded."

"Then you admit to the crime?" Spittle flew with his words, and I made a show of pulling a kerchief from my sleeve and dabbing the offending fluids from my face.

"As you are not among your company's writers, and as those you employ fall some short of my art, I will forgive your mistaken thinking, as you evident hold little command of your own language and, language being the stuff of thought, thus think false. I will instead offer such schooling as you clear require, in particular in the matter of tenses, there being many – past, present, future, and then those each being either simple or perfect, the past being sometimes pluperfect, and there being the additional complication of conditional phrasing. But I see by your slack expression that I already have taxed your limited faculties, so I shall simplify my instruction. Tenses in simple terms allow us to tell those things that have happened from those that are happening and those that will or might yet happen, and this seems to lie at the heart of your confusion. You say you have bought this property, which would be true, were your transaction complete, in which case you could produce title and make this conversation moot. But what you should say is that you will buy this property. You say you have claim to these materials when, again, you mean to say you will have claim at such time as you do hold title. Or, rather, you should say would have had claim, the conditional now raising its troubling head, as, by such time as you do hold title, the question of these materials will be settled in our favour."

Henslowe was now much red in his face. And though he opened his mouth as though to speak, he articulated nothing beyond some grunts.

"Being unable to discern any meaning in your utterance, I will assume you are now clear as to those matters of tense that concern this instant case. Therefore, I shall shift our lesson to matters of law. In this area I claim no special schooling, but there are some simple facts of it that I think I know complete. Namely, that law is at heart a matter of contracts, and that I have in hand a contract with this land's current owner – that owner not being you, as we have already demonstrated. This contract gives our company full right to remove all improvements to this property for our own use. That owner being here present and speaking no protest on the matter, and you already having called him honest, I can see no dispute. I have also such lease that said owner has agreed remains in force until such date as this sale does final close, making us this property's legal tenants and putting you, sir, in trespass. So, your bailiffs, in my view, cannot arrive soon enough, as I will have you off my land of your own accord or in irons, though I do admit to preferring the latter."

Henslowe turned now on Miller. "Does he have such documents as he claims?"

Miller now stammering, "Recent days have seen much confusion in this matter, my addressing both your issues and such as Shakespeare's lawyer has raised both at once, and I think I may have granted such right as he claims. But only in confusion and through some trickery, as his lawyer did much cloud the air with his contesting."

"Then I call fraud!" Henslowe shouted.

"Fraud is the one word about which neither you nor our friend Miller requires instruction," I said. "And I would advise you each to hold its meaning and consequences close in mind."

There was then some shouting and general tumult, little said by any party being heard by any other until Webb arrived with Jenkins on foot from one direction, Burbage and the teamster on his cart from another, and Henslowe's summoned bailiff on horseback from a third. Finally the bailiff gained some control by saying the next to speak without his assent would be the first to jail. He then heard from each in turn, and read those documents available, and then turned to Henslowe.

"This sale you claim, do you have any proof for it? Any title?"

"It completes some few days hence. So, as yet, no. But I did contract for both this land and this theatre."

"Having had chance to read your contract," Webb said, "I would suggest you have your next drafted so as to reflect the facts and not just your wishes. Your contract is at best unclear concerning this property's improvements, and, said contract being drafted by your own lawyer, such ambiguity will, by law, be read in your opponent's favour. But in any case, that contract is with Miller, as is ours, and so your quarrel is with him at such time as your sale is concluded; while we have no quarrel, our contract being clear and in force now."

The bailiff nodded, holding up our agreement with Miller. "Having only this to read and it being plain in its meaning, I can conclude only that the Lord Chamberlain's Men are within their right to remove these materials. There is no matter of theft here, at least not of any kind I can rightly judge to breach the Queen's peace."

"No theft you can rightly judge?" Henslowe screamed close into the bailiff's face. "When carts bearing my property make such plain and regular exit? I know not whether to think you blind or simple!"

The bailiff looked hard at Henslowe. "I will once forgive your temper, sir, you being clear distressed. But such property as you think yours is by all evidence theirs, and I can be of no further service to you in this matter. You have need of a court and not of me, and so I will retire and leave you... gentleman," the last spoke with some edge, "to settle your matters as you will, trusting that my return will not be required. Good day."

With that speech, the bailiff swung quick back astride his horse and spurred it off.

Henslowe stamped in a narrow circle, clear chagrined that this foray he had envisioned ending in my arrest did now end in his shame. "Oh, I will to court," Henslowe raged. "With you," looking at us, "and you," now at Miller.

"And I welcome the contest, sir," said Webb, "you having had these many weeks to concoct your scheme – which, I warn you, stinks plain of fraud and is rotten at its heart – and having used varied lawyers to fashion in papers such trap as you considered inescapable. And yet I took but a day to find ways fully legal to deflate it entire, leaving you here blustering your empty threats in an attempt to win now, by acting, what you have already lost. But the present company knows an actor's art full well and can see in both the poor quality of your lines and in your faithless delivery your admission of defeat.

"I do warn you to remember, Henslowe, that your plot as to this theatre is but a small wart of fraud on a larger canker rich with it – one by which you already have profited. I would suggest you make home and lick those wounds you have. For, should you entangle your Somerset friends in your failings, you like will find the next wound your lies have brought upon you to be mortal."

Henslowe sputtered, his voice growing louder as his faith in its contents shrank. "Lies? Do you now call me a liar, sir?"

"Now?" said Webb. "I thought sure I had previous. But to be plain, yes."

"A liar and a coward, sir," I added. "As you could not defeat us in the open combat of commerce, you tried instead to undermine us with guile. And you have failed flat in both attempts. We have bested you on stage, we have bested you in law, and we have even, reluctantly – as we hold our honour dearer than do you, we being better acquainted with its virtues – bested you in scheming."

"Honour, sir?" He stepped close to me, puffing out his chest and drawing himself to his full height, him being some few inches taller than am I. "You dare question my honour?"

"To question it, I would first have to find it," I said. "It being smaller even than that worm you hide in your codpiece."

"You go too far, sir!" Henslowe shouted, his spit flying once again onto my face and its small weight tipping final some balance in me that had quivered too long between caution and action. The chests holding our store of costumes lined the road, those being the last load that we would send to Bankside. I kicked open the lid of the chest that held our stage armoury, snatching out quick two swords and tossing one at Hemslowe. It bounced off his chest and fell to the dirt.

"If your too little honour is too dear offended, then there is your remedy. Pick it up and be a man or let it lie and be that foul coward we have long known. Defend the honour to which you pretend, or scurry back under the skirts of the law, where my lawyer will carve you up instead of my steel. But enough words today. Be a man or be gone."

Henslowe glanced down at the sword a short moment, but then turned to leave. "This matter is not at its end," he called back.

"Because you lack the spine to end it," I called to his back.

Miller now stood alone, seeming in such pose he had held the entire time, his mouth agape.

"Well?" I asked him.

"I… I feel I have been ill used."

I slid the tip of my blade into the hilt of the sword

that Henslowe had left on the ground, and lifted it up to Miller in invitation.

"If you have been used ill, I invite you to use this better."

He held out his hands and shook his head, then backing away many steps, before turning into a mincing run.

Our company now alone, Burbage threw back his head in laughter, and then clasped me by my shoulders. "By God, Will, you do act the lion well. But methinks you were perhaps too sure of Henslowe's nature, for what if he had taken up that blade?"

"Then I would the lion be," I answered.

He looked hard on me a long moment. "And in your eyes I see the truth of that. Can it be that this heart we have long known wise is now in equal measure stout? Your recent adventures have made you into a lion! Jenkins!"

Jenkins stood to the side, slack jawed.

"My God, lad," Burbage cried. "You pick this moment to be without a bottle?"

I looked down Bishopsgate toward the receding Miller, knowing that road would be the route from which, in one day's time, Carey's coach would fetch me to our meeting with Topcliffe. And, while my earlier resolve did hold, it was flavoured with a sick tickling in my belly that seemed to foretell the path of some future blade.

"Be quick with the bottle, boy," I said. "For I am soon a lion into the lion's den, and I must fortify my newly fierce nature."

CHAPTER 27

By the morning next, the theatre and our stores entire were at Bankside, and such small work as was needed to adjust the foundation to fit our design was complete. In the early hour at which I arrived, Burbage was already in his element, directing the raising of the timbers that would frame our stands. I watched for some minutes, marvelling at that easy congress he made with any, whether our own actors or the simple tradesmen he had contracted for this raising, being all at once cajoling and profane and a happy companion and a stern master so that each party was to his task and most willing. As skilled as he was in an actor's art, he seemed almost happier in this role.

I remembered suddenly fond those days in my youth when I was under my father's tutelage at his glover's shop, and that unalloyed satisfaction that came when first I made whole a product he deemed worth sale. They were simple gloves of only little adornment as would suit the purse of one mean in station, which were sold quick to a man who worked at the livery. And I still note, each time I arrive at Stratford and there board what horse I have rented for that passage, that he wears them still. I am always disproportionate happy to find them continuing in good service. I think there is some joy attendant to those real things we make with our hands that I cannot find in the more abstract products of my work, as my words can please only the mind and thus leave the body wanting.

Burbage finally noted my presence. "Gads!" he shouted. "It seems even the foreman of this enterprise falls under some eyes." And he walked over to my place.

"It seems to go well," I said. "Not that you've had much benefit of my sweat, nor am I sufficient schooled to know."

He nodded. "Most well. We will have it this day complete, even if we must again work into the night. Jaggard was by, and offered free printing of such bills as we might need to promote our first performance at this new location. While we will sure tell him "yes", I told him I had first to seek your consult, as it is your offense to forgive."

"I find myself of late so burdened with insult that I think it will lighten my load to be rid of one. And so yes, and my blessing."

I heard a high, sweet voice singing, and noted Jenkins perched light atop the highest beam and pounding hard at the peg that would join it to its cross member. "I had not known his ear for music," I said.

"Like a bird, he seems happiest high up and, once there perched, graces us constant in song. Had I not grown fond of the boy, I would make him a eunuch and preserve both that voice and those womanly charms for which our stage has use."

"His new fondness for the bottle does not put him at risk at such heights?"

Burbage drew a key and dangled it before me. "I have the sack under lock until our work is done, for fear the boy might take wing either in accident or in liquor's fancy." He slipped the key back into its pocket. "So, will I have use of your hands today, or must the Lion of Shoreditch again be on the hunt?"

"To the hunt," I said. "And I will have you know that I must some deplete the company's purse in the effort, though such will be spent on costumes, which we must refresh before we next appear at Court in any case."

He nodded his agreement. "I pray this means your own costume today will be finer, and so you also will be armed? For I would not have my lion loose amongst the jackals without his claws."

I smiled. "I shall wear both our finest clothes and our finest sword. But I fear I shall not return hence until after tonight's congress with Topcliffe, at which time I will like find the theatre complete and ready for my benefit, it having benefitted only little from my labours."

Now adorned well, I made to the mercer's shop with the morning still only little commenced. Such early hours were still unusual in my custom, but I did recognise in the morning a certain fresh charm.

The day, like a child, seemed to greet the world unmarked. But while this sight lent some faith to the heart, I knew I did still prefer the evening. The hours from dawn until dark take the day entire through the sweep of human experience, so that in the night's darker confines I can see those scars and blemishes of the day's passing and commune with those conflicts and sufferings and even comedies that are meat to my quill. I knew that, once this matter was settled, I would not change my habits and play the rooster where I had long played the owl.

It was early enough that some other shops in the lane were just taking down their shutters, but I found the mercer's ready for commerce. And as I made my way in, I had to admire his art at costume. For while his was dressed much fine, so as to display such wears as were his to offer, those clothes still were cut in such way as did make him seem clear your servant and not your master.

"A good morning to you, sir," he said. "I assume you come on some other's behalf, as I cannot hope to improve on your appearance with my humble wares, though in truth you are a man of such fine form as to compliment any garment."

I smiled and bowed, thanking him, though noting some concern as his eyes passed over those injuries I still bore on my face.

"I assure you, sir, that my face is usual as fair as my form, except that I made unfortunate acquaintance with some of our fair city's lesser beings just recent past."

The man's own face came sour. "For shame, sir. You did suffer dear at their unkind hands."

"Not so dear as they," I said, putting my fist firm to the hilt of my sword, thinking it best that he hold some little fear of me.

He nodded. "But it is too fine a day to dwell on your travails, sir." He swept his hand graceful in an arc over his offerings. "Pray, how can I make your world more beautiful?"

The shop was arrayed such that the counter displaying samples of his wares cut the room in half, the floor on my side covered with an ornate carpet and there being several chairs richly carved and dressed in fine fabric. The wall behind the mercer opened on my left to a room in the back, where I presume he kept his stores and where his cutting and tailoring were done. In that opening hung a curtain well embroidered in reds and golds, which would be as fine a sight as such opening could hope offer except that Mary Norton's face did brief appear at its edge, and in that moment make the curtain seem just a painted harlot.

"I am an owner in a troupe of players which does perform regular at Court for our good Queen, and as we have just received notice of several new performances there, we will refresh our costumes to include such as appropriate to this occasion," I said.

The mercer bowed slightly. "I do common make attires for nobles at court and for her Majesty, too, and am well versed in such styles current to her liking. And as our shop is mercer and haberdasher both, you can secure such fabrics as you need and have them shaped to your design."

I nodded. "Then I place myself in your skilled hands. Pray, give me some sample of what current pleases my noble audience."

The mercer bowed, and then called into the room behind. "Lucy, bring out such goods suited to court as we have near done. And Mary, be so good as to model for this fine gentleman that gown that awaits the young duchess, for whom you have proven such a fit example."

An older woman came out immediate, and laid forth on the counter several doublets, blouses, and gowns of varied design, but all rich in fabric and ornament. She then took her leave to help young Mary into that gown her master would have modelled. I passed some minutes complimenting the mercer on his wares and inquiring as to ways in which they might be made seem both older and more foreign, as our plays were usual set in times past and in lands distant.

"This last gown, sir, may be of particular interest, as another of the exact same save in colour and detail will be made for the Queen herself, her household having commissioned their making for some pageant soon upcoming. I would show you hers, sir, but such ornaments that on this are made through embroidery or bauble are on hers made with actual jewels, and so I keep it well secure."

And then the curtain parted and Mary came forth, and while it was the dress the storekeeper would have me notice, her beauty seemed steal all light from the room, as if each beam was jealous to alight on her person instead of his product. On her fair face, which though almost alabaster pale seemed somehow also dusted as though with some spice that made that fine skin more rare, or on her eyes, which were a rich hazel flecked with emerald and some little exotic in their shape, or on the pursed bow of her lips, her small mouth making the impression of a waif but her lips being sufficient full as to make any man wish they made congress with his own. She was past average tall for a woman, her shoulders being just broad enough to make perfect the proportion of her frame, but still of that lean and willowy grace that blesses the young. Her breasts, pushed into prominent display by the nature of the garment, woke in me both hunger and shame as I remembered that girl now dead who in form Mary did much resemble, and made it too easy for me to picture what wonders the gown concealed.

"Sir," I said, "I would have this dress exact as seen on this form, except I fear I am so moved by the model that I will find the dress some faded when seen on any other."

I noted a slight blush colour Mary's features, and even the rich hillocks of her breasts, as the mercer smiled and made a slight laugh.

"Mary is only recent in my employ and, while some skilled, is still learning her art as seamstress. But I can sell off her back any clothing of my design to any woman who sees it, each imagining that

it is the gown and not the girl by which they are
so moved and all too embarrassed to later say so.
And so the child is dearer to me than gold, though
I would thank you not to say so to the man who
recommended her."

"You mean some man had such in his clutches and
instead looked to place her elsewhere?"

"A minister at some parish nearer the river. She
had lost her position in some household and was
orphan, and so he made from shop to shop asking
if any had need. As our commerce is growing and,
frankly, to be rid of him, for he was most persistent,
I agreed to meet her. And having met her, well..."
And he turned up his hands as though to conclude
his argument, its logic being plain.

He turned to the girl. "Mary, do come around the
counter so this good sir may admire the gown more
close."

At which I saw a little shame flicker in her features.
For while she was not in this made whore, she was
clear used as an instrument to inflame in men lust
and in women jealousy, and in either case to gain
their commerce. But she moved dutiful to the end of
the counter, although somewhat awkwardly, likely
being unused to such involved costume. She caught
a shoe on the edge of the carpet and stumbled, so
that I reached out and took her hand to steady her
progress, surprised to feel a small square of paper
pressed into my palm as she righted her balance.

"I thank you, sir," she said, looking into my eyes
direct and communicating more.

And I made good show of examining both gown and girl, this clear being the mercer's intent, and left his shop only after placing an order as would deplete the company's purse by many pounds.

Back on the street, I opened the small paper the girl had passed to me. It bade me meet her one hour hence near the market two streets north.

CHAPTER 28

Even from a street's distance and with her dressed now in the plainer garb that fit her station, I could mark Mary easy as I waited at the edge of the market.

She walked to me direct. "Pray, sir, walk with me as I buy my master's supper, as it is my daily duty and I have little time." And so we made into the crush of stalls, and she performed her office.

"You are Shakespeare," she said.

"I am, and would like to think my fame such that you know this, but suspect other."

She shook her head. "I did see you brief at Somerset just short after the Lord Chamberlain's passing, as you were admitted to meet with the new Baron. Immediate after, we were all by him informed that we should talk plain with you concerning his late father, as you would draft some work to his honour."

"That is my charge," I said.

"I must mark you most diligent in its execution."

"Diligent how?"

"To take such pains so as to talk with a woman only short in the late Lord's service, for I cannot count your appearing in a shop where I am only one week employed as an accident."

She seemed suddenly some hostile. I thought to make her mood other with flattery.

"Your being blessed with such beauty, I should think you well used to men taking pains to make your acquaintance, be it their charge or no."

She reddened again, her skin being so fair that it did colour easy, but by her face I took this blush to be in anger.

"Blessed, sir? So that I feel the crawl of every man's eyes across my body like a corruption of spiders? So that I can think no man's intention true, but only such false designs by which he might gain access to my favours? So that every woman sees me first as threat? Is this how you mean blessed?"

I remembered my Anne's harsh speaking in which she had coloured my lordship over words that I had always thought my blessing instead as my curse, and felt now some ashamed at having tried to ply this girl with flattery.

"Every gift we have comes at some cost. I do know this true."

She calmed, the red gone from her face. "But how can I know you true? When you are today yourself, or some version of it, but were just yesterday a beggar who gained my pity as I watched you suffer hard at the hands of some brutes just below my master's windows?" She looked to my face. "For I know how you gained your injuries, sir." And then a weak smile, "And how dear you made suffer those who caused them."

"In truth, I do think they suffer for them in their souls," I said.

"Their souls being God's province, such suffering is not of your agency."

"But I am told he oft works in mysterious ways. So, could we not, any of us, be each day his instrument?"

She smiled light again, but this time with some little mischief. "I fear conversation with you, sir, as I think I might find myself led into some maze from which I would have to rely on your mercies to be out. And, in truth, I doubt your mercies. And so I will be plain so that I can remain clear on the bounds of our discussion."

I nodded in invitation for her to continue.

"I believe you have some mission from Baron Carey, but that a play is not the thing. And I will ask you plain to tell me that mission and my place in it, for I am a young woman alone and by that station already at some peril. If I face some other, it is best that I know it."

I thought careful on my words next, for while I was not at liberty to reveal Carey's mission, I was charged to learn what truths I could and by what means I may. And I had learned at the cost of not little recent suffering that my duty had to be to truth first if I hoped to faithful serve myself or any master second.

"I do make inquiries on the Baron's behalf," I said, "and will ready admit that my fortunes and those of my company do much depend on his favour, so I am diligent in that office. Whether the end of that office be such work as you were told commissioned or some other hardly seems matter. I swear that this be true and will have you know that I have recent resolved to serve truth better, but, now trying to be better true, must also admit that I have served it poorly in the past and am only little acquainted with its practice."

"That may be as true as I have been spoken to by any man. And in hopes our congress can remain true, I will ask how, given the family Carey's august circles and circumstances, I came to be such a spur to your curiosities."

"My lady, I have found much curious in these few weeks past, so do not imagine yourself alone in that circumstance. But the manner and timing of your leaving from Somerset, coming at just such moment as to put you past my questioning, this did give me pause."

"As though no lady has before left a household's employ upon her master's death?"

"Or was made leave."

She coloured again. "Made leave, sir? By whose word? For my leaving was of my choice and for my reasons alone."

"The Baron's brother told me he had you transferred to his service on his father's passing – as he found you lovely and, to be plain, planned to use his station to have use of you. But that you bore some pox that made him fear for his health, and so he discharged you."

Her colour deepened, and she took some moments to answer. "I must guard my tongue, sir, for such as the Baron's brother can say of me as they will and at

no consequence while such as me must either speak
false or not at all. And while you may have only late
made truth's acquaintance, I do hold my virtue most
dear. Men have much to claim in this world and can
pick their treasures, but for a woman, virtue is all
she is granted."

"I have no affection for the younger Carey, I
assure you, and even his own brother holds him in
low regard. While you might imagine me of some
station, sure you realise that I am no more at liberty
to impugn a Carey than are you. And even so I will
call him as vile a man as I have known."

Which seemed to calm her some. "I will call your
words again true, and will have you know this plain.
The younger Carey did on my very first day in his
charge trap me in his rooms and attempt to press
himself on me, at which I drew his dagger. Not in
threat, but instead I did hand it to him and tell him
that, would he have my honour, he would need
take it immediate and from my corpse, for I would
fight him to my last and, if I lived, immediate leave
those rooms and that household's employ. As it
seems his taste for rape runs only to such as can be
accomplished by threat and not to such that would
require his actual effort, I was left to leave and so I
did."

"But what of this pox? For the chambermaid did
mention it, too."

"You mean of my hand?"

"The same."

"I am at least by that relieved, for I thought from

your telling that Carey had claimed to see such portions of my person that no man has, and such seeing would imply my assent to his advances, or at least my insufficient resistance."

"Then I am sorry for your alarm, as even Carey claimed the hand only."

She turned both arms up to me. "I am very fair of skin, and it is tender and easily offended. I am frequent with some rash, and was so often at Somerset, such lyes and other agents as they use in their laundries and cleaning being much hard on me. So, yes, my hand was that day some reddened, but hardly poxed."

She seemed now vexed. "Sir, I am past my time and must be back to the mercers. I have answered you plain and do pray this can conclude your interest."

Time being now short, I had to make best use of it.

"You are Catholic," I said.

At which, instead of colouring, she looked more pale.

"Sir?"

"You attended this Sunday morning past a mass held secret in the cellar of that building where your late father lived. It was from there that I marked your progress."

She regained herself quick. "And so your costume as beggar, as it better fits that district where I live than this one where I work."

"Which does not answer my question."

"Which question you have not asked, but only for yourself answered."

"Then I will ask it plain. Are you Catholic?"

"And now having been asked direct, I will answer plain. I am. I do not brag my faith for my peril, but I will not deny it for my virtue."

"Having been so raised by your father?"

"He did teach me to be true in all, but in my faith most."

"And your mother?"

"She died at my birth, so I have only the example of her sacrifice and not her teaching."

"And is the mercer, also, in secret, Catholic?"

She made a small laugh. "The mercer, sir? He has no God but his purse. Why would you think thus?"

"Him saying you were hired through the intercession of a cleric. You being Catholic, I thought perhaps the cleric was, too, and the mercer part of his congregation."

She shook her head. "Services to the poor are run by the Queen's church through its parishes, and I considered it no insult to God to ask help there to find a position, it being my duty to God and Queen both to find work for my hands."

I could think of no question further.

Her face was now set hard stern. "So, we come final to the truth of your mission. It seems, sir, you hold my life in your hands, and that of my congregation. Did you suppose you would have something for it? Use of my person? For I will grant nothing. I do not pursue martyrdom, but neither will I dodge it. If my virtue cannot be my shield, then it will instead be my reward."

I shook my head at her. "I ask nothing, for my office is only as I have claimed: to make such inquiry as I see fit and to report to Carey that which pertains to his cause. I see no cause in your faith, nor, in truth, harm in it either. And I see in your character such better person as I might be and in your beauty a reminder of some past sins that do haunt me deep. So, go. As you have been true to me, I will be true to you. I will trouble you no further."

She turned as though to leave, stopped, and then turned back to face me, drawing close near. "Do you know God, sir? For I sense in you such man who does seek good but has no map by which to find it."

"I'm afraid he does elude my understanding."

"There is peace in his company, sir, and if you would have it, I pray you seek me again. Know that what I do now, I do not in lust, but in his name and in blessing."

She leaned forward and kissed me gentle on my cheek, and then stepped back, gracing me with her full smile. And then she turned and was gone.

I set off toward Somerset, having sent word to Carey that I would be near to there on his business and so would meet his coach at that junction where we did confer upon my return from Stratford. I was making my way there slow, having still some time, when I saw ahead two men in rough congress with a cripple who begged alms, and I recognised those same Puritans who had so sore abused me the Sunday just past.

Drawing near, I could hear the same threats of bailiff, these courageous fellows also slapping this fellow as they had me, though he had to accept their blows on his knees, as it was there his legs ended.

"What trouble here, good sirs?" I asked, now immediate behind them. And they turned brief, seeing only my dress and manner and taking no note of my face, turning immediate back to their rough work.

"Trouble, sir? None. We are just making plain God's lesson to this sinner so clear out of his favour. For God would have all earn their keep and not beg it."

"The earning being some complicated when one's legs end at one's knees," I said. "Though I can imagine, being so blessed he does better pray than do you, as he is all day on his knees, and may thus know God's lesson already in full."

At that, the men turned to face me.

"That being the case," I continued, "he requires no schooling from you. Perhaps you will instead offer it to me."

The men looked at me puzzled, saying nothing.

"As I am today in my true garb and armed, you seem less keen to threaten your steel," I said. "Perhaps your honour is only a Sunday thing."

Only then did their eyes grow wide in recognition.

"As you are a gentleman and thus in God's love, I will forgive your short temper, sir," said that man who had first struck me on our last meeting. "And will not even ask on what business you were late in these quarters and in disguise, as I will assume your honour and pray that you will assume mine."

"Oh, I will glad tell you what business. The Crown's business, sir. Topcliffe's business."

It seemed, in some company, my recent commitment to the truth did ready fail me. At the name Topcliffe, they both blanched, knowing well he did have some agents who worked disguised and in secret.

"Topcliffe's business," I repeated, "but not yours. Except on Sunday you chose to make it so. I could not then oblige your offer to make whole that honour that you did swear I had offended, so I do so now." I put my hand to the hilt of my sword and pulled it the first inches clear, my eyes hard and unblinking on the man's own.

At which both men backed away a step, their hands clear of their swords. "For such offence as we did unwitting offer, we do sincere apologise," said the second man.

"To me only?"

"Sir?"

I nodded to the beggar they had current accosted. "What of my fellow agent whose report I am here to take and to whom you have now drawn such unwanted attentions? Does he, too, not deserve your apology?"

They looked to the cripple and then back to me. "Him, sir?"

"Do you question my word? For, like you, I would have such insult answered immediate."

"Question, no, sir. We are but surprised."

"Then gather yourself and offer your apologies. For you see, this fellow does in fact earn his keep and not beg it. He earns it in vital service. A service that you have now twice interrupted."

At which they turned to the beggar, both now fulsome in their apology.

"As our congress here has drawn such attention to our presence that we do not welcome," I said, "your making gift of alms might some explain your interruption and reinforce his disguise. Consider it a donation to the Queen's service."

At which both men dropped a crown into the beggar's cap and beat a hasty retreat. Them gone, I added tuppence to the man's hat, and he looked up at me with a toothless smile.

"I know you, Shakespeare," he said. "For I did see you perform many times when I still had use of my legs."

I smiled back. "And how do you rate my performance?"

"Your finest, sir," he said. "For I have never before been paid to watch theatre."

CHAPTER 29

"Any news of Mary?" I had met Carey's coach at the appointed location, and he quizzed me as we made way to Topcliffe's house.

Now that I cared more deep for truth, I found its nature more troubling. The truth of Mary was plain enough, and I could relay it easy and in seeming clear conscience. For I had sought that truth in Carey's service and so did seem to owe it to him in debt to that service, or to his patronage, or even as he had late saved my life. What is more, I believed Carey honourable – or at least a man who made effort to be.

Yet, now knowing the truth of Mary, I felt the weight of its consequence heavy in my hands. I could share it with Carey plain and hope to convince him that she seemed only a small tool in this plot, already ill-used, and that she deserved no further injury. But I feared that he would have the matter more fully exposed, and that not only Mary but also her small and secret congregation would likely then suffer dire and to no purpose, but, still, at my hands. My mind flashed to the baker and his wife and their happy home and shop, all at peril because I had wandered to their door. I pictured them at Tyburn, the ropes around their necks, them then hoisted high. And I decided quick that such flag of truth as I might serve could not be woven from innocent flesh flapping at the end of a hangman's ropes.

"What news I've had seems say she is but a girl, and full innocent in nature," I said. "I fear any attention more toward her is attention away from those hands true stained with guilt."

Carey nodded. "Though my company with her was small, that was my sense, too. But the matter of our ill-nosed fellow may have yielded more fruit."

"If it be such fruit as we must harvest from Topcliffe, then it is not such fruit as is happy in my diet."

Carey nodded. "Topcliffe is like unto a fierce dog that you might trust to savage any that cross unwelcome onto your estate, but a beast whose savaging is a matter of hellish appetites, not of loyal service. And so you employ the beast and feed the beast but never full trust it – that dog never admitted in evening to lie by your fire and keep your company with the steady and loyal affection for which dogs are known. Instead, it is kept chained out of doors, where its dreams are as like to be of your throat as of any other."

"And yet we make our way to his kennel," I said.

Carey nodded. "As you suggested, I asked some close in congress with the players in this Somerset scheme whether they have knowledge of a man similar in description to our late assailant, making particular note of his much injured nose. They answered unanimous no, but news of my inquiry reached Topcliffe, who sent word we should have his congress on the matter."

"Such word being passed to him by some agent in his service?"

"It seems little happens in London to which he is not quick made privy," Carey said.

I watched for a moment out the coach's door. The city passed at such speed I usually would have envied, making my way most often afoot, but I wished now instead to be on foot so as to slow our progress. Or, in truth, to be in this coach, but headed away from, instead of toward, Topcliffe's door.

"To be true," I said, "I much fear this meeting and could easy have lived happy had Topcliffe never made my company."

Carey grunted. "If it makes your mind any more at ease, your name likely is already full known to him – as the Puritans attempting to use the Queen's instruments to further their religious ends constant seek his inquiry into supposed Papist or Spanish plots they believe are hatched among your kind, theatre being always included in those devilish ills they think put our fair kingdom at Satan's use. At least now it will be known to him in my service."

The coach slowed and then stopped, and I could hear the driver stepping down to come and open our doors.

"That is not the type of ease my mind imagined," I said.

"Are you surprised to find so plain this chamber that is the subject of so much myth?" Topcliffe asked, ushering us into his lair.

On entering his home, after only quick introduction, he suggested that, as our talk would involve his art, we hold our discussions in that room where his art was practised. He thus ushered us down a narrow stairway to a cellar room. The stones of the room's walls had been well smoothed and then whitewashed, the floor, too, being stone and smooth. There was no window, but only the door through which we entered: heavy oak, banded with iron, so that, once it was closed, the room was sealed entire. A single chair of heavy but complex construction sat fastened fast to the stone floor in the centre of the room and facing the far wall, along which ran a long table on which sat a series of chests. To the left were three simple chairs and a small table hosting a claret jug, three cups, and a plate of cheeses. Topcliffe motioned theatrically to the chairs.

Every monster, in our imagining, exceeds its true form. I don't know how I had pictured Topcliffe – huge and heavily muscled, perhaps. Or maybe lean and pale with a hawkish face. But instead he was short, old, soft, almost feminine in his aspect, an air he seemed conscious to emphasise in his foppish dress and his lisping speech so that, at first, I was some amused to credit him such evil that had haunted my thoughts since I had first learned of this meeting. And yet slow that same manner did begin to feel as a disease, as if it bore some pestilent strength that the healthy could not recognise, as if the sibilance of his talking by some charm eroded my will.

Us all seated, Topcliffe poured a measure of the wine into each cup and then offered a smile that slithered across his face like Eve's snake. "I shall let you each choose your vessel, as I find those in my company too oft suspect that I will try by guile to practise on them some vile art."

Carey reached direct for the cup closest him, took it and drank a long measure, and in doing so partly broke that spell Topcliffe seemed so easy to cast on me. I did the same and Topcliffe, making his serpent's smile, reached toward his own cup, but then instead took a piece of cheese.

"We are here at your invitation, sir," Carey said, "as your note indicated you might offer some insight into the matter of this man by whom we were late attacked."

"In good time," Topcliffe said. "I so rarely have chance to entertain guests save those who make use of that other chair," he nodded toward the construction in the middle of the room, "and so I'm afraid I will impose on your good graces first to converse." He finished his cheese and then drank from his cup, and looked at me direct. "You never answered my question."

"Question?" I asked.

"Concerning the room. Are you surprised at its nature?"

"I am," I answered. "I did picture it arrayed with larger engines of your art, of varied and horrible design."

"A rack at least, I would have thought," said Carey.

Topcliffe drew his hands together in a soft clap, and then squeezed them, beaming. "Precisely," he said with some excitement. "And so the room seems less horrible than you imagined?"

"Much less," said Carey.

"And so enters in hope," Topcliffe answered. "It is hope, and not pain, that is the lever of truth." He turned toward me. "Shakespeare, you could not know this – as I do keep my activities secret so to serve the common fears that I might be anywhere at any time – but I make pains to attend the theatre, and think you and I have similar knowings in our divergent arts."

"How so, sir?"

"When you tell a tale, does it serve your art well to tell it direct so that its object and endings are in plain but distant sight from the first, merely growing closer and clearer as the story progresses?"

I shook my head. "That idea suits the human mind, for it is our desire always to have clear known to us what we may. But stories must learn from nature's way of things. The way a river will, at its start, its power being small, meander in the path that least resists it. It becomes some straighter as it gathers its waters and their force but even so being subject to some turning. In the end, it will to the sea, as all rivers must, but I will have the audience take that full journey before the story finds its home."

"Exactly," Topcliffe said, seeming pleased with my answer. "And what do I do in this room but help others to tell their stories? Just as every river must to the sea, every story here must, eventually, to the truth. But my authors hold jealous their truths and would have me believe other, and so I must, too, take them through such meandering journeys by which they understand the primal nature that controls the flow of their story so that the water of their truth might final be reunited with its brethren. For is not all truth of God's sea and in his service? And so I collect for God such truths as have wandered into the use of the Papists and his other enemies."

Topcliffe got up and walked to the elaborate chair in the room's centre. "Some men come subject to my ministrations having in their own imaginings made such horrors that I need only ask and all is revealed." He turned back to me. "And so, Shakespeare, men such as you with minds that can ready create do usually resist my efforts least, as they have the wit to discern the story's inevitable end and have already in their own minds suffered such twists and turns in it as are beyond even my capacity to create. They do my work for me in advance in the nightmares of their own beds and reach my company full ripe.

"But there are others," he turned now to Carey, "who are blessed not with a creative mind, but instead one hard in will and courage. Them I must lead on this full journey so that they can see that such truths as they think their own are not theirs to possess, but rather waters from God's sea of truth that were theirs to carry for some time only and that they must now release into the river of my story so that these truths may again find their righteous home."

"I had not imagined so much philosophy in your arts," said Carey. "I had supposed it a simple thing to cause a man pain."

Topcliffe shook his head as though a master disappointed in his pupil. "As I told you, my instrument is hope, not pain."

Carey looked about the plain stone room. "I see no hope here."

Topcliffe raised a finger. "But you forget your expectations. You had said you did expect a rack at least. So, what if you were now here, but as my prisoner and not as my guest? While you do not have Shakespeare's gift for imagining, you would of course have contemplated on such that you might expect at my hands. And so your mind would turn to those instruments common ascribed to this practice – the rack, the wheel, perhaps some boiling cauldron. And you would attach your fears to those objects and so have steeled yourself to resist them. But arriving here, you would see none of them. None of those things of which you had been most afraid. And in that moment, you would have hope. And you would be strapped into this chair feeling stronger than you had been even at the door to this room."

Topcliffe pulled down on the back of the chair, and through some elaborate design of hinges and joints, the chair became instead a kind of table – now lying flat at the height of Topcliffe's waist, the wings of the chair to which the victim's arms would be secured having swung out so that any strapped to it would now lay supine and spread beneath him.

"This would be your first lesson," Topcliffe said. "That which you thought a chair – in which, while bound, you might at least sit in something like dignity – is instead the table on which you will suffer, full spread, any indignity I might inflict. And you understand even in that instant, there being no pain in it, that nothing in this room is what it seems, but is instead what I will it to be. And so I do offer first the false hope that this room holds fewer terrors than my subjects imagine, and then replace that hope with the knowledge that it holds whatever evils I might conjure."

Carey scoffed. "Such tricks might play hard on a mind as supple as dear Shakespeare's, but I'm afraid you would find me little moved. Coming here, I would have steeled myself for torture, not for tricks with your furnishings."

"Little moved to be sure," Topcliffe said. "But little is all I need. You mentioned the rack. You know how this works, of course? The victim placed upon it, both wrists and ankles bound to its engine, and then the cranks turned so that he is stretched, first to his normal limits, and then beyond them to his pain, and in final to such degree as his joints are sundered?"

Carey nodded. "I know of it."

"You are a soldier, yes?"

"I am."

"And so you have seen such horrors as might befall a man in battle?"

"I have."

"And who suffers more? A man so cleaved as has no chance to live, but instead spends whatever few minutes his mortal wound takes to claim him, or a man more lightly injured, perhaps pierced through but in such location as may not prove fatal, or perhaps slashed deep but not mortally?"

"The less injured man usually suffers more, for such wounds as prove mortal often seem to shock the body into a kind of stupor. Methinks, perhaps, it is a small grace God grants to those so afflicted so that they can keep their wits sufficient to make their final peace instead of being mad with pain."

"And yet consider the rack," Topcliffe said. "There are sure long moments of suffering as the victim is held in its embrace, but the pain is constant and of the same nature, and the body does adjust. And when the victim is stretched final to that point where the joints give way, often he is suffused in that stupor you have seen befall those most serious injured in battle."

Topcliffe now turned back to me. "Shakespeare, you are no soldier, but I have late learned you are some schooled in the art of seduction."

He paused, clear expecting an answer. When I did not give one, he raised his eyebrows in question, and so I nodded.

"And in such pursuits, does it profit a man to ask a woman outright to surrender her virtue immediate?"

I shook my head, not wanting to speak words on this matter in this room, which seemed the fouler

the longer I was in it, and full closer to evil than any
I had encountered. Not wanting, too, to long reflect
on what similarities there might be in such wiles as I
had used on women and those evil arts Topcliffe had
used on his victims.

"Of course not," Topcliffe said. "Carey thinks as
a soldier, and wants to bludgeon his foe immediate
into surrender. But even in wars, surrenders are
most usual won through a series of small victories.
As Shakespeare well knows, virtue is surrendered
in pieces, the first seeming innocent beyond
consequence. But it is through those little surrenders
that he can drive a girl first to his bed and then to her
grave."

Topcliffe now scurried to the far wall and the table
lined with chests, opening each. The chests opened
such that their tops swung up, their fronts folded
down, and then a panel on the inside tilted upward
so that the various instruments secured to those
panels could be easy seen by any strapped to that
table. The chests held knives of varying sizes and
shapes, hooks of some kinds, awls and needles and
many other instruments of unknown nature that
seemed almost more sinister as their purpose could
not ready be discerned.

His smile at me now was most cruel, and his eyes
shone with a light much like lust.

"And so, with this or this or this," Topcliffe snatched
varied instruments from his chests, first a pointed
awl, then a curved blade, then what looked like a
bird's talons, "I can extract through little injuries

– that, in their small natures, do not so offend the body that it seeks stupor to still its suffering – some small surrenders, little truths the victim thinks of no matter, the first meanderings on our journey. But with each surrender, the force of the river builds until its ending in the sea is inevitable. It is hope I use. For with each change in instrument, the victim hopes the next will be less terrible. But I have studied long on my art and know full how to build on the effect of each insult, how a small injury here makes more raw some nerve there so that the pain suffered is worse, always worse, the suffering growing just as Shakespeare's plays build to a climax. Until finally, such false hopes as I have offered having been all put out, hope itself is full extinguished."

He turned to face us, almost like an actor at a play's end facing the audience to receive its applause. "I kill hope, gentlemen, not bodies. For in hope's death dies every man's last strength and leaves unguarded his truth."

It was not our applause he received, but instead our silence.

"I could never be so sure of any cause that I could, in its name, kill so fine a thing as hope," I said finally, "for to quash it even once in error would, I think, leave me damned."

Topcliffe looked hard at me, that curious light burning the brighter in his eyes. "Certainty is more precious than any tool in my chests," he said, "for stood I not certain that my work be God's will, I would have no stomach for it. But if there be treason, then I will have it out. For I know Satan to be at the root of it, and the Pope and his minions and his allies in Spain and France to be at the heart of it. I am called Priest Hunter by some, and I relish the name as I would have every Papist in England dead, their confessions first secured at my hands and at the price of such suffering as will make them greet welcome their eternity in hell. Cruelty is not sin in God's service, but rather his avenging fire making clean this nation that alone he has clutched to his bosom and called to his greatness."

Another silence.

"If you had us here only to tutor us in your art and your theology, then we thank you for the foul lesson and will be gone," Carey said at last. "But I had been led to expect some assistance in the matter of our mysterious assailant."

Topcliffe sighed like a singer who finds his song falling on deaf ears. "Yes, yes, yes. The matter of the nose." He returned to his chair in our midst at his small table and nibbled at another piece of his cheese, took another sip of his wine. "Could you explain in detail the nature of its injury?"

Being better with words and also noting that Carey much tried Topcliffe's spirits, I answered.

"The man's nose had been most grievous harmed," I said, "such that it seemed to be made now almost entire of scars."

"You say scars and not a scar," said Topcliffe, "so the effect was not one of a single insult but of varied injuries?"

"Yes and no," I said. "Many scars, yes, but when scars on a body age, they fade or whiten so that one can tell those older from those newer. These seemed all aged the same."

Carey nodded. "I have known men to have noses cut off, or even bitten off, but had never seen the like."

Topcliffe smiled, rose, and returned to his long table, drawing an oblong object with a handle at its bottom from the chest to the far right. As he turned the crank on the bottom, the object that had seemed solid began to open, revealing that its sides were in fact a series of four blades that could flower into these sharp petals.

"Do you know this?"

"The pear of anguish," Carey answered.

Topcliffe nodded eagerly. "The first of its kind had dulled blades. It would be inserted into the mouth and opened sufficient to serve as a gag to keep a victim silent, or, with a sufficient lever for a handle, be cranked open full enough to break the teeth and separate the jaw from its hinges. Then smaller versions with the sharpened edges were made that could be inserted into, shall we say, more intimate crevices, so that men and women both might suffer the agonies of their blooming."

He returned the device to its case and took forth another that appeared to be the same but shrunken down to a small size, and with the pear shape split in two, the rounded sides facing out with a flat space in its middle.

"We are vain of our faces and suffer injuries to them harder in our minds than we do such insults that leave scars others might never see. The human nose offering two orifices, I created this device." He turned the crank on its bottom, and the separate, half-rounded sides opened in three sharpened blades each, small spikes protruding out into the flat space between them. "The spikes hold fast to the septum, while the blades then spread and sunder the nostrils entire. I have used it with great effect over the years, though not on so many who have lived. For as you know, my gentle offices here frequently are only preface to those sterner ministrations that the Crown does impose. While I am charged only with collecting truths, the Crown can collect heads. From Shakespeare's description, it seems certain I have past made your assailant's acquaintance, for such injury as you describe is exactly as this would have made, and I can think of no other likely cause. To your fortune, I keep detailed records of who has enjoyed my congress, on what charge, when, those instruments used, and the truths gained. As those records are kept in my office at court and not here, I shall review them when I am next there and let you know those persons who fit your charge."

Our session ended, Topcliffe led us out of his cellar and to his door, taking Carey's arm just as we would leave. "I know that revulsion in which you and your fellows hold me, sir. You nobles who first profit from that knowledge that my inquiries gain and then damn me for the methods by which they are made. But I forgive you, as I understand your revulsion to be at heart a kind of fear. So many of your fellows have, over the years, due to their weak service, ended up subject to my ministry, and so you do all fear me, and then hate me, as it is man's way to hate most what he most fears. And so God's true service is ever lonely."

Carey tugged his arm lose and turned on Topcliffe, taking him by the front of his doublet and pushing him hard against the threshold of his door. "Fear you, sir? Call me coward again and we will see what courage you can manage with a foe not bound at your mercy. For it is only fear you know, and no courage, and if you are not more careful of your tongue with me, then I shall instruct you full in both."

Topcliffe attempted his serpent's smile, but it was weak at the corners.

"Review your records quick and have word to me immediate as to your findings," said Carey, releasing Topcliffe from his hold and looking down on him with scorn. "Imagine yourself God's servant if you will, for that imaging offends God, not me. But do not imagine that I would ever stand in fear of you, for that gives me offence, and I will have it answered."

We left, and the door closed behind us.

CHAPTER 30

The coach left Carey at Somerset, but he instructed his driver to have me home. Instead, I directed the driver to Bankside, alighting to find a complete theatre where that morning I had left bare timbers. From inside the stands, I could see the flicker of torchlight and hear the banging of hammers, and so I made my way in to find our company nailing the last boards to the floor of the stage, all else seeming done.

Burbage noted my arrival. "You have an actor's timing, sir, arriving for our applause, the work of things being finished. But, as you come from Topcliffe's and seem still entire, I do rightly welcome your company."

"Entire in person, Burbage, but some afflicted in spirit. Though my spirits are lifted to be among these fellows and to see our stage so nearly done." I removed my hat and swept it in a deep bow. "I do thank you all, and humbly, my hand having lent too little to this enterprise."

"Drop your hat and sword, sir, as you are among friends," Heminges said. "But do take a hammer to these last, so that, on such occasion as one of our feet passes through the stage, we can call it your work."

And so I did, and happy. And in short minutes, the last of the stage nailed tight, Burbage stood in its middle, turning slow with his arms outstretched. "Gentlemen," he said in such strong voice as any in audience could hear, "I give you the Globe!"

"Will you give us her in name alone, or shall we drink to her fortune and to ours?" called Jenkins from the stage's far side. "For you have kept locked the sack all this long day, and this workman's life is a thirsty one."

"Keep you sack secured, Burbage," I answered. "It is time we scout this neighbourhood for some tavern close. For as the theatre is the cathedral of our art, such tavern will be that chapel in which we will frequent pray to the saints of our lesser appetites. Besides, Jenkins has drunk from your purse enough. Tonight you shall all drink from mine so that I might contribute in ale what I could not in sweat."

"Oh!" cried Jenkins, now running across the stage to join us. "I am well blessed in the matter of masters!"

It was no long search to find a tavern, Bankside being rife with them. And so we started in one almost direct across from our new home, and then another more toward the bridge, Jenkins then calling on us to try yet a third, him thinking Bankside a new Eden and he would have all its wonders known.

"Do you like Will's ale as well as my sack?" Burbage asked, Jenkins having drained another tankard.

"As they are equal free, they are equal loved," he answered, his words followed hard by a long belch. Jenkins smiled. "Although ale does give me the airs and seems to love me less as it will not stay long. If you sirs will excuse me, I shall visit the alley and make room for more."

Burbage waved to the girl to refill our tankards as Jenkins made through the crowd to water the cobbles. "Do you suppose the boy has yet had his codpiece aside in a woman's service?" Burbage asked.

I smiled at him. "I suspect no."

"He is of the age for it," Burbage said.

"He is of the age where he is all for it," I said, "but knows not where to find it."

Burbage waved over a girl near the door, who, through her comings and goings with assorted fellows, had made clear her trade. And, being still young and in a darkened tavern after long drinking, she was still some comely.

"What is your name, my lovely?" Burbage asked.

"Michelle, at least for the part you would have me play. You are those actors who have taken new residence," she said, bending over our table such that her ample orbs hung nearly free for our inspection.

"A graceful name," I said, "but short by far of the grace of that it graces."

She smiled. "I offer no discounts for poetry, sir, but I do love an actor. Or two, if you are an ensemble."

"Alas," said Burbage, "we are old and sufficient in our charms so as to secure for free those few affections our shrivelled members might still require.

But perhaps you noted our young player?"

"That makes such regular acquaintance with the alley?" she said.

"The same," Burbage said. "The boy has not yet known the wonders of a woman, and having first confused you with Aphrodite until you drew near and I could tell you even more beautiful, I now pray that the boy might baptise himself in your font."

She blushed a little and stood straight. "Baptism is it? I would never deny a lad his sacraments. But as Jesus did drive the moneychangers from his temple, how can I expect the lad pay me, us being about the church's business?"

Burbage pressed a crown into her palm. "Such a lovely lad would never have cause to pay, as I'm sure you will find his charms such that your flower does open full ready in the light of his fair sun. But, this being church business, I do make my offering."

She looked careful at the crown, it being more than she would usual hope from a full night's steady commerce, and it already being such hour that her future custom would be thin. "You must love the boy well to pay so dear."

"I do, and would have you pretend so, too."

She made a slight bow. "Unlike we poor children doused as infants, the boy will long remember his baptism and will never question his faith."

Jenkins was just back in the door, and she turned and made toward him, seeming accidental to bump him in passing. Then she was accepting his apologies, and offering hers, her hand already light on his arm, and the two were soon deep in congress, her pressing closer, the hand that rested on his arm now against his chest, its fingers curling and uncurling light in teasing. Jenkins looked some stunned, but his hand made its own awkward foray, first to the side of her bare arm, then to her waist, it creeping toward her haunches like a frightened child, the surprise on his face growing as she turned her hip toward him, so that his hand now lay flat on her rump, He looked toward our table, and Burbage raised his tankard in salute. The girl then leaned in close, her lips pressed to Jenkins's ear as she made a whispered offer, and the two turned toward the door.

Burbage stood. "Come," he said. "We must see the boy off!"

Rising, I watched the girl put her arm around Jenkins – half in pretended affection, but half also to keep the unsteady lad on his feet. "I fear his furnace may be so soaked in ale that she may find it hard to stoke," I said.

"Will, do you forget the insistence of those fires that burned in your youth?"

And I thought for a moment of Anne and the urgent and passioned hours we long ago had shared. "I have not forgotten," I said, feeling sudden cheapened to be party to this ploy, even knowing that Burbage made it from affection only and sure that Jenkins, even if he knew the truth of his lady's attentions, would now, being full in lust's tow, most happy continue. This new conscience of mine, it seemed, was intent on clouding in question every action.

Burbage and I walked clear of the doors and into the street to mark the progress of Jenkins and his new love, Jenkins's stumbling having taken them only some few yards distant.

The girl would at least spend some few moments in more gentle embraces than common to her experience and would for those moments be far better paid. Jenkins would find in her false but willing arms a new corner of Bankside's Eden that would likely please him even more than his bottle. There was only pleasure and no harm in this staged encounter. But even as I formed these thoughts, I was consumed by the knowledge that they were the lies of my old habit, as my Anne had charged – my way of letting words be my master by having them paint some false truth that I could believe for my convenience. For, in truth, we had stolen the lad's chance to have a woman's fair sun first shine on him in true affection, and I started toward the couple to stop this unholy play, which I knew now I should not have authored.

"Will!" Burbage shouted in alarm, crashing hard into me and knocking me toward the gutter, me staggering unbalanced so as to see not entirely clear the caped man that flashed past, his sword extended and missing me by only little.

Burbage had the man by his free arm and hurled him past, my hand going to the hilt of my own blade and drawing it clear. The man's sword flashed back at Burbage and cut him along his arm, Burbage gasping in alarm, the swordsman gaining his release and now free to face me.

I raised my blade, setting my feet, but deflected only barely his first flurry of swipes and thrusts. His was a more nuanced art than Carey's, one of speed and deception, but no less sure deadly, and I was alive to this point by chance only. My vision had shrunk to his blade, attempting to mark its progress, when I heard an animal roar and the man turned, Jenkins almost upon him.

The man raised his blade in instinct and it passed clean through Jenkins near under his heart, the combination of the man's thrust and Jenkins's foolish rush bringing the boy full to the sword's hilt. Jenkins clasped that hilt hard as the man tried to pull the weapon free, and I drove my own blade into the man's side, the blade stopping first after only a few inches, the man being still and my not having his skill or strength to thrust deeper. But I braced my feet and pushed the blade hard into him, and after a grudging budge felt it drive deep into his chest.

The man gurgled up blood, releasing his grip on his own sword, sinking first to his knees and then collapsing to his side and rolling onto his back. Something that was not a breath bubbled final in the blood that pooled in his open mouth.

Jenkins stood for a moment still, holding the ornate hilt that basketed the offending blade's handle, and then started his own, slow fall. But I stepped to catch him and laid him gentle to his side.

Kneeling by the boy, my first thought was to have the blade free of him, and I reached to grasp the handle, but Jenkins's hands wrapped around mine.

"I pray you don't, sir, as I fear the sword is all that holds me together."

Burbage knelt now, too, at the other side, blood running down from the gash to his left arm. "He's right, Will. We should have some surgeon's word on this first."

"He'd best be quick if I am to hear it," Jenkins said, and then there was a light cough, and some blood, too, flowing from his lips.

"You shall hear plenty," Burbage said, "and from me. God will not allow you so soon gone for fear I will drink all my sack alone."

"So far as God is concerned," Jenkins said, "it will please him some that I die with my virtue unspoiled." He turned his eyes to look at the girl, who stood at his head, her hands to her mouth, and her face wet with tears. "But I cannot say it pleases me."

At which she knelt at his head, taking his face gentle in her hands, and, leaning down, pressed her lips soft on his. Jenkins reached up his hand behind her neck and pulled her mouth tight to him, and they held their kiss a long moment before his arm went slack and his hand fell away, the fingers curled up gentle on the cobbles as the flood from two bodies pooled and framed it crimson in the faltering torchlight.

CHAPTER 31

It was near to an hour since Jenkins was soft transported to that undiscovered country on the lips of a kindly whore, and I sat on the threshold of the tavern, an empty sack of skin in the stinking bowels of the night. It seemed no sun could ever again grace such a world as this, but that we would instead stagger in the Stygian dark, tearing each at every other for any small advantage and in constant service to our greed, our pride, our lust, our wrath, our gods, our crowns. And to no end save to reduce the world to that valley of bones that Ezekiel did witness, save this valley being in service to none and not dry, but instead swamped in the blood and slippery with the guts of any we did ever love.

At Jenkins's death, I was a flurry of action, sending Heminges straight to Somerset to have Carey hence immediate and to brook no argument. I was not sure even what need I had for Carey's presence, though I was full sure I had no standing to require it and did not care. As I knelt by that ruined cage of bone and flesh that had late held that sweet boy's spirit, I knew only that he had died in service to the mission to which Carey had set me, and so I would have Carey's thinking on this immediate, or at least have him, too, as witness to his handiwork. I had dragged forth the tavern keeper and sent him after the bailiff responsible for Bankside, it being at liberty and not of London, and me not full familiar with its governance. And finally I had asked that girl, her lips stained still with Jenkins's blood, to fetch for Burbage what surgeon near she thought best.

Those tasks done, I had but to await arrivals and did dear wish for some task further that could divert my mind, for it drew back constant to Jenkins and raced in that helpless thinking of every little variance that would have had him other than at the end of this dead stranger's blade. If we had not introduced him to drink, if we had not bought him this whore, if I had been less consumed in my revels so as to note my own danger. Even if we had never taken him into our company, choosing instead some other, and so he would still be... Still be what? I realised I did not know.

Where I could say that, had I not come to this player's life, then I would be a Stratford glover, I could say nothing of Jenkins save what we knew of him in our company, for on no occasion had we asked after his circumstance either before our meeting or when out of our congress. I realised I was not sure even to whom else we should send word that he was dead, and then did sour recall his earlier saying he had been well served in the matter of masters. He had been foul served indeed to have made so dear a sacrifice for us, who had loved him so poorly. And the oppression of these knowings weighed so heavy that I was true glad when Burbage, the surgeon done with him, sat beside me.

"How with the arm?" I asked.

He held it before him, now tight wrapped in linens. "The blood washed off of it, it did seem less fearsome. If it does not corrupt, then a scar only. Though a scar I will bear at the cost of some hard remembering. If it does corrupt," he shrugged, "then you will need write more parts for a one-armed man."

"This falls to my account," I said.

"To ours," said Burbage. "By what perverse greed do you seek to own to yourself every sin entire?"

I nodded, having no energy then for more words.

Burbage looked toward the stranger's body. "Do you think Henslowe? A coward's belated answer to your challenge?"

"I did first," I said. "But have late made myself party to evil in so many directions that I feel fogged in it and can see no sure cause."

"He did lay in wait, clear," Burbage said, "and made for you direct. For he could have had me dead easy, me having no arms."

"My arms served me little good in this contest, for I would have been dead sure and in moments save for Jenkins."

I heard Burbage swallow hard and, looking to him, saw that his tears flowed freely. "My God, Will. He was a fine boy. Sweet in his disposition, sure in his talents, generous in his spirit, and in the end braver than us all. Even in his drinking there was never that dark spirit in most who seek to drown some world they cannot abide, but instead only that full innocent joy of a world he did rush to embrace. What a loss we have suffered to never know that man he would become."

At which I could feel burn my own tears, and was glad to hear the ring of hooves on the cobbles. Carey on horse from Somerset. He swung from the saddle, seeming in ill spirit.

"Have our stations reversed, Shakespeare, that you feel free to summon me to the scene of any actor's drunken brawling?"

I stood and walked to him direct, pointing down at Jenkins, and spoke hard in my voice. "That boy, sir, died in my service and yours and as brave in his end as any soldier, rushing headlong onto this assailant's blade. Even having accepted it full through his person, he did hold it tight for my safety as I sent this stranger to greet his god. I will have you call him hero only. And if you think other, then I call you ungrateful and untrue, and you can have me answer that as you will and leave me, too, here dead. For I am in truth full tired of this world and will have it either changed or be quit of it."

Carey looked down at me stern for a long moment, but then his face softened some. "I am, at my age, ill tempered when disturbed from my slumbers, and, to be true, slept not easy after our time with Topcliffe and was already sour of mind. My apologies, to you and to this good servant."

I could only nod, having no faith in that moment

in my words. As Carey stood at Jenkins's back, he now walked round to see him full.

"My God, he is but a boy," he said.

"He died full a man," Burbage said from his seat.

Carey squatted down, and being more accustomed to those dead at violence and there being no possible injury now to Jenkins, pulled the blade clear from the boy, taking some interest in its hilt. He then walked closer to the torch near and looked close at the blade.

"This is Toledo steel," he said. "A Spanish blade. I have taken enough from dead Spanish hands to know."

"Does it matter?" I asked. "Jenkins would be equal dead in any case."

"It may," Carey said. "Some think Toledo steel finer, though I have had no complaints of my English iron. Toledo blades cost dear and, as we current have no trade with Spain, they are rare in English hands. They are more common in those of our enemies."

Carey clear had no qualms near the dead, as he did now bend over my late assailant and tore open his shirt. At the man's neck was a fine silver, which Carey snatched quick loose, holding up the object the chain held. A small crucifix of the Catholic fashion.

"I half expected this," Carey said, "as Spaniards seem happier in battle having their God near with them. You cannot trip over a dead Spaniard in the field and not find such."

"Then you think him Spanish?"

Carey shrugged. "By the cross, Catholic sure. And by the blade Spanish."

I was now true confused. "But would this point toward or away from our Somerset friends?"

Carey shook his head. "In matters of commerce, money holds its own allegiance and knows no boundary, cross or crown – so toward Somerset mayhaps, meaning only the scheme be broader. But if away, then to what? Some recusant mischief? This matter is a weed that grows denser the more we cut at it. Perhaps Topcliffe's records will yield some light. As your man had me awake, I saw no reason Topcliffe should slumber, so I sent your man to his quarters in my name to summon him to court to examine his records immediate."

Even on this present sorrowed stage, I could not help a small moment of humour in picturing Heminges's face at Carey's order that he go and chase Topcliffe from his bed.

At which the bailiff did final arrive, armed and with a few armed factors in tow. He was much dishevelled and stunk clear of ale. He had taken no care in his appearance as most often such matters as might have him to Bankside at this hour involved only those whose favour toward him counted little, being most likely drunks or whores or actors or keepers of the bear baits, all being held about equal in his esteem. Carey, being in the street and near the gutter opposite the tavern, was behind the bailiff as he near tumbled from the sorry nag that had borne him hence – Burbage, myself, and such others still present being more near and to his front.

"There being two dead, the Queen's peace has been plain breeched," he blustered, "and I'll have no congress on fault or cause at this hour, but instead you all to custody, and this then better addressed in the light of day." At which his factors advanced toward us.

Burbage stood. "This good gentleman," pointing to me, "for you will note his arms and he does have full licence to carry them, was cowardly attacked with no warning or provocation and saved only by my small intervention and by the fatal sacrifice of that boy, who is our friend. And I will not bear the insult of custody, the matter of this being so plain and witnesses here abundant."

To which the small crowd still gathered muttered their assent.

"Insult?" the bailiff said. "You call my exercise of the Queen's office insult?"

"A fool can turn God's mercy to insult and with little effort," said Carey from behind.

The bailiff spun. "And what have we here? Some gentleman come across the bridge to dip his prick in some whore and now thinks this gives him leave to instruct me in my business?"

"What you have here, sir, is your better. In station, in manner, in thinking and, should it come to it, at arms. And you will not have these men to custody, as what ills they have already suffered they have suffered in my charge."

"Oh, well," the bailiff said, now feigning obeisance, "I must humble beg thy favour, as I do always swerve in my duty easy at only the word of any well-dressed stranger at the place of any murder." His acting now over, the bailiff made straight to Carey, his chest puffed. "I would have your name, sir, as you will be joining your fellows in custody."

Carey pulled off his glove and held up his hand so that the bailiff could see his signet. "I am George Carey, the Baron Hunsdon, son of the late Lord Chamberlain and soon to assume those duties. And on the subject of your office, I would ask how, on word of these events, I could be here from Somerset before you," Carey looked down on the bailiff in clear disgust, "me having taken time to be properly attired whilst you seem to have rolled first through a puddle of ale and then a sack of filth."

The bailiff stood, his jaw slack. "I do true beg your pardon, sir, as I did not know."

"I should think your not knowing to be a common enough occurrence that you would have better practice in its management." Carey brushed past the man, put his foot to the stirrup of his horse, and swung easy into its saddle, nudging the horse near up to the man. "All present here are at liberty to leave if they will or return to drinking if they must, both the slayer and the victim in this case being clear known. As you seem little able to manage your own dress, much less the matters of your office, I shall handle any further inquiry this matter requires. It would bode you well not to draw yourself to my attentions further, as I will like be sufficient distracted by more vital duties so as to soon forget your sorry performance. But, if reminded of it, I shall bring it immediate to the attention to those in power to remove your office."

"I am at your service, sir," the bailiff said.

"You are in my way, sir," Carey answered, spurring his horse and knocking the bailiff to his arse.

CHAPTER 32

"Your answer when last I questioned you concerning Mary Norton was all summation," Carey said, an edge to his voice indicating some knowing past that of our last congress. "I would now have the whole truth plain."

I was back in that larger room that had set scene to our first meeting, having been summoned early from my bed back to Somerset. Topcliffe was seated behind a table toward one corner, many papers I could only assume being the accountings of his unholy arts scattered before him.

"My lord?" I answered.

"That is a question and not an answer," Carey said, now more stern.

"And a first sign of guilt," added Topcliffe, "for those in my inquiry do often answer question with question, trying to find such news with which they can careful frame their answer next more to my liking."

Topcliffe was to me this morning less fearsome. Perhaps on account of his being out from his sordid lair and seeming in the environs of Somerset House, which was now some familiar to me, less an exotic nightmare and instead plain that diseased creature he true was. Or perhaps the real horrors of the night past made any imagined ills grow pale. If he expected my fear, this day he would not have it.

"If Baron Carey doth chose to question my honourable exercise of such offices with which he has charged me, as I have found him honourable, then I will learn from him how he comes to hold this new opinion," I said. "But I will have none of it from you, sir."

Topcliffe's face reddened some and he prepared to respond, but I turned from him to Carey and spoke quick. "I will gladly answer about Mary, but ask only why such answer today holds consequence that it yesterday did not, for I do true think her innocent and will not be careless with her."

"Tell him," Carey said to Topcliffe.

"My lord," Topcliffe said, "as matters Papist now seem to cloud your father's passing, I would be most careful of our news, as we know not yet this plot's scope or true direction. I advise that we share nothing with this scribbler, but instead have from him direct what he was summoned here to provide. The more time I am in his company, the more I suspect him, for it seems his faith – or at least that of his father, sure – can be thought in question. The Papist faith has a stench," he now turned to me, "and he does make my nose twitch."

Clear, Carey had shared much with Topcliffe in recent hours, and only then did I note that Carey was dressed still in such as he wore the night past, and so had been not to bed but to here direct and likely in Topcliffe's congress for long hours.

Carey brought both hands to his face and rubbed it slow in the fashion of one much wearied, and not in body alone.

"I have, I think," he said, to Topcliffe, "heard sufficient from you on matters of faith. We are called to faith not in God only, but also in one another, at least as we have earned it. And Shakespeare has earned mine. So, tell him." Carey sank hard into the chair nearest him, his hands again to his face, speaking through them. "And I would warn you both that I am wearied of having my orders questioned."

"Very well," Topcliffe answered, his face flashing shame, and he then turned to me. "What know you of the Rising of the North?"

"Little," I said. "A Papist rebellion when I was a but a boy, some few dukes and earls hoping to strike down the Queen and have England return to Rome's fold."

Topcliffe nodded. "The late Baron Carey was general to those forces that quelled this foul business. And he helped collect for our good Queen, whether on the field or after, such heads as made their vile allegiance to Babylon's Whore instead of our sweet crown – Darce, Percy, Neville, some others," at which Topcliffe paused to shift through his papers, bringing one to fore. "The rebellion being in the north, where even today the stink of Papist still scents heavy the air, I will note that Stratford is some little north and the name Arden, your mother's name, carries no small Papist taint. But the rebellion was near to York, and the family Norton was deep involved, having at the time many holdings in those districts."

"Mary's family?" I asked, remembering now the Yorkshire accent.

"The same," said Topcliffe. "At the rebellion's end, I was summoned to York to assist the late Baron in such investigations as needed to ensure we had this weed of treason out by its root. We found that weed was flowered thick with Nortons, some few of whom did pay full with their lives. One man questioned was a Harry Norton, some attached to the family but in that branching way of cousins and latter-borns so that he was a distant twig to the treasonous tree and had shared little in its fortunes. But he did prove stubborn as I exercised my arts. His right hand suffered true terrible to no avail, so I was little surprised to learn he did later lose its service. As his own suffering had not the effects I wished, I had brought forth his son, aged a decade perhaps at the time. And when I applied full to the boy's nose such instrument as I showed you this night past, the father did finally break and offered what little secrets he had – which were only scare helpful in our mission. It was my thought to have him hanged, but the Baron – being of a merciful bent, and we having found no direct support of the rising, but only that Norton may have kept secret some he should have shared – ordered him freed."

"The son being near ten at the time of the rising would be near to forty now," Carey said. "The age to match our late, foul-nosed assailant."

"And so this Harry was Mary's father, and the son Mary's brother?" I asked.

The serpent smile that too oft did decorate Topcliffe's face new appeared. "To be sure, no," he said. "For in my ministry to Norton the elder, I employed another instrument of my design that attaches in full circle to the sources of man's seed and crushes them slow but entire if the subject does not relent. As he did not relent. Any children he might have sired, all would need be seeded before that night. And had he seeded Mary then, she would number near thirty years now at least."

"But our nosed friend, being forty at his dying, could easy have a daughter of Mary's age," Carey said.

It was my turn to sink to a chair, being sudden unsure in my legs. "This all, then, revenge? The granddaughter seeking service in Somerset to have your father dead to avenge his role thirty years past?"

Carey breathed out a long sigh. "If that were all, it would be enough. But sure you cannot think it all, not with some Spaniard at you last night, and with your friend dead. For if my father had been the sole aim of this plot, Mary and her father could have been easy gone these days past. Instead, he died trying for your life and she tarries near still."

Topcliffe waved a hand over his papers. "We have been long hours over reports from my varied intelligencers as to these Nortons. Mary seems curious absent in any records prior to her sudden arrival in service at Somerset only this winter past, and her father – famous to you as the ruined nose, but John by name – more absent still. That absence is true puzzling, him being remarkable in appearance and marked in our files early as such Catholic as would bear scrutiny. And yet of either John or Mary, until her Somerset service, nothing. Or almost nothing." And he drew out a single sheet. "A letter from a man I keep in my employ to report on comings and goings or any curiosities of note in those districts nearest the river where we suspect the rot of recusancy still festers deep. It concerns an aging father, lost of a hand, new to the district, supposed from Cornwall. His village having been burned by the Spanish in that raid of this summer just past and his family there lost, he was now dependent on his daughter for care, them having travelled to London, where she might seek better fortune in the city."

"I recall the raid, of course," I said.

"The Spanish are sometimes curious in their intrigues," Topcliffe continued, "and, being Papist, they do love to plot foul. Not a few English who still suckle at Rome's bosom have found refuge in Spain, and we have seen them at times returned to our shores as Spain's agents. Having looked hard and found no evidence of these Nortons over long years, and finding it now easy and sudden in only these recent months, I do suspect the Nortons were to Spain short after the rising. Mary was likely born there and schooled from birth to this purpose. I believe they were returned to England under cover of this Cornwall mischief but in service to some larger and darker plot."

Carey now pushed himself up from his chair, standing purposeful with the stature of his office.

"And so, Shakespeare, innocent as you might think the girl to be, and full admitting that I, too, held that opinion, I will now have a full accounting – as it seems she may in truth be an arrow aimed to England's heart."

CHAPTER 33

"We can assume that last night's Spaniard was dispatched at Mary's hand to still your tongue, you having traced her to her new lair," Carey said after hearing my account. He had, at my request, excused Topcliffe that I might have his ear on this in private. For I had now to share with him in full all I had learned, but I wanted still to shield from Topcliffe any that I could. I was honest with Carey in all details save the baker and his wife – having told Carey instead that I had returned to near to the building that I had previous marked as Mary's father's home to continue my investigation, only to chance upon Mary's entry to what I soon learned to be a secret Catholic mass, and that I had marked her from there to that shop where she now served.

"It seems sound thinking," I said, "and yet feels false. When you first sought my service in this matter, you did so on your belief that I could see the truth in others, even that they would keep hidden. I cannot see the truth of this in Mary."

"But neither did you see in her Spain's agent."

To which I could only shake my head. "I did not. And yet I can believe her such, but still not see her send some secret assassin. I cannot say why, except that I true believe she would hold her service to Spain – really, to Rome – to be in congress with her virtue. She would not so hold that assassin's work."

"You can think thus knowing she poisoned my father, who had been only kind to her, and in such manner that he died in long suffering?"

I nodded. "I can – giving account to his station, so that she could see him a soldier in her secret war on the Queen and her heretic faith, and also knowing your father's history with her own. For while it was Topcliffe's hand on the instrument of her father's suffering, and her grandfather's, it was your father's office that gave it force of law. She would not consciously admit such motive, it being simple wrath and thus sin, but we often find in God's name convenient excuse for such actions we could not otherwise call right."

Carey shook his head in dismissal. After hearing my initial account, he had ordered assembled some armed men and meant to lead them to the mercer's shop to make Mary's arrest, their numbers being guard against any additional swordsmen she may have at her disposal.

"You have too much philosophy, Will," he said. "There comes time when men must act in their person and not just in their thinking. We will short have Mary, and then short have the truth." Carey strapped on his sword and sash, and turned to leave.

I grabbed his shoulder to still him. "I fear that your plan may have too much action and too little philosophy, and that if you make to the mercer's shop in such large company, you may lose her instead."

"How so?" he asked.

"Whether by her hand or no, the assassin was plain sent. Mary and any in her congress would know by now that he has plain failed and that her lair may no longer be safe. I think she will have fled the mercer's shop, and will again have to be ferreted out. If you take to those districts in force, any whose help I might by more gentle means secure will like turn silent at the clear peril of your arms."

Carey huffed. "Your ways do vex me greatly, for having my foes known, it is my instinct in my every fibre to confront them immediate. I am suspicious of guile."

"I think we each trust most such as we have best talent for," I said. "Your talent is in war and its arts and so you would have all settled in battle. This war, though, is not of open combat, but instead of secret plottings."

"You would be sent alone, then?"

"I would."

"And if she has more Toledo steel in her employ?"

"Then I will likely serve as its unhappy scabbard. But I do not think she could long harbour some Spanish battalion secret in London's bowels. If you could have your men close, I will send word when they are needed."

Carey paused for a moment. "You should know, too, that the Spaniards will not be your only peril."

At this, I raised my brow in question.

"Should you go alone, and then Mary escape, Topcliffe will like charge you as accomplice. He already is making whispers in any ready ear to claim credit for uncovering this threat. And if Mary cannot be held to account, he will need some other in her place or else be thought a failure. Do not count too greatly on my powers, Will, or on my honour. Should you fail, his designs will turn to you. As I would be unlikely able to stop them, I most likely would not try, lest I, too, end up their victim and to no end. I have seen battles enough to know that discretion is sometimes valour's better part."

I thought on this careful, but at the end knew Jenkins deserved the truth of things. I would be my own worst company what days I had left if I failed him in cowardice, knowing how well he had served me in courage.

"I thank you for your honest congress, sir. And I true bide you to take no action on my behalf that would bring you ill for no gain save honour. I think honour serves us best when it spurs us to make the world some little better. But it would serve the world poor if it drove a good man, for I do hold you such, to sacrifice for no reason save his conscience. And you are right. I am too often philosophy's friend when it is action that is needed. So, let me go now, as I have only recently made courage's acquaintance and should be gone before it moves on to better company."

"My good sir!" said the mercer in his practised cheer at my entrance. "Dare I hope your company's success has grown such in only this day past that you require further service?"

I drew on my actor's art for an easy smile and manner. "Alas, no. But being in this district on other business, I did wish to ask if such garments as already ordered could be made ready some few days earlier, as the Court has added yet another date to our schedule."

The mercer now drew on his own acting, which in truth was at least equal my own, pursing out his lips as though in some distress. "In truth, sir, such timing as to which I already have agreed will sore tax our little shop. How we could manage sooner I do not know."

"Of course, we would ready pay for such difficulties as our request might cause," I said.

And his smile returned. "In which case, I might hire temporary such hands as to meet your need. I did not first offer such as it would offend my honour to try to shift such price as we had already set, and I do offer it now only at your suggestion."

After some short haggling, we set the new date and price.

"Can I assist you with any else?" the mercer asked. "I have only today received by way of Venice new silks."

"If you will have Mary model them, then I will happy inspect them," I answered with a small wink.

"Alas, we have lost her service," he said. "For I arrived this morning to a note that she must away to tend to some dear friend in such need as she would not deny and still call herself Christian in her duties. I do think she thinks on Christian duty much, as she clear first stayed late into the night to finish such chores as I had thought would take her all today – namely some sewing yet left to be done on chemises and corsets for the Queen herself, those being due to court today with that jewelled garment I had previous mentioned. Mary's hand was sufficient skilled for these simpler items, and the Queen of late has favoured some fabrics of mine that lay soft on her person in these more intimate uses."

"I am true sorry to hear Mary gone," I said. "Sorry for us both. For I did plan to return often if only to look on her."

The mercer shrugged. "It seems she was such flower that, being so fine, could only short bloom." He lowered his voice some. "To be true, sir, I had hoped eventual to better know her petals, and, being in recent years a bachelor, my wife having died of plague, had even planned to offer her marriage in the bargain."

"Had she known such, she might well have stayed."

He turned up his hands. "I will never know."

"Come, man," I said. "This seems almost from a play, and so in my art. Do not surrender the chase! Have word to her! Surely she did not go in secret."

He smiled a small smile. "Had I a place to send word, I would. But alas, she did."

"If you come for bread, sir, you are welcome, but if you come other, I bid you gone," said the baker as

I entered his shop, for he was clear unhappy of my company.

"I come other, sir." I shut his door behind me, and then fitted its bolt so that we might have our congress uninterrupted.

His wife came from the room to the back, taking her place beside him.

"We can tell you no more than we did at our last talking," she said, but unsure in her speaking.

Only a fool thinks that every lesson comes from an agreeable voice, for the wise learn from their fears as well as their fancies. Having reflected on Topcliffe's philosophies on torture, I considered his thinking on hope, but considered it reversed. To kill hope was to invite despair, and in despair there is nothing to be gained. With nothing to be gained there is no reason to answer. But if you can seeming kill hope, and then offer its resurrection, what would a man then deny you? As I had not Topcliffe's tools to use but only my words, I would have them do to these poor souls what his instruments would do to their bodies.

"No other? Nothing of the Papist mass you attended in secret this Sunday past in the very building where Mary Norton's father did late live?"

"No sir, we never–" the man started. But seeking to leave his hope no room to turn, I cut him off.

"Save your lies, sir. I watched with my own eyes as first your wife, and then you, did make quick across this very street and into the cellar door on the side of that building most near to you. As you do attend mass in secret and prayed by some priest in hiding

from the Crown, you both stand already subject to
the Queen's justice. And as you have just denied
your faith plain and will in arrest have no priest
to cleanse your soul, you will stand, too, subject to
God's justice as you know it."

"I pray, sir," the wife now in clear pleading, "if you
be a good Christian of any stripe, do not deliver us.
For we seek only to pray in such fashion as God calls
us, but stand also clear obedient to our Queen in any
but this."

"And what if your congregation plots against the
Queen?" I asked.

"They do not," the man said.

"At least one does, and I will tell you this now
clear plain. I am current in the Crown's service in
company with many, including Topcliffe, and on my
word alone can and will have any I feel party to this
treason immediate to his care, and from his care to
Tyburn. By the knowing of my own eyes, you both
stand current damned, and this will be your fate
unless you prove that, at least today, you love your
Queen more than your God. Do remember that, by
your own creed, you can later seek his forgiveness. As
I am the Queen's minister in this matter, I can assure
you that you will have none from this quarter."

At which they clung to each other, both in weeping,
and I could see hope clear dead. I wondered from
whence would come my own forgiveness, and when,
if at all.

The woman some regained herself.

"What would you know, sir?"

"Where is Mary Norton?"

"If I knew, on God's eyes, I would lead you there by the hand," she said. "She is only recent in our congregation, though clear much in favour with our priest, and must live near to choose this place to worship."

"Who is your priest?"

"What will befall him?" the man asked.

I looked on him stern. "Will it ease your conscience to hear some lie? Why else would you ask a question to which you already know the answer, save in hopes that I might say other than you expect so that you can pretend it truth?"

"Father Ignatius," the woman answered. "He came to our congregation at the same time as did Mary Norton, and is, I am certain, foreign born. If there be treason afoot and it involve her, then he is party to it. And so I will damn him easy as he did easy risk those in his flock such that either their souls or their persons fall harm, if not both."

"How do I find him?"

"Why, at Sunday mass next," she answered.

"For which I cannot wait. How do I find him immediate? For priests must administer, too, such sacraments as do not mind any calendar."

They looked to each other, being at the final, uncomfortable moment of treason where, by their own words, some other would suffer hard.

"I do fear that such sin as we might soon make will weigh dear on us," the man said, as though giving speech to his torment might relieve it. But I wished to offer no pause for him to consider his honour.

"If you do not answer, and true and immediate, mark this promise: You will watch first all such torments as your wife will suffer under Topcliffe's hands, entire unto her death. Consider how heavy that might weigh on your soul, sir."

He hung his head. "Take this road straight to the river. At the left on the river's verge is that long market given solely to fishes, above which are some poor rooms. These are his quarters."

"Lift your head, sir," I said.

He looked up at me.

"Know true that I am much grieved to have so pained you both, but also true was every threat I uttered. For I am clutched within much desperate business and am trying to have it ended at the cost of as little innocent blood as can be. If you are true, then your worries on this are ended, for none will have your name from me. As to your God, your creed says he will forgive. And if he will not, even though it was his own priest that helped carry this evil to your door, then I call him a god unworthy of your worship."

I unbolted the door and walked quick toward the river so that I was into the alley nearest before I vomited hard onto the cobbles there, too close in spirit to Topcliffe in that moment for my own stomaching.

CHAPTER 34

Reaching the river, I could plain see the building the baker had described, mongers of fishes, eels, and other aquatics making commerce at the level of the street. The building had been first only one level, but in the manner common now to London, a second storey was late added, it being accessed from stairs laid in a galley to the side nearest me. There seemed some commotion in the rooms upper, as I could see persons moving rapid past the windows. And twice in short minutes since my arrival, men made down those outside stairs carrying chests, stacking them on the short dock at the road's end.

At the dock was tied a pincke, those being common to the river for their shallow draft, as they could make easy up the Thames in varied tides and still be sound enough for the channel or the nearer seas. The ship's crew was busy with the rigging and other such matters that made clear they would soon sail.

"Boy!" I called to me a lad of perhaps ten who was coming from near the dock.

"Sir?" he asked.

"Do you know today's tides?"

"I should hope, being as I serve the chandlers near.

Those making to sea today will be off within the hour."

"Do you know that ship?" I asked, nodding to the dock.

"The pincke? I've been on and off all morning, helping load her. Once the couple from the rooms over the shop has their luggage aboard, she'll be away."

"I think I know this couple," I said, "the wife being young and remarkable fair."

The boy blushed a little. "To be true, sir. I may be but a lad, but I will admit I was some scolded by her husband, him feeling I played my eyes on her over much and on my work not enough. He said my eyes did offend me, and I would better heed God's Bible and have them out than continue in my foul habits and risk hell's fire."

"Do you know this street well?" I asked. "Not just this district, but those finer shops nearer to Threadneedle and the grocer's market there?"

He nodded. "I do, sir."

I took a half crown from my purse and held it up for his inspection. "Take this and be fleet. At the edge of that market will be several men at arms on horse. Tell the man at their head that Shakespeare bids him meet me here, and with all haste. Have them hence before this ship makes sail, and you shall have a full crown, too." I pressed the coin into the boy's hand. "Go!"

The minutes marking the boy's absence ground heavy, each chest carried down from those rooms and stacked to the dock like sand from a glass that timed my own life. Either Carey would arrive in time to have Mary, or Topcliffe would have me.

The ship was clear ready – several others already being at sail on the river, both the tide and the winds in their favour and taking them rapid to sea. Now the ship's crew was boarding those chests from the dock to the ship's hold. None more were coming from the rooms, that frantic traffic I had seen in the upper windows was now stilled. Should the pincke make sail before Carey came and lose itself in the Thames's heavy commerce, I was likely doomed.

Anxiety makes us a poor judge of time, but the boy seemed too long gone. The last chest now aboard, a member of the crew made up the stairs and then back. He was almost immediate followed by a gaunt man of middle years in plain dress of almost Puritan fashion, and by Mary, whose dress tried also for plain, but on her form and in the company of her aspect failed in its attempt. I looked hard up the street, hoping to catch some hint of Carey. Seeing none, I thought that if the boy were faithful Carey must short arrive, and that any delay I could affect might buy me short minutes now and then long years later. In any case, such life as I would live in failing would be little measured but hard suffered. I might as well try to buy those minutes at risk of my life now.

I drew my blade and stepped into plain view, moving rapid toward the dock.

"Mary Norton," I called.

She turned and seeming almost smiled. "My good

sir," she said. "I cannot call thee false to be here
having first said me safe, as you did say you would
be as true to me as I was to you. I would have you
know, though, that I did hold you at your word.
That man at whose hands you did almost suffer was
sent by another against my will, as wiser heads than
mine called my trust in you an insufficient shield."

"But I did suffer at those hands, Mary, as they did
take a dear boy wholly good in spirit who did ready
trade his own life to save my own."

She closed her eyes and breathed long. "I will
pray on his soul, sir, as I would have none innocent
suffer."

The gaunt man called into the ship. "Gentleman!
We are accosted! A brigand threatens the good
Mary!"

At which several crew bolted from the ship,
variously armed with staffs and other such weapons
handy and made hard at me, spreading into an arc
that I might face only few of them at once.

"That man is a priest secret in this country and the
woman an agent of Spain," I called loud, hoping to
sway them to my side or at least to stall their advance.

A large man to my front, thickly muscled and much
weathered from long years at sail, laughed. "And I
am some dainty mermaid come to shore to find your
love," he said, and he swung hard at me with a staff,
which I ducked under, hearing his fellows laughing
as they closed. I swung my blade in a circle, some
surprising them at my crouched level and catching
one of them below his knees and cutting him deep

so that he fell. Then I felt a blow fall hard across my back just as I rose, my sword almost coming from my hands. But that blow thrust me forward, and past the swipe of a short cudgel such that I was able to swing my sword up, cutting the arm which held that weapon, and could then step past him, escaping the crew's closing circle for a brief moment – except that I had broached it toward the river, them all arrayed now to my back and blocking any escape. I ran onto the dock, thinking that, on its narrow confines, my assailants would be able to confront me only in ones or twos. But then, turning back, I could see Carey closing hard at the front of his men, the horses crashing into the crew, his sword flashing down on my muscled mermaid and having his arm near off at his shoulder.

"Stop!" screamed Mary. At which the melee paused. "My defeat clear, I will have no more suffer in my cause. We are your prisoners, sirs."

"And I am a one-armed mermaid," the large man said in a shocked voice, seated now in his own blood, "and ruined for the sea."

CHAPTER 35

The chests taken from the ship lay scattered open across the dock in the lowering sun. I had been with Carey some hours as the chests were unloaded and broken open. They were solid and careful locked, and we found in them the priest's vestments, chalices, Latin bibles, and the other accoutrements of his religion, and also several bottles of that good port for which the Spanish are rightly known. Now I sat with Carey on the dock's end, looking out on the river, each with a bottle of that rich Spanish wine.

"I must admit you looked surprising fierce in your battle, Will," Carey said, "though unschooled, to be sure. Still, two men cut and you untouched."

I felt across my back a hard reminder of the blow I had suffered – which reminder, come morning, would be felt harder still. "I would not say untouched, sir, but as my goal was to stay alive until your arrival, I will call my action a success."

He raised his bottle to me in salute. "You have been brave and true in my service, sir, and your company can count me your faithful patron all my days."

I nodded. "I have learned much of myself in your service and would count me in your debt for that knowledge alone, save for much blood and suffering that has fallen to my hands in this exercise."

"A hand unstained is a hand unused, sir. Who will try will fail, but who will not can scarce be counted a man."

We drank some moments in companionable silence, hearing behind us the sounds of the day's commerce drawing to its end, the mongers trying to entice some final custom in their last minutes, some shutters already slamming closed.

"Even knowing her religion and her cause, it harms me some to think of young Mary in Topcliffe's care," Carey said finally, "understanding her history and knowing that, were I her, I might easy have reached a similar end."

That thought cut hard, and I had a long pull at my bottle to still it. "We think ourselves loyal to a crown or a god, but in the end, I think, can only true serve our own hearts."

"She has served her own and brave," he said. "Still, I cannot say I am ungrateful that we ruined what further mission she must have had. Sad as I am for my father's suffering at her hands, I cannot think that her entire purpose."

And I knew sudden that I had watched this tale unfold as does an audience – swept up in its events and in that strong current, watching only each scene as it played out instead of thinking on the story's whole.

"Your father dead, she still stayed long in this country, even early suspecting that we questioned her role," I said. "And yet now, nothing new accomplished, she would bolt for Spain?"

Carey shrugged. "And to your credit, sir, as it was your investigation that made plain her mission."

I shook my head. "Yours as much as my own, and Topcliffe's, too, as I would never have suspected Spanish mischief. But no, something is amiss. That she might bolt to some new hide, that I could credit. But she seems too stern in her character to quit the country whole with some task undone due only to threat, for that smells of coward, and she does not have that scent."

"Sir!" One of Carey's men called to us from the dock's opposite end, where they made inspection of the final few chests, which seemed to hold only clothing and other such unremarkable things. "I would have you see this."

So, we made to the man, a small chest of Mary's things open at his feet, the chest filled with mostly those items most intimate in their nature.

Carey snorted. "Did her beauty so inflame thee, Snellings, that you would have your nose in her drawers?"

The man stuttered a moment, then answered. "Look here, sir." And he pulled down from the chest's side a false lining, behind which were secreted several small bottles in varied colours, as one might find at an apothecary's shop.

And I sudden knew whole the danger in my mind before I could find even words for it, so I grabbed Carey by his arm and pulled him to his feet and toward the horses. Swinging myself into the saddle of the closest, and Carey, too, swinging aboard his own, I spurred my horse away from the river with Carey in pursuit.

That Mary might leave note for the mercer explaining her absence rang true, for that explanation would forestall his searching for her or raising any alarm. But that she would stay late in the night to complete her sewing, and for a Queen she did clear despise, here was that moment in the play's progress that I should have noted and did not.

I explained the threat to Carey as we rode.

CHAPTER 36

The mercer's shutters were closed when we arrived, and his door bolted. But Carey hammered hard at it with his fist, and the mercer opened the door some alarmed.

"Mister Shakespeare, sir. What matter could have you here so alarmed, and outside our normal time?"

"Those items Mary completed for our good Queen," I said. "I would have them immediate."

"You actors have a reputation for your drinking, and I can smell it on you," the mercer said, his voice now hard, "but this prank does not amuse."

"It is no prank, sir," Carey answered, "and we have not time for long congress. I am the Baron Hunsdon and I tell you plain that you are either party to or have been sore used in a plot against our good Queen. You will either fetch out those garments now or I will strike you down where you stand and take them."

At that moment, the rest of Carey's company – having noted our alarmed departure and so given chase – arrived, reining in their horses to our back.

"But those are gone, sir," said the mercer, near blubbering, "delivered to the Court this very day.

What plot can there be in them?"

Carey leapt back to his horse, me following, and turned it to his men. "Keep secure this man and building until I send word, and touch nothing."

And we rode hard for Whitehall.

Our ride left many sprawled in our wake. Carey's horses were large and trained for war and so not shy of crowds, and the streets being thickly peopled at that hour. But we arrived quick at Whitehall's gates, and I watched amazed as Carey cleaved hard such protocols that would usual long delay our progress further.

Challenged first by the guards at the gate, Carey leapt from his horse and drew close to them. And where I thought I had heard him stern previous, I heard now such voice as I suppose a man learns in war as he makes himself entire a weapon.

"I am George Carey, the Second Baron Hunsdon, son of your late Lord Chamberlain. Your Queen is in dire peril, and you will have me to her immediate or I will hold bound to any consequence all who impede me."

The guards looked to one another, their officer finally answering.

"I know you, sir, and make full note of your urgency, and will have my man quick to make congress with the household. But I can assure you no threat has passed this gate, not this day, sir. Not on my watch."

At which Carey quick drew his sword and had the tip of it to the officer's throat before any could make move.

"This threat is one of guile and poisons, and it is already by you unknowing. You may let me pass and even keep my company, but I will immediate to the Queen's quarters. And if you think other, then let us settle it here in blood."

There was a short pause in which those other guards present did all draw their swords and, not knowing where to point them, pointed them all at me. I hoped Carey's argument would win the day quick or I might, as my father had long wished, end holy.

"If you will put back your sword, sir," the officer answered, trying hard for a voice stern, but its timbre instead much unsteady, "I will have you hence, but in our company only."

Carey sheathed his sword and walked hard past the man toward the palace, the guards now scrambling to form around him and me trailing the procession.

"But what of him, sir?" the officer asked, pointing back at me.

"He is in my service, and I in his debt."

Our assembly burst into the castle proper, Carey clear being familiar with its rooms and making direct toward the Queen's quarters. The train of our company grew as we pressed toward her apartments, until finally we approached her door, Carey calling from some yards distance that he would see the Queen immediate and not be stayed.

"But the Queen is dressing, sir!" the attendant there stationed said, rising to block Carey's path.

Carey planted a hand to the man's chest – the Baron's muscle and momentum sending the attendant far down that hall and to his backside – and burst through the first door, some of the Queen's lady attendants there gathered and shrieking at this intrusion. But Carey was unswayed and burst through the second door, through which I could glimpse our good Queen. She stood in her stockings, farthingale and chemises, her lady holding her corset and ready to place it on her.

Carey sank immediate to one knee, his head bowed.

"Your Majesty, I do most humble beg you forgive this intrusion, but must ask that your lady stop immediate with your dressing, as you are at grave peril."

"Carey?" she said, looking down to confirm his identity. "It is you. Your father's manners were at times some rough, and we see you do surpass him in his lesser habits." Looking past Carey to the larger crowd beyond, she raised her brows. "While we do enjoy an audience, we would have it see less of our person."

Her gaze passed over those faces present, passing by me, but then snapping quick back.

"And who is this man who you have brought to witness your Queen in her nakedness, Carey?"

"Pardon, your Majesty?" Carey said, still on his knee and his face still to the floor in bow.

"Oh for God's sake man, stand. You are curious in which manners you observe and which you do not."

Carey stood, and the Queen made a questioning face, her hand pointed clear to me.

"William Shakespeare, your Majesty," he said.

"The playwright?" she answered.

"The same, ma'am."

She beckoned me with her hand, and I made into the room next to Carey, dropping to my knee and bowing too.

"Your Majesty," I said.

"And are there any others we should greet in this multitude you have brought to observe us in our dressing? A tavern keeper? A bear baiter, perhaps?"

Carey's face blushed full red. "No, ma'am."

"Well," she said, waving the guards and courtiers back, "having all the players present, we suppose we needs hear this tale. Shakespeare's reputation being as it is, we pray it be a good one, as a fine play does oft soothe our temper, and it current does run some hot."

The crowd excused and the door to the room immediate closed, the Queen looked hard at Carey, having dropped the mask of patient amusement she wore for the larger audience and now speaking clear harsh.

"Explain yourself, sir."

"Your Majesty, that chemise and corset, were they today delivered from your mercer?"

She snorted, "Do you suppose, Carey, that we trouble with details of the source and delivery of our garments – taking council on that issue, perhaps, between matters of the treasury and our varied foreign entanglements?"

"These are new today, your Majesty," her dresser answered, "you having preferred such that we late received that were of this finer silk."

"I ask only as I fear them possible poisoned," said Carey, "we having late uncovered much serious Spanish mischief, and this seeming to be its object."

"We?"

"Myself and Shakespeare, your Majesty."

She looked at me and gave a wicked smile. "Well, sir, you having joined Carey in this unassigned office as our new intelligencer, it seems you will share equal in either his reward for saving us or his punishment for interrupting our dressing."

"Ma'am," Carey said, "I beseech thee, careful remove the corset and chemise that we might make their inspection. If I am wrong, then I will glad suffer as you require. But if my thinking be true, then your life could short be forfeit."

"Carey, on such occasions as we may have claimed to hold our people close to our bosom, you may have took our speech too literal. If we are to be further disrobed, you and your apprentice spy shall have to be excused." She motioned to another door past, to which we made hence and quick, it closing behind us and locking us in her closet.

The chamber having no window, it was dark entire. After some minutes, Carey spoke.

"The threat being so immediate, I never stopped to

credit your thinking. I hope your wits be true."

"I think my argument sound," I said, "though I would not have played it for these stakes."

After another pause, Carey spoke again.

"I do wish they would hurry with their dressing."

"In truth," I answered, "I can wait longer, as I do not rush to peril as seems your habit."

Carey's breath seemed to grow laboured. "May I make you a confession in confidence?"

"You may, sir."

"Since I was a boy, I have always been greatly feared of such spaces as this, anywhere small and dark, and I am close to panic."

And I was shocked to think this man, who I had late seen fearless play mortal at swords, and who had with no thought to consequence breeched not just the palace but the Queen's own rooms, now quailed by a simple closet. I could not contain a short laugh, Carey then smacking me hard to my chest and the closet door then flying open, the Queen standing in its space full dressed.

"Do we amuse you, sir?" she asked.

And I sudden thought charm my best defence and so answered, "Only if that is your intent, your Majesty."

At which she smiled a little, and I was a little relieved.

CHAPTER 37

"While the plot be infernal, the design is ingenious," said the Queen's apothecary, he and most high members of her council now present in some larger room to which the items from the mercer's shop had been transported. The chemises had proved free of taint, but the corsets were true deadly.

"The stays have been sharpened at their ends," he continued, "and treated with the poison late developed in Venice from castor beans from which death is sure and for which no antidote is known. I have checked, and did also find such in those bottles in this Norton's chest. The stays were then tempered so that, with only little urging, they would snap inward, being held to their place by only some light sewing. When the corset laces were pulled tight, your Majesty would have been several times pierced and mortal poisoned."

The Queen cocked an eyebrow. "We do for fashion's sake daily suffer at our corset's hands, but never this dear."

She turned to Carey. "You are true forgiven, sir, and true loved, for we think few in our service would have been so reckless for our safety. You are named immediate Lord Chamberlain in your father's place, as the safety of our Royal Household falls chief in those duties and you have already performed them well."

"I am true grateful, your Majesty."

She turned to Burghley, a minister much in her confidence.

"Any further from Topcliffe on this? Can we be sure we have the entire threat?"

"From the girl, nothing, as she has suffered his complete efforts with no word save her praying. The mercer, we think, was none involved but simple used, as he confessed all immediate on only making Topcliffe's company and we have been at some trouble to stop his talking since. The priest suffered hard, but then broke. He seemed little schooled in her mission, being sent as her spiritual support. We do have from him such names as counted in his congregation, and those are now in our custody and will be examined."

Which news troubled me dear, me thinking on my word to the baker and his wife that they were safe in this.

"And you, Shakespeare. You have served us well. What will you have for it?"

"There is a boy, Jenkins, who died in this service. I would have his family cared for."

"Done," she said. "None other?"

There was much other that such a man as I had been at this matter's start would have ready asked, but I was now instead troubled more by that accidental evil done at my hands.

"These Catholics arrested on the priest's confession. I have had truck with some in their number on this matter who did serve you well, your Majesty, and am pained to have them suffer."

"It being Catholics also who made this plot," she said, "and these all having ready prayed with a secret and foreign priest, knowing this full well a crime."

"I do not argue that, your Majesty. But without their service, this plot would not be known and you likely would now be dead." And I told her all concerning the baker and his wife, there being nothing left I could do to protect them save pray mercy.

The Queen sighed long. "In truth, Shakespeare, we have been long vexed in the matter of religion, and did try for some years toward tolerance – our tolerance met with rebellion and calls from the Pope for my death, as matters of religion are now close tied to matters of state. And yet Christ calls us all to mercy."

She paused, looking about the room as though seeking counsel and none meeting her eyes.

"It seems only the playwright has any courage in his tongue today. Very well, those two, in recognition of their service, can be freed, needing only swear their loyalty. We will have word sent immediate so that they are not subject to Topcliffe's art."

"If it please your Majesty," I said, "I will take word to them direct, as I am certain this august assembly requires no further council from me."

She nodded and turned to her clerk. "Have immediate drawn such papers as he needs."

The clerk made for the door, me following.

"Shakespeare." The Queen spoke again when I was at the door's verge.

"Your Majesty?"

"We alone decide whose council we require. Do not be surprised if yours is required again."

CHAPTER 38

Topcliffe was much discomfited to be deprived of the baker and his wife, thinking the Queen too ready with her mercies.

"That they betrayed their fellows to you in fear proves their hearts false, even to their own religion," he said. "And you now would have the cancer of their false hearts free in our midst? Do you think they will hold their promised loyalty to our Queen dearer than their promised faith to their own God?"

"I think I hold my own word dear, and I promised them no harm from helping me."

"There is no harm from you, sir. It was their own priest who betrayed them."

"The priest being in your hands through my agency, and so from me."

Topcliffe snorted in disgust. "You are either weak in your heart and have thus released our enemies as salve to a conscience too easy bruised, or else are too clever in your sympathies. I warn you I have not forgot the Papist stench that surrounds your name. They and you will be watched. Perhaps we can continue this conversation on such day as you are not hid in our Queen's skirts."

He looked me hard in my eyes and seemed true surprised that I held that gaze unblinking. Carey was right. Topcliffe was just a savage dog, and current held firm on her Majesty's leash. The dark power I had invested him with in my imaginings had much paled in recent days, thrown into shadow in the light of such true horrors as I had late witnessed.

"I am easy watched, sir, as I am on the stage most days. You need only leave the company of the vermin in your cellar to find me."

He tried his serpent smile, but it now held no charm over me. "You should take more care in choosing your enemies, Shakespeare."

"A man can be as judged by his enemies as by his friends, so to count you my enemy can only serve my honour well. Besides, as you could not even break the girl, I stand less in fear of your arts than once I did. There is, I think, more strength in her than in ten of you."

Topcliffe's face quivered in rage, yet I still held his gaze, and he used his rage as an excuse to look away. He turned to call his guard, a ferret-faced man with animal eyes and a mouth that never quite closed.

"Take this scribe to see Norton that he might understand my strength." He turned back to me. "I have more Papists to question, as you could save only two. I do hope to make your company again, Shakespeare, and soon." And he turned, hurrying down a hall, his mincing steps tapping light on the stones.

The guard gestured in the opposite direction. "This way to the fair Mary," he said in a dripping voice. And I observed in his manner and aspect every corrupt evil I had seen in Topcliffe, but stripped of the pretence of intelligence and manners and so shown truer in its nature – a simple hunger for human suffering, a hunger Topcliffe had wrapped in pretend service to the Crown, so as to excuse the ill and misshapen desires that even his own shrivelled heart must rebel against in the nightmares that I prayed infested his sleeping. This guard was merely a carrion bird that fed in Topcliffe's wake, sharing his inhuman appetites but having himself no talent for catching his prey.

The guard left open the door to Mary's cell, it being immediate apparent that there was no risk of her leaving. She lay on her back on the stone floor, her late modesty poor served by the short shift of rough fabric that reached not even to her knees, the fabric variously spotted through with blood. Beyond its hem, her legs were mottled complete in bruising, even the soles of her bare feet, and so, too, her arms and hands, all of her fingers clear broken. But though her hair was matted with sweat, her face was unmarked.

"You will forgive me if I do not rise," she said, her voice soft and her breath catching as though to draw it caused pain. "But I fear my legs no longer do me good service, and I would save such strength I have as to walk with what dignity I might muster unto the scaffold that short awaits me."

I knelt on the floor next to her. "I will forgive it," I said, "if you will forgive me your state."

"You served your conscience as you understood it, sir. And I served mine. What sins we might either have committed in such service, they are not ours to loose or hold bound." She stopped and swallowed briefly, closing her eyes a short moment. "But I do ready forgive you for any sin you imagine you have done me, and do humbly beg that you forgive me my lies to you, and your friend's blood, which stains me more deep than these bruises."

I nodded, unable at that moment to speak, having recent wanted vengeance for Jenkins so dear and, now seeing it, wanting it only erased.

"Your queen's interrogator knows his art well," she said, "understanding immediate what we treasure and not. And so has left my face intact, so that, even on the scaffold – as I will there, I am told, be better dressed and these other insults hidden – I shall have to bear men's eyes upon me. Until the axe closes them."

"My eyes are upon you now," I said, "and I say true that your ruined body speaks your true beauty current more full than your untouched face."

She closed her eyes again, swallowing again. "Oh, my body is true ruined, sir, as I was immediate stripped and bound and made prey complete to Topcliffe and then to his guards all, and so will not bring with me unspoiled that virtue I have so long protected." Her face now ran with tears. "In truth, had he made threat of that act longer and not been so hurried to complete it, I do think I would have told him all, and thus sinned in my pride. But his lust saved me that decision, and, having taken a virtue that could not be returned, he left me able to bear all his other foul arts, having first borne that."

And I, now, had to close for a moment my own eyes, for I could too ready imagine that scene.

"You still hold entire every virtue," I said, "and in truth now hold more. For a virtue cannot be taken, only surrendered. Do trust me in this, as I have ready waved a white flag over all my own these long years, and have seduced others to do the same, and do true understand that pain. You will go to God as unspoiled a creature as he has yet received."

She moved her hand the few inches to mine, covering it and squeezing such little as her ruined state allowed. "Do you now know God, sir? For you did not when last we spoke."

"Know him, no. But do true believe that any such God as there might be would hold you dear."

"I will pray for you, Shakespeare, that you find him. For there is peace only in him, and none in you. It is in the constant survey of that empty tumult that broils within your heart that you create your own ills."

"And I will pray for you, though I know not where to direct it."

At which the guard shouted in the door. "Have your arse out, scribbler. That's time enough."

I lifted her ruined hand and kissed it. Then set it gentle back to the floor and left her to her short and unhappy future. Walking home through the darkened streets, I wondered on that peace that Mary wished for me, knowing true I had seldom felt it. But knowing also that Mary's peace stemmed from the sure knowledge of her God's will, which will had set this good woman on this foul course that was now littered with the dead and the tortured, the blood of the guilty and the innocent running together toward whatever eternal sea might receive it. It was the tumult of uncertainty only that checked our appetites – and so I was comfortable only not sure knowing God but stumbling instead in the unsure light of such knowledge as he had granted me and hoping that that faithful effort would prove faith enough.

CHAPTER 39

It was some days later when I sat in the tavern outside which Jenkins had died, our first performance at the Globe behind us and the tavern crowded full with both our company and many from the crowd. Our spirits tried for high, but were still some haunted by Jenkins's ghost. Burbage was lecturing Taylor, our new boy player, on the many faults in his performance.

"I am at some wonder the crowd did not run shrieking before the first act was over in horror at Taylor's wants," I said, finally, Burbage's litany of failings seeming to have no end, and Taylor not yet sure enough in his place to counter Burbage's bombast.

"He is no Jenkins, Will," Burbage said.

"Tell me which of you would claim to be, and I will have him outside to answer it," said a voice from behind. We turned to find Carey. "I have come to ensure you do not too much abuse your patron's good name."

Burbage popped from his seat and attempted a deep and theatrical bow, but, he having been some hours into his cups, overtaxed his balance and fell flat at Carey's feet.

"Come now, Burbage," I said. "The good Baron may have been some stern in his demands, but bootlicking is not required."

As Burbage made to rise, Carey placed one foot to the back of his neck, pressing Burbage's face full onto his other boot. "But I think I am growing a taste for it," he said, Heminges and I laughing hardy, Taylor seeming afraid to take any merriment.

"Come, boy, laugh," Carey said. "Your patron commands it."

This pushed Taylor to hysterics, at which Carey released Burbage but claimed his seat, so that Burbage tossed Taylor from the stool next. Thus the boy was on the floor, still unable to quiet his mirth, and Burbage finally smiling, too.

"Was my boot to your liking, sir?" Carey asked.

"Like any good Englishman, my face has oft been pressed close to many royal arses, and I can tell you sure that your boot smells equal of shit," Burbage said.

"Then I shall stand you to a round to cleanse your tongue," Carey said, "as I would not have any think the stink that comes from your mouth be mine."

We were at the tavern long hours, and on leaving Carey bade me to his coach, as he would have words.

"As you were instrumental in its unravelling, I would have you know the disposition of this Somerset Company business," he said.

"I have been curious."

"The Queen found no laws clear broken, but found

also such laws as there might be insufficient. And so she has named a commission on matters of securities and exchanges that such might be better governed. Your Webb has been named to this, I would have you know."

"And so the parties to this will escape with their profits?" ·

"The Crown required some expansion in its debts, and those profited from the Shoreditch episode were gently requested to finance those bonds and at such rate that will, by the end of the bonds' terms, leave their purses at approximate such standing as they had at the matter's start. Or so I am told, the mechanics of this all being beyond my ken."

We rode in silence until the coach neared my rooms. Above us, a distant thunder gave herald to a storm I had smelled brewing, and the night, which had been still, began to stir.

"And you, sir?" I asked. "Are you at peace?"

He snorted. "Peace will be in short supply at Somerset, I fear. I have sent my brother to my northernmost holdings, a dreary place that tries even my rustic temperaments, having told him should I ever look on his face again, he will answer immediate for his insult to our father's name. As he was my mother's pet, she counts that unreasonable. But finding such holdings equal dreary, she has not decamped in his company but instead remains to torment me." Then he slapped he seat of the coach hard and adopted a happier tone, "But there is mischief again in the Netherlands, and we may soon have a fine war. So, at peace current? No. But once at war I shall be."

I stepped from my rooms the morning next feeling some lightened and wondering by what alchemy, as I had made witness these past weeks as some had some died, some had suffered, and some had gained – none seeming through their own merit or earning, but all greater or lesser, whether by intent or accident, at my hands. I was myself lost a son, estranged a wife, a grief to my father, known more a sinner to many than I wouldst be – though not so much a sinner as I was known to myself – and witness at the death of a boy I called friend, and not witness only, but in truth the cause of it.

Yet the sun blessed this day, which was much fair and framed in a sky washed clean in the night's thunderings so that such scents as the breads made fresh at that baker near did have their rare chance to clear present their small glories above the usual effluent attendant to man's greedy agencies. And I did suddenly know the sun shone on us all even, and under its grace we chose whether to trudge weary as toward dusk or dance lively as toward dawn, it being such greater or lesser weight as our personal secrets did press upon us that decided our direction. But our secrets were of our own fashioning, and such weight as they bore of our own deciding, and mine own all having been made plain before eyes both common and noble, I did this once have none to carry.

And so I decided to turn east, toward dawn, and step light for those minutes or hours or days before I was anew cursed with their kin, knowing any promise to avoid such new burden to be a naïve and false hope, but knowing too such evils as we suffer are as random and as fickle as such blessings, and that to bear each in turn with such grace as we can muster – ready to forgive our fellows such weakness as we can, and ourselves such weakness as we must – this is all we can do.

And the baker's was near, and the bread did smell sweet.

ACKNOWLEDGMENTS

This unexpected foray into Elizabethan mischief sprang unbidden from an unusual direction. I was on the phone with my daughter, Shannon, who was off at college and taking a Shakespeare course, and she asked me what would have happened if Shakespeare wrote noir. My immediate answer was *Othello*, but that conversation gave rise to a literary itch I decided I had to scratch. Shannon stuck with me through the scratching, reading along as I went, and both her audience and her insights made this a better book.

The book didn't come first, though. First came a short story, *The Bard's Confession on the Matter of the Despoilment of the Fishmonger's Daughter*. I sent an early draft of that to my friend and fine writer, John Hornor Jacobs, whose enthusiastic encouragement to continue with the story and to undertake the novel are much appreciated. Thanks also to Steve Weddle for running the story in *Needle*, which you ought to be reading. And a tip of the hat to the good folks at Snubnose Press, who included the story in my short fiction collection, *Old School*.

I had a layman's familiarity with Shakespeare's plays when I undertook this project, but only a cursory understanding of his life and times. Tom McBride, English professor extraordinaire at Beloit College, was kind enough to answer a few questions and point me to the right sources to fill in the gaps. Gaps remain, I am sure, as I am no expert on either Shakespeare or Elizabethan history, but those sins are mine to bear. Where I have referenced historical events, I have tried to be true to them. The one liberty I have knowingly taken is to move a few years earlier in history the story of how Shakespeare's troupe moved (literally) the Theatre from Shoreditch to Bankside, where it became the Globe.

As always, thanks to my agent, Stacia Decker, who encouraged this departure from my usual, provided her customary insightful editorial direction, and then found it a home.

And, of course, to the good folks at Exhibit A – former editor Emlyn Rees, who bought and edited the book; new editor Bryon Quertermous, who shepherded it through production; their art staff and Nick Castle Design for another stellar cover; and their diligent copy editor, who has again saved me from my lesser angels.

Dan O'Shea (for Bartholomew Daniels)

An enigmatic, unsettling thriller that never
lets you get your balance
CheffoJeffo

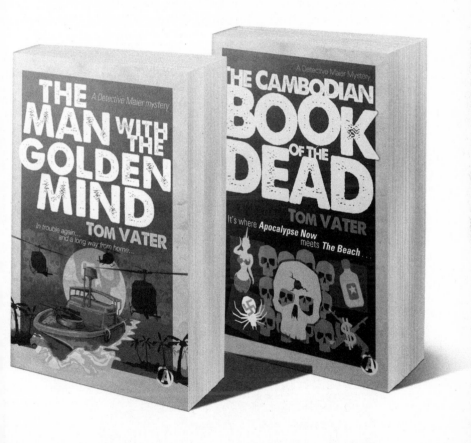

**Your worst nightmare just
went viral...**

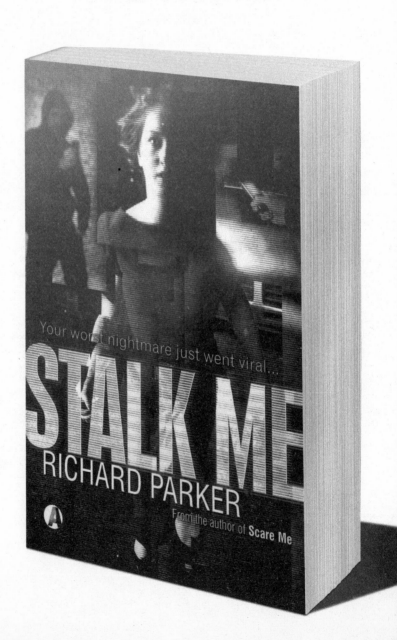

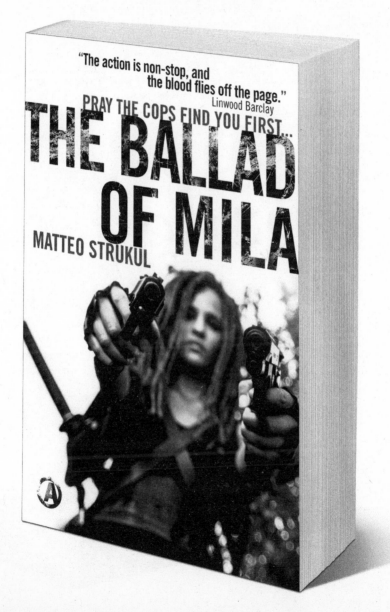

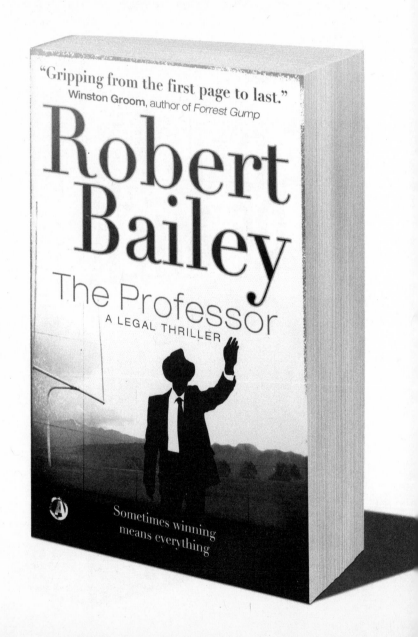

Robert Bailey

The Professor

A LEGAL THRILLER

Sometimes winning
means everything

DAN O'SHEA

Introducing Detective John Lynch

PENANCE

One dark secret is
about to rip a
whole city apart…

DAN O'SHEA

A Detective John Lynch Chicago Thriller

GRID

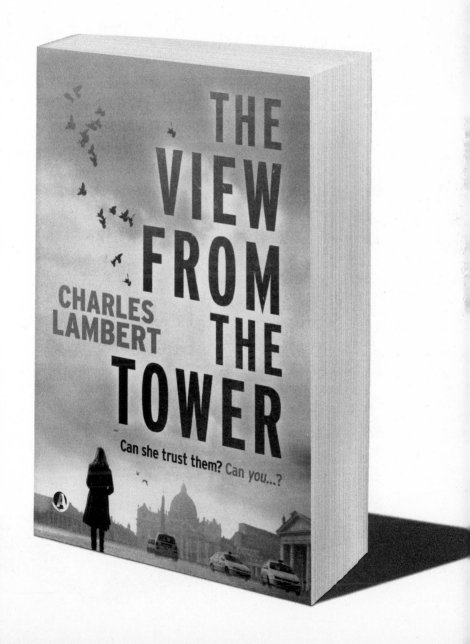

A gripping psychological thriller about love and betrayal.

THE VIEW FROM THE TOWER

CHARLES LAMBERT

Can she trust them? Can you...?

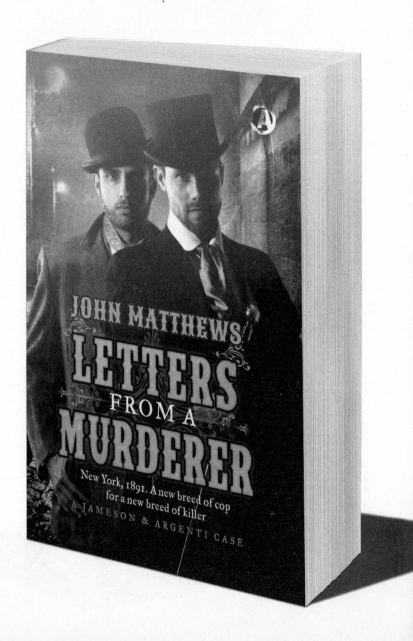

JOHN MATTHEWS
LETTERS
FROM A
MURDERER

New York, 1891. A new breed of cop
for a new breed of killer

A JAMESON & ARGENTI CASE

A taut, timely thriller ripped from today's headlines. Blisteringly paced, authentically told, here is a novel that demands to be read in a single sitting."

James Rollins, New York Times bestselling author of The Eye of God

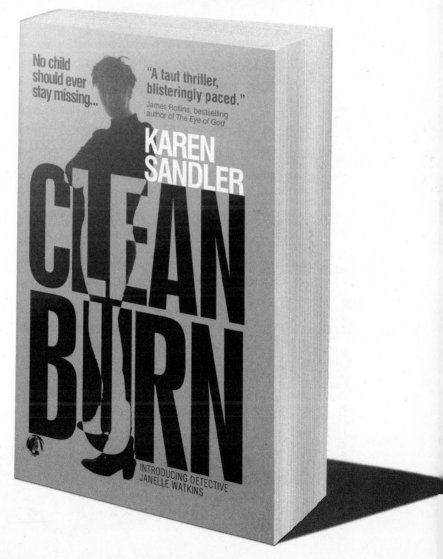

No child should ever stay missing...

"A taut thriller, blisteringly paced."
James Rollins, bestselling author of *The Eye of God*

KAREN SANDLER

CLEAN BURN

INTRODUCING DETECTIVE JANELLE WATKINS

Murder. Vice. Pollution. Delays on the Tube. Some things never change...

WILLIAM SUTTON

Lawless And The Devil of Euston Square

"First-rate Victorian crime fiction"
The Herald